Nothing Sung AND Nothing Spoken

ALSO BY NITA TYNDALL

Who I Was with Her

Nothing Sung
AND
Nothing Spoken

NITA TYNDALL

An Imprint of HarperCollinsPublishers

Nothing Sung and Nothing Spoken
Copyright © 2022 by Nita Tyndall
Translations copyright © 2022 by Nita Tyndall
All rights reserved. Printed in the United States of America.

Library of Congress Cataloging-in-Publication Data
Names: Tyndall, Nita, author.
Title: Nothing sung and nothing spoken / Nita Tyndall.
Description: First edition. | New York : HarperTeen, [2022] | Summary:
"In World War II Berlin, under the shadow of the Nazi regime, a group of
German girls become involved in the Swing Youth resistance movement"—
Provided by publisher.
Identifiers: LCCN 2021063006 | ISBN 9780063087446 (hardcover)
Subjects: CYAC: Swing (Music)—Fiction. | Lesbians—Fiction. | LGBTQ+
people—Fiction. | Family life—Germany—Fiction. | World War,
1939-1945—Underground movements—Germany—Fiction. | Berlin
(Germany)—Fiction. | Germany—History—1933-1945—Fiction. | LCGFT:
Historical fiction. | Novels.
Classification: LCC PZ7.1.T9652 No 2022 | DDC [Fic]—dc23
LC record available at https://lccn.loc.gov/2021063006

Typography by Corina Lupp
22 23 24 25 26   PC/LSCH   10 9 8 7 6 5 4 3 2 1

❖

First Edition

Zweites Buch: Lamentationen: 'Gedächtnisfeier' by Heinrich
Heine (Author), A. S. Kline (Translator), Copyright © 2004

For all the queer teens throughout history. Your stories matter.

And

For my parents, without whom this book would not exist.

Keine Messe wird man singen,
Keinen Kadosch wird man sagen,
Nichts gesagt und nichts gesungen
Wird an meinen Sterbetagen.

Not a Mass will be sung then,
Not a Kaddish will be said,
Nothing sung, and nothing spoken
On the day when I am dead.

—HEINRICH HEINE, "GEDÄCHTNISFEIER,"
TRANSLATED BY A. S. KLINE

Nein, das Nazi-Regime konnte meine Liebe
zum Swing nicht brechen.
No, the Nazi regime could not break my love of swing.

—GÜNTER DISCHER

PROLOG
10. August 1945

ALLIIERTEN-BESETZTES DEUTSCHLAND

IT BEGAN the summer before the war. An urgent, thrumming summer, the summer we were fifteen, the summer Geli was obsessed with Heinrich. Not some boy we knew, fair-haired and porcelain, but the Jewish poet Heinrich Heine. She'd found a book of his poems, and despite the fact that his words had been forbidden since 1933—or maybe because of it—she clung to that book like a lifeline.

War was coming, but we didn't know it yet. We were too young to remember what it had been like before. We grew up in shadows, threats looming overhead, and by the time we paid attention to them, it was too late.

We were often together, she and I, staying awake late into the night. Our bodies close, our arms touching, her voice softly reading those verses.

"Do you think," she whispered to me one night, "that it's really possible? Being so in love with someone like Heine was?"

"Ich weiß nicht," I replied. *I don't know.*

But I did know, because Heine's longing was spelled out plainly in every word she read me, reaching inside me and threatening to expose my own longing for her.

"What about you?" I asked her. "Do you believe it's possible? That kind of love?"

Her breathing was deep and even; I assumed she was asleep, for she did not answer me.

It was only later, looking back, that I realized she never had.

She dragged me to the club first, before Minna and Renate joined us. She took me because out of all of us, I was the one who was by her side.

I was always by her side.

To the very end, I was by her side.

I promised her I would be.

Part 1

APRIL 1938–AUGUST 1939

April 1938

IT BEGINS with a secret.

It begins with Geli's hand in mine, pulling me along Fasanenstraße, the two of us practically running, the April air biting through the thin fabric of my jacket.

"Geli, slow down!" I say, but she either can't or deliberately doesn't hear me, because if anything she picks up the pace, letting go and running ahead of me. We pass couples on the street, SA guards in brown uniforms, who scowl as Geli breezes by them.

"Geli!"

"Komm schon, Charlie," she says, finally slowing enough to allow me to catch up to her. She takes my hand in hers again, laces her fingers through mine. "We don't want to be too late."

"And what exactly are we going to be late for?"

"You'll see," she says. I look up. We've finally stopped on Kantstraße, in front of a large set of stairs leading up to an imposing building with the name *Delphi* written on it. Around us are adults in glittering dresses and furs, immaculately made up and precise.

I shrink back. This has to be a joke, Geli bringing me to a Tanzpalast like this. I don't belong here like she does.

But from the look on her face, I know it isn't.

"Geli, was ist?"

She smiles, shakes her head. "Ask me in English, Charlie."

"What?"

"They don't like German being spoken here."

"Geli, you know my English isn't as good as yours—"

"Just try," she says, smiling that dazzling smile at me, the one she uses whenever I have her full attention. The one that makes me feel special.

I take a breath, try in English, because I need to feel special. Because after next school year our paths will split; Geli will continue on at her Gymnasium and I will have to work, and we live in two completely separate districts and she's not going to have time for me anymore.

I almost didn't come tonight. It's a Tuesday, and tomorrow is the Führer's birthday, tomorrow I have duties and responsibilities to my family and the Bund Deutscher Mädel group to which Geli and I are both required to belong, and I almost didn't come.

But Geli has those same responsibilities, and yet here she is. Here *we* are.

"What is this?" I ask carefully, the words heavy in my mouth. She laughs.

"You'll see." She throws her arms out and spins before turning back to me, her eyes wide. "Charlotte Kraus," she says, drawing out the syllables of my name. "I need you to pick a different name."

"What?" I ask.

"When we get inside," Geli says, "German names aren't allowed—well. It's better if you have an English or American one." She smiles.

"And what is your name going to be, Angelika Haas?" I say, and her nose wrinkles at my use of her full name.

"Nancy," she says immediately.

"Nancy," I repeat.

Geli stifles a laugh behind her hands. "Let me pick your name," she says once she's recovered, and I nod, content to let her. She circles me, studying. I try not to shiver under her gaze.

"You look like a Peggy," she says in English with an air of finality.

"Peggy," I repeat.

"It's a nickname for Margaret," Geli says.

I frown. "How do the English get 'Peggy' from 'Margaret'?" I ask, and Geli shrugs.

"Are you ready, Peggy?" she asks, leading us up the stairs toward the entrance to the Tanzpalast.

"Ready for what? What *is* this?" I ask, frustration creeping into my tone.

"The surprise," she says, and then I hear it.

Music.

Not the Goebbels-approved songs from the radio, not the Volkslieder I grew up singing. I realize with a start that I *know* this music like a memory: Papa playing it on the record player when I was young, dancing around our small living room with Mama while my little sister, Greta, and I watched, laughing.

It's jazz.

But it feels different from Papa's records, most of which were in German. I can't make out the words of these English songs, and this music feels like a living, breathing *thing*, not something coming out of the speaker of our small Koffergrammophon, the record player that lives in its own suitcase house.

It's also forbidden. Outlawed. Not "German" enough.

"Geli . . . ," I whisper.

"Nancy," she corrects. "We're American now."

I frown, but at the look on her face, I play along. "Nancy, this is . . ."

"I know," she says, and pulls me inside.

I can't help but stare. There are people dancing everywhere, some our age, some older—eighteen or nineteen—all flailing their arms to this music, which is coming from a group of boys onstage. Geli pinches my arm and I realize I'm gawking, blinking before turning my attention to the rest of the room.

It's magnificent, and against it, I feel even smaller. The ceiling is lit with lights like stars, the columns like something from ancient Greece rising up to meet them. I watch as Geli drops a Reichsmark in a tin by the door.

"Geli, I don't have any money . . ."

"Don't worry, Peggy, I'll cover it," she says, and drops another mark in like it's no big deal. "Besides, it's just a suggestion."

I think of the torn skirt lying on my bed at home that I will have to fix myself because we cannot afford to replace it, and wish money were just a suggestion.

But I don't have time to linger on this, the sharp sting in my chest at her words, because Geli shrugs off her coat and motions for me to do the same, then tosses them both in a heap by the door. She pulls her lipstick out of her dress pocket and touches it up before turning back to me and grinning.

"What do you think?"

I try not to stare. She looks like an American flapper, golden hair curled, lips painted that bright red, the absolute antithesis of what a good German girl is supposed to look like. My fingers play with the fabric of my dress; when Geli told me she had a surprise for me, all she'd said was to wear something nice. But my nice isn't her nice, and compared to her, I just feel plain and small and unremarkable.

Why did she bring me here? Renate's more outgoing than I am, Minna more musical, so why did she bring me, of all our friends?

As if she can sense what I'm thinking, Geli takes my hand. Her nails are the same bright red as her lipstick. I have no idea when she had the time to paint them; it's not like the BDM allows us to wear nail polish, and Liesl would have commented on it earlier at our meeting if Geli had been wearing it then.

"Charlie," she says, and I tear my attention away from our intertwined hands. She leans in closer so I can hear her over the music. "Come dance with me."

I look around the magnificent room, try to ignore the feeling of her hand in mine, and I do what I always do—

I let her lead, and I follow.

At first I don't know what to do. This music doesn't follow a strict rhythm, and I have trouble trying to move and dance to it. The people around us are flailing their arms, bodies twisting this way and that, and I awkwardly try to copy them for a song before Geli cuts in. She dances with me for a few beats before laughing and pulling away again, always dancing and swirling at the periphery of my vision, the sight of her hazy through the smoke-filled room. She dances with a boy with hair longer than hers, catching my eye and winking when he dips her. One of his friends takes my hand and, on my nod, spins me around the room. We dance for two songs—or is it three? Or four? I lose count so quickly, each melody blending into the next.

Boys have never danced with me like this before. No one has. We sing songs in the BDM and sometimes we have approved dances with boys from neighboring Hitlerjugend groups, but nothing has ever felt like—like *this*. This electric.

The band takes a pause and I'm finally able to catch my breath as the boy—Jimmy, he said his name was, though I know it wasn't—gives me a bow and heads off to rejoin his friends. I look around, but I don't see Geli. I'm about to go looking for her when a shout from the stage stops me where I stand.

"Swing Heil!" one of the boys onstage calls, throwing up his arm in a mock Hitler salute. I freeze. A few of the other people around me laugh nervously, but other than that, none of them even give this boy a second glance. His blond hair is long, longer than a boy in the HJ would be allowed to wear it, his nose crooked in a way that suggests it's been broken before. His friends onstage jostle him, and I recognize him then as the boy Geli was dancing with earlier. As I look closer, I realize none of the boys look like ones I would know from the HJ—not just their hair but their clothes, suspenders and trousers and hats I've only seen in some of Geli's British fashion magazines. The girls standing around me, too, all look like Geli—curled hair instead of braids, lips painted outrageously bright colors, skirts above their knees.

My heart hammers faster, as if trying to keep up with the desperate tempo the band has struck up again.

I need to find Geli. She'll be able to—to explain this. If she tells me I belong here, then I do. If she tells me this is safe and exciting, even though it feels forbidden and dangerous, then it is.

I turn, trying to spot Geli in the crowd, finding her after a minute. She's sitting at one of the tables pushed against the wall, her legs on the lap of a different boy who looks much older than us. A lit cigarette dangles out of his mouth, and I watch as she plucks it and takes a drag off it before handing it back to him.

"We have to go," I tell her, ignoring the thudding in my chest at the sight of her with this boy. She opens her mouth like she's about to argue but stops at the look on my face. She stands and kisses the boy on the cheek, her lipstick leaving a bright mark.

I turn away.

Outside the hot haze of the dance hall the world is sharp and clear; outside, you can barely hear the music.

"Didn't you love that?" Geli says as we stand on the sidewalk, quickly reverting to German. "Oh Charlie, please tell me you loved it."

"Yes," I say, breathlessly, before I can even think about what it is I'm saying. "I loved it, but Geli—how did you hear about this? How—how is this allowed, how have the SA not found it, what . . . what *is* it?"

"It's jazz," Geli says, again in that American accent she's perfected. "Hot dancing!"

I frown. She grabs my hand and starts humming one of the songs, laughing, trying to spin me around. I dig my heels into the cobblestones.

"Geli, I'm not playing. The—the boy doing the mock salute, the music, I just—"

"Relax, Charlie," she says. "It's nothing serious."

"How did you even find out about it?"

"Tommy told me," she says.

"Tommy?"

"The boy from onstage. That's not his real name."

"I know that," I say, frustrated. "How did you even meet him?"

She shrugs. "The boys' Gymnasium isn't so far from mine. I talk to them sometimes," she says, giving me a wink. "He asked if I liked music, I said yes, and he brought me to this club a few weeks ago. And I wanted to show it to you."

"But—"

"It's just dancing, Charlie," she says. "It's fun. It's a way to relax. You had fun, didn't you?"

God, she knows me so well. I don't even have to answer; she can see it on my face—yes, I did have fun, my hair loose and skirt flying. I liked how the music filled my body, how it made me feel.

How dancing with *her* made me feel.

It's just dancing, she says.

But it feels like something much more dangerous than that.

◆ ◆ ◆

Geli and I part ways at the U-Bahn stop by the Zoo. Her home isn't far, but mine is a few stops away in Kreuzberg, near Renate's flat. She briefly hugs me before pulling back.

"Let's go again," she says. "Soon."

"When?"

"I don't know—they meet at least once a week, but not always at the Delphi." She smiles. "Once I find out the next meeting place, I'll tell you—you can draw me one of your maps. We could even bring the others! You can invite them tomorrow before the induction ceremony, right?"

Something in my chest tightens when she says that. The others. Minna and Renate.

"Sure," I say, hoping she doesn't hear the jealousy in my tone. I know they'd love it, the music, the dancing, but I want it to just be me and Geli, just for a little while longer. "I can invite them then."

"Perfect!" she says, and hugs me again. This time when she pulls back from me, her hands linger on my shoulders.

"Thank you," she says.

"For what?"

"For coming with me. I wouldn't have wanted anyone else by my side tonight."

"Oh," I say, because I'm not sure what to say, how I'm supposed to respond to that.

Warum ich?

14

Why me?

Before I can stop her, Geli leans in and kisses me on the cheek, then flounces off to her side of the street.

I place my hand to my cheek as if I can keep her kiss there. As if I can keep her with me.

The lights are off when I enter our flat, Mama and Papa's door shut. I head down the hall, trying to tiptoe past my little sister Greta's room to my own.

A whisper in the dark. "Charlie."

No luck.

I go into Greta's room, shutting the door before I turn on the light.

"What are you doing up?" I ask her, perching on the edge of her bed, careful not to mess up her new JM uniform that's neatly folded at the foot of it. "Mama will be cross with you tomorrow if she thinks you didn't sleep."

"I was waiting for you. Where did you go?" She frowns. "You smell like cigarettes. If Mama finds out . . ."

"Keine Sorge, Gretchen, I didn't smoke."

"Then where were you?" she asks. "You told Mama you had to go help Fräulein Schröder for the induction ceremony tomorrow."

Tomorrow is the Führer's birthday, a national holiday. Tomorrow my little sister is being inducted into the Jung-mädelbund, the little sister organization of the BDM. I helped her memorize her induction speeches, took in her uniform so it fits on her small frame.

Greta's eyes narrow. "You were out with Geli, weren't you?"

"Yes," I say, and the frown on her face deepens.

"Why didn't you invite me?" she asks, pouting, folding her arms across her chest.

"Because you're ten, Gretchen."

"So? That doesn't matter to Geli. Geli likes me," Greta says, her voice matter-of-fact. I sigh. It's no use arguing with my sister when it comes to Geli. She idolizes her, has since she was old enough to follow the two of us around. There are times I think she'd prefer it if Geli was her older sister rather than me.

"I'm sorry," I say. "Geli and I went to the movies. She only had two tickets." It's a poor excuse, but hopefully my sister buys it. "She said she misses you."

"She did?"

"Mm-hmm," I say, and swing my legs up onto the bed. "Scoot over."

She does so, and I lie back, thinking of Geli, of her kiss on my cheek, until Greta's voice cuts into my thoughts.

"Will Geli come over soon?"

"I can ask her," I say, and Greta nods.

"Good. I want her to braid my hair."

"I thought you hated it when I braided your hair."

"She's better at it than you," Greta says, and I sigh. She snuggles down farther into her bed, looking up at me with big eyes.

"Will you tell me a story, Charlie?"

"You just told me Geli was better than I am at braiding your hair. Why should I do anything for you?" I say, and move like I'm going to stand up. Greta reaches out and clutches my arm.

"I didn't mean it, Charlie, bitte?"

I pause just a second longer to really make her think I'm still angry, then lie back down.

"What do you want to hear?" I ask. I haven't told her a story in a while. I'm forbidden to tell her any more of the Grimms' Märchen, ever since I read her "Von dem Machandelboom" and she had nightmares about cannibals for months, even refusing to eat Mama's potato soup, claiming the tiny pieces of Wurst in it looked like fingers.

"Can you tell me a story about Sisi?"

"Again?" I ask, but I already know I'll tell it. Greta has been obsessed with stories about Kaiserin Elisabeth of Austria since she was old enough to understand them. When she was younger, she'd beg our father to tell them, her eyes lighting up whenever he mentioned his home state of Bayern, where Sisi was also from.

"Yes, again," she says, and snuggles in closer to me. "Please?"

"Very well," I say. "There was once a princess named Elisabeth—"

"She wasn't a princess, she was an *empress*," Greta says bossily.

"She was a princess before she was empress, Greta," I say. "Are you going to let me tell the story or not?"

She pouts, but relents, laying her head on my chest. I run my fingers over her hair, the curls left by her tight braids.

"Elisabeth was very free-spirited," I say. "She loved horse-back riding and poetry and wanted to join the circus. But when she was my age, fifteen, she met the emperor of Austria, Franz Joseph. He wasn't supposed to marry her," I say, and Greta draws in a breath. "He was supposed to marry her sister, Helene."

"But Elisabeth was so beautiful that Franz Joseph fell in love with her immediately," Greta cuts in, and I let her, because this is her favorite part of the story. Right when I'm beginning to tell her about Elisabeth's wedding, she drifts off the way she always does, and I gently extricate myself from her before leaving her room and shutting the door.

Geli loves the story of Elisabeth, too, if only because she is so much like her. But as I'm getting ready for bed, I think, *What about Helene?*

What about the sister who worked hard, who studied, who wanted to be empress, and was passed up for someone more beautiful? Girls who wield their beauty like a weapon, who charm boys and emperors, those are the girls stories get told about. Girls like Elisabeth, like Geli.

No one tells stories about girls like Helene.

No one will tell stories about me.

Greta wakes me early, running into my room before Mama has even come to get me up. She throws open my door with such enthusiasm I'm surprised our downstairs neighbors don't bang on the ceiling to complain.

"What, Gretchen?" I say as she rocks on the balls of her feet. I let her pull me out of bed, wondering sleepily why Mama hasn't come to get us ready for school.

But of course, there is no school today, just the scent of something delicious and fragrant wafting from the kitchen. I frown. Normally we do not celebrate the Führer's birthday so thoroughly.

But it's Greta's induction day, of course. Mama must be making her something special.

"Mama made Kaiserschmarrn, and if you don't hurry I'm going to eat all of it," she declares. "Come on!"

"Greta, wait—" I call after her, but she's already disappeared down the hall, her footsteps loud. When I'm sure she's gone, I hurry to my vanity and pull out the present I've been working on for her.

It's a map, not unlike the other maps I've drawn that now hang on the walls of my room—routes to the church we attend on Christmas and Easter, to Viktoriapark where Greta and I used to spend summer afternoons. Drawn in charcoal on scraps of paper Papa took from his job at the post office, on the backs of my school assignments. I've drawn maps since I was a child, marveling at the feeling of being able to create entire cities with my hands, reducing the complex sprawl of Berlin to charcoal lines and curves that I can follow. Maps and routes so I never get lost, so even when the street names change, I can find my way back to places I love.

Greta's map is from our home to the building where her JM meetings will be held. It's the same building where I have my BDM meetings, so more often than not we'll walk together, but I want her to be able to find her way without me.

A piece of hair falls in my face as I bend over my work, and I tuck it behind my ear, wondering if I could get away with cutting it as short as Renate's.

I think of the boys from last night, their hair down past their shoulders and their fashionable clothes. How were they able to get away with wearing them? And the girls, wearing makeup! Mama would never let me, and the BDM wouldn't allow it, either. We're all supposed to look the same: perfect German women.

I sigh and go ahead and shrug into the white blouse and navy skirt that is our uniform, the fabric stiff and starched. I flip up the hem of my shirt to check that my stitches are holding, the tiny bit of embroidery I did during one of our evening meetings, my initials sewn in to mark that this is mine.

Last night was a dream. A beautiful, loud, ecstatic dream, but my life is not Geli's, it isn't dance parties and short skirts and that music invading my body. It's careful, neat stitches in my blouse and watching after my sister.

Still, though. Is it bad to want such things? To enjoy them?

I know what the BDM would say, what the Führer would

say. We good German girls are supposed to only want three things: *Kinder, Küche, Kirche.* Children, kitchen, church.

And I do want those things—some of them, at least. Children, a safe home.

But what if I want other things—freedom, music, Geli's smile that lights me up from the inside?

Charlotte shouldn't want those things. Isn't *allowed* to want those things. Peggy is. And until last night, I never even thought I *could* be a girl like Peggy. It was never a possibility.

Today I have to be Charlotte. I have to get Greta through her induction.

But all I can think about is how much I want to be Peggy again.

When I enter the kitchen, Mama has the Kaiserschmarrn in a pan, and I watch her deftly flip the batter until it's light and puffy. A bowl of applesauce sits on the table, and Greta sticks a finger in, then catches me watching and laughs. The radio plays in the background; national hymns and music and a replay of the Führer's speech from last month when we absorbed Austria back into Germany.

"Do you know why they call it Kaiserschmarrn?" Greta asks me as Mama sets the pancake in front of her. I sigh, indulge her.

"Why?"

"Because of Franz Joseph," she says, just as my father makes his way into the room. "Because he loved it so much, they named it after him. Do you think Elisabeth loved it, too?"

"I'm sure she did," my father says as he sits down. He gives me a wink over Greta's head. "I'm sure they had it every day."

"Papa, can we go to Austria sometime?" Greta asks. "I want to see the palace where Sisi lived."

My parents glance at each other before turning back to Greta.

"It's Ostmark now," Papa says. "And certainly, Greta— perhaps now that it is part of Germany again, I'll be able to take you. We can all go together, as a family." He glances over at Mama. "We can visit Bayern while we're at it."

She huffs, pouring a cup of coffee for him, then a small cup for me, as it's a special occasion. The Führer's loud, impassioned voice continues in the background.

"Mama, is it all right if Greta and I go over to Renate's before the ceremony?" I ask. "Greta can change into her uniform there; otherwise we'll just be sitting around the house all day and I think Greta will burst if we do."

Mama looks over at us. For a second I think she's going to say no, but then she looks at Greta, so nervous she's alternating between pushing the pancake pieces around on her plate and shoving six of them into her mouth at once.

"Of course," Mama says. "Tell Frau Hoffmann we'll meet them at Aschinger after the ceremony."

"The Aschinger at *Alexanderplatz*," Greta cuts in. "Right, Mama?"

My mother sighs. "Yes, Gretchen, the Aschinger at Alexanderplatz." She shares a look with my father over Greta's head. "Not as if they don't have the same food as the Aschinger down the street."

"But we go to that one all the *time*," Greta whines, something that would normally earn her a sharp look or word from Mama. Today, though, it's clear she's allowed to get away with whatever she wants.

Mama is happy Greta is being inducted, happy my shy little sister will have a chance to make new friends. But secretly, I worry. While I've loved my own time in the BDM, loved the songs, the hikes, the chance to learn new skills and spend more time with Renate and Geli, Fräulein Schröder makes it easy to enjoy our time there; she even lets us call her Liesl. Frau Köhler, the sour, pinch-faced woman who leads the Jungmädelschaft, will not make it so easy for the younger girls.

The BDM, to me, has never been anything more than a chance to see my friends, to sing some songs, to perfect my sewing because it's a skill Mama appreciates. To draw my maps while Liesl talks. Sometimes there is that nagging feeling of guilt that I am supposed to be doing more with my time there.

Sometimes there is another feeling, one I can't name, a spark in my gut at the thought that Minna and her sisters aren't allowed in because they're Jewish.

But I can't think about that too much. Especially not today.

I take a sip of my coffee as Mama runs Greta through her

induction oath again, my hands itching for my sketchbook so I can clean up the final lines on Greta's map.

She can't follow me forever.

Renate and Minna live on the other side of the Landwehrkanal, in a residential building on a tree-lined street. Greta and I cross the Admiralbrücke, my bag bumping against my hip. Inside I have my sketchbook and Greta's uniform, carefully folded. Greta runs her fingers along the rail of the bridge as we walk.

"Do you think Hans will be there?" she asks as we turn onto Freiligathstraße, Renate and Minna's street. Hans is Renate's older brother by two years, fair-skinned and golden-haired and the crush of pretty much every girl I know, my little sister included.

"I'm sure he will. He's a leader and Fritz is being inducted, so he has to be," I say. Fritz, Renate's younger brother, is Greta's age. Like Greta and the Jungmädelbund, he's being inducted today into the younger branch of the HJ, the Jungvolk. Mama keeps trying to push them together.

Greta makes a face. "I don't like Fritz."

"You must start liking him, Mama thinks he'll make a great husband for you," I say. Greta looks up at me, eyes wide.

"Nein, Charlie, she didn't say that—"

"Doch, she did," I say, and wait a few seconds before I can't help it and bust out laughing.

Greta's mouth turns down into a scowl. "You're so *mean*."

"I am not," I say. "Come on, you only have to be around Fritz a little. I bet Minna brought the twins over, so you might not even have to see him at all."

"Fine," Greta says, and we push open the door to Renate's building and begin to climb the flights of stairs to the Hoffmanns' flat on the fifth floor. As we pass the fourth floor, I stop and look over the rail. Herr Neumann, the Hausmeister in charge of the upkeep of the building, is mopping the floors outside the Kochs' door.

Or at least, he looks like he is.

I pause. Normally I pay Herr Neumann no mind; just like with our Hausmeister, Herr Lang, he fades into the background—though our Hausmeister has always had a kinder face than Herr Neumann, whose sunken eyes and thinning hair make him look almost skeletal, his skin pale and translucent like he'll fade away at any moment.

I don't know why he catches my eye this time. He doesn't see me, hasn't even glanced my way. But the more I study him, the more I realize he isn't actually mopping, not in a way that would be considered effective. The look on his face is the one Mama accuses me of having when she finds me daydreaming instead of cleaning, wiping the same spot over and over.

Herr Neumann doesn't look like he's daydreaming, though. He looks like he's listening.

For what?

I bite my lip. If I were a braver girl, I'd shout, let him know I see him. But what would that matter? Maybe he is just cleaning and doing a poor job at it.

"Charlie, hurry up!"

Herr Neumann's head snaps up. He makes eye contact with me and I swallow, quickly turning and running up the stairs to catch up to Greta. When I reach Renate's floor, I steal a glance over the railing.

Herr Neumann is already gone.

It only takes Greta one knock on the Hoffmanns' door before Hans opens it. He's not in his uniform; in fact, he's barely dressed, in a button-down shirt and tan shorts. If Geli were here, she'd swoon. Greta *is* swooning, her face turning a bright pink.

"Hallo, Hans," she says quietly, and I roll my eyes. Hans notices and smiles.

"Tach, Greta," he says. "Are you excited?"

She nods, but doesn't say anything else, her gaze downcast. Just when I think I'm going to have to prompt her, there's the squealing of girls, and Minna's younger twin sisters, Ruth and Rebekah, come flying around the corner and wrap my sister in a four-armed hug. They nearly knock into Hans, who quickly steps out of the way as Minna appears behind her sisters. The twins are a smaller copy of her, all three with the same curly chestnut hair.

"I told them to slow down but then they heard Greta

and—whoosh," Minna says, laughing. She pulls me into a hug, her tall, willowy frame enveloping mine so my nose is pressed into her shoulder. "Hallo, Charlie."

"Minna," I say, and hug her back. The twins and my sister have already disappeared down the hall, the three girls drowning out Fritz's annoyed shouting. Hans rolls his eyes.

"Better go settle them down them before Fritz complains," he says. "Good luck, Charlie."

I give Minna a quizzical look, and she laughs. "You know how Renate gets when she has to dress up for anything."

"Is it that bad?" I call after Hans, and he merely looks back at me with a grimace on his face. I laugh. Between her two brothers, Renate's always gotten along better with Hans, who is far more easygoing and quicker to crack a joke than Fritz.

"Lead on," I say to Minna, though it's not like I need her to, not like I haven't spent most afternoons at Renate's flat since we were in Grundschule together.

If I were to draw a map of Renate's flat, here is what I would draw: her room, shoved into the corner but with a view of the courtyard down below; the wall separating her room from Hans and Fritz's; the narrow hallway leading to the kitchen which only one of us can walk down at a time; a small box for the living room and then another for her parents' room. All laid out in clean straight lines.

Here is what I would not be able to draw: the coatrack in the corner with the family's shoes piled up beneath it, the pots perpetually on the stove from Renate's mother trying to teach her how to cook. Her father's chair in the living room, where he often sits when I come to visit, his cane leaning against it, the stiff way he moves even now, almost twenty years after the war. The chaos of Fritz and Hans's room, the way the courtyard smells whenever Renate opens her window. How this place feels like my second home, more crowded than our own flat but still comforting.

And directly below Renate's flat, Minna's, her voice sometimes carrying up through the window—the day we discovered her flat was directly below Renate's, the three of us made Hans teach us Morse code so we could tap out messages on the floor.

I knock on Renate's door only to hear a grumbled "*What?*" from behind it. Minna covers her mouth and laughs.

"Has she been like this all day?"

"All day," Minna says. She pushes open the door. Renate stands in front of her mirror, scowling. She's almost as tall as Minna but stockier, her dark hair cut in a short bob.

"Charlie," Renate says, turning this way and that in front of her reflection, "please tell Minna that I look like a Wurst stuffed into a casing."

Minna giggles again. I look Renate over.

"Stimmt nicht," I say. "You look fine."

"I do not. This uniform isn't made for girls who like to run."

"I thought it was," I say, setting my satchel down. "Aren't we supposed to be able to do sports for the Führer?"

"The Führer didn't take my legs into account," Renate grumbles, then sighs. "I'll have to get you to tailor this sometime."

"I'm sure Frau Koch could do it better," I say.

"Oh yes, that'll be a lovely conversation," Renate says, flopping back down onto her bed. "Hello, Minna's mother who I've known since childhood, can you please let my skirt out for the BDM? Because I appear to have eaten one too many of your latkes and now it doesn't fit."

Minna laughs. "You know she wouldn't mind, though," she says, sitting down next to Renate. "Though she might make me try to do it, to practice."

"I've seen your sewing and it's atrocious, so no thank you," Renate says. "Is she still trying to get you to take over the business, though?"

"She is," Minna says, making a face. "And she knows it's not what I want to do, but it's not like any hospital is going to let me apprentice as a nurse or anything." She sighs.

"But you're good enough," I say, and both Renate and Minna turn to look at me. "I mean it. You've got some of the best grades in science out of any of us—"

"That doesn't matter, Charlie," Minna says gently. "You know it doesn't."

"But maybe we could talk to your mother—I could apprentice with her instead, it would get Mama off my back, and you'd be free to—"

"Charlie," Minna says again, firmer, and I bite my lip. "It's not Mama not letting me do it. It's—it's everything else," she says, and her gaze lingers on my uniform before she turns away.

I press my lips together. I don't know what to say, how to respond.

Renate does, though, cutting the tension as easily as she used to beat me at marbles. "What about you, Charlie?" she asks. "What're you doing once school is over?"

"Mama actually does want me to get an apprenticeship for sewing or tailor work," I say. "It's a stable enough job. But I thought . . . I don't know, I want to do art school, but without an Abitur . . ."

Renate and Minna both nod. Unlike Geli at her Gymnasium, destined to get the Abitur that will allow her to attend a university, the three of us are in Realschule and have to settle for our Mittlere Reife next year. We are not destined for university; we are destined to be Hausfrauen or go on to apprenticeships and work to support our families.

It is not something we discuss in front of Geli. As an officer's daughter, she's expected to be in Gymnasium; she speaks French, English, and Latin fluently. Yet every time she mentions her school she does it with a frown on her face, and I've seen the glances Renate and Minna give each other when she does so.

Doesn't she know we'd kill for such an opportunity?

Doesn't she know *I* would?

"I wish Mama would push an apprenticeship on me," Renate

says after a moment. "Though I doubt she will, once she finds out."

"Finds out what?" Minna asks, looking at her with wide eyes. Renate bites her lip.

"I'm not coming back to school in the fall," she says. "With the two of you."

"What?!" Minna and I cry in unison, and Renate juts out her chin.

"You know I've never liked school," she says. "I'm not—not good at science like you and Minna, or art like Charlie. It's just—it's pointless. We all know what kind of job I'm going to get when I leave, even if Mama thinks I'll be staying home otherwise. What's the point of even getting a Mittlere Reife? It's not like I want to sit at a desk all day. Plus, trying to concentrate with this . . ." She tugs on her left earlobe. She can barely hear out of that ear due to a childhood fever but tries to hide it as best she can. More than once I've had to cover for her during our BDM meetings. If they knew, she wouldn't be allowed back.

"But you can't just—you can't just quit," I say, and Renate sighs.

"There's no point in struggling through another year for me, Charlie," she says. "Besides, I'll be happier this way."

"Your mama isn't going to like that," Minna says.

"Mama doesn't like anything I do that isn't related to staying home and becoming a Hausfrau," Renate says sourly. "She should be glad I'm working; Hans won't send any money back from his labor service, and Papa can't work." She shakes her head. "But she doesn't think it's proper for a girl to enter the workforce. The only things I should be doing are staying home, learning how to cook and clean and make babies." She makes a face. "Not like that last one's difficult—"

"Renate!" Minna gasps and throws a pillow at her. Renate catches it and tosses it to me, grinning. It hits my chest with a *thwump*, and I'm about to throw it back at her when the door bursts open and Greta, Ruth, and Rebekah come flying in, all talking as quickly as a waterfall.

"Fritz won't let us play," Rebekah says, pouting. Greta tugs on her arm.

"We don't need him anyway," she says bossily, but the other two girls shake their heads. They're their own little group, the three of them, though Greta's more the ringleader than the others.

"They're being obnoxious," Fritz says, coming up behind the girls, who squeal and run farther into Renate's room. His dark hair is shorter than Renate's, though not by much, and shaved on the sides. He's already in his uniform, a smaller copy of Hans. The sight of him in it makes me uneasy; he looks much older than he is, a miniature soldier. "They keep bothering me about my records, but they're *mine*."

"Fritz, just let them listen to one," Hans's voice calls from the hallway. "And besides, they're mine anyway."

"Records?" I ask, thinking of my father's own records, tucked somewhere in my parents' bedroom, the music from last night.

"You can't listen to them either," Fritz says to me.

"I wasn't . . ."

"Fritz, don't be rude," Renate says. His scowl deepens further.

"Fine," he says. "We can listen to something, but *I'm* picking the music."

"As long as you let one of the girls pick something after," Renate calls after him, but he's already disappeared down the hallway, the twins trailing after him.

"If Fritz is mean again, we're coming back in here," Greta says to me. She looks up at Minna. "Can you do my hair before we go?"

"Of course, Greta," Minna says. "Go change and I'll do it now, all right?"

Greta beams at her and hurries off. I bite my lip, look at my friends. Here would be a good opening to tell them about the music, the club, the freedom. Geli wanted me to tell them tonight, and I could ask Renate if Fritz has any jazz records.

But I think of the warmth that filled my chest when Geli initially invited me, saying she wanted it to be just for the two of us. And I don't want to let go of that feeling, not yet.

Greta bounds back into the room then, changed into her

uniform. Her blouse, though it's one of my old ones, is clean and starched; her skirt neatly hemmed. Seeing her in it, much like seeing Fritz, causes a knot to form in my stomach, one I won't be able to easily undo like my stitches.

But her hair is still loose, and that, at least, makes her look more like my little sister and not a girl about to enter the JM.

Greta sits on the floor, craning her neck to look at the three of us as Minna begins to braid her hair into two plaits.

"Hold still, Greta," I say, and she sticks her tongue out at me before turning back around. The four of us sit in silence until another knock sounds on the door, and it opens to reveal Frau Hoffmann. I watch her take in the scene, her face much sharper than my mother's, far more angular and hard, though I think between the two of them Mama is the stricter one. Fritz takes after Frau Hoffmann; Renate and Hans, with their large, wide-set brown eyes, look more like their father.

"Hallo, Frau Hoffmann," Minna and I chorus, and Renate laughs and covers her mouth. Her mother glances at her before turning back to us.

"Charlotte, Wilhelmine," she says, and both of us grimace at the use of our full names. "Charlie, you look nice. Renate, why haven't you done anything with your hair?"

"Oh, what am I going to do with it?" Renate says sourly. "It's too short to braid."

Frau Hoffmann sighs. "But you're almost ready, yes?"

"Yes," Renate says. "I think so."

"And you, Greta?" she asks, just as Minna finishes the last of Greta's hair. Greta stands slowly, turning so Frau Hoffmann can see her uniform.

"You look lovely," she says, and Greta beams. "You're going to do fine this evening."

"Danke, Frau Hoffmann," Greta says, and runs out of the room.

"Don't mess up your hair!" I call after her, but she's already gone. Renate's mother lets out a small laugh before turning back to us.

"Minna, would you and your family like to join us after the ceremony? We're all heading to the Aschinger at Alexanderplatz. I know the twins can't be inducted"—her mouth twists at these words—"but if you and your family would care to join us, you're welcome to."

"Oh," Minna says. "I'll . . . I'll ask Mama. But thank you, I appreciate the gesture."

"Of course, Minna. You're family," Frau Hoffmann says, and Minna smiles for a moment before her face falls, her eyes once again flicking to me and Renate.

"I should go," she says, standing and collecting her bags, her curly chestnut hair falling in waves down her back. "But— danke, Frau Hoffmann. We'll meet you at the restaurant at eight if we decide to come."

"I'll walk you down to your flat," Frau Hoffmann says, to my surprise, and she and Minna leave.

I turn to Renate. "What's that about?"

"What's what?"

"Your mother walking Minna back to her flat. She lives just below you."

Renate frowns. "She started doing it last week. I think she's just being cautious, though who knows with Mama. I'm sure Herr Neumann is none too pleased with it."

I think of Herr Neumann, lingering outside the Kochs' door. "I . . . I saw him today," I say, the words coming slowly. "I mean, when Greta and I arrived. He looked like he was just cleaning outside their door, but something about it—"

"I know what you mean," Renate cuts in. "Mama's noticed it, too. Maybe that's why she walks Minna back sometimes."

"But isn't it dangerous for—for her, to be walking Minna back, then? If Herr Neumann is . . ." I trail off. If he's what? Listening in? Spying?

"More dangerous for Mama, or for Minna?" Renate asks, but she doesn't let me answer. Instead she stands, deliberately turning her left side toward me so I can't interrogate her about it further.

Renate's words echo in my head as we walk. But the closer we draw to the building, the more they're punctuated with thoughts of Geli. Of how she looked last night, of the excitement of seeing her again so soon. Greta walks beside me, her own brow furrowed in thought.

"What if I forget everything, Charlie?" she asks as we round the corner to the building where the induction ceremony is being held, joining the streams of families heading inside, their children in uniforms identical to our own.

"You won't, Gretchen," I say, and she nods, though she doesn't look entirely convinced.

"Is Renate mad at you?" she asks.

"Ich weiß nicht," I say. I smooth my hand over her braids, try to smile down at her. "But let's just—let's just forget it for now, all right? You know how Renate's temper is. She'll have forgotten all about this by the time we end up at Aschinger."

Greta nods again and we head inside.

As soon as we enter the building, Greta leaves my side to go huddle with the other girls in her Jungmädelschaft. Unlike our normal meetings, tonight's induction ceremony includes groups from all of Kreuzberg. The sight of so many people makes me think of the club last night, but where that was a swirl of haze and color, here the dizzying effect comes from the sea of black and brown and white cloth.

I immediately look around for Geli, scanning the crowd of sour expressions on pale faces. She's easy to spot, even without her usual makeup. Her hair is pulled back and tightly braided, her lips their regular pink color. She sinks her teeth into them occasionally when no one is looking. She stands next to her father, a man I have only met on a few occasions, despite the fact that I've known Geli since we were small. His hand is firm on her shoulder.

I wonder if he braided her hair. And if he didn't, who did, if it was her stepmother, Mathilde, or one of her father's servants.

My palms sweat, and I resist the urge to wipe them on my skirt. I want her to see me. Will her to see me. Like two connecting points on a map.

"Angelika!" I say, but my throat is dry. Somehow, she hears me anyway, and her head turns toward me. Her face lights up in a smile that makes my insides twist.

"Charlie—Charlotte!" she says at a stern glance from Liesl. She does not bound over to me like she normally does, but instead walks over calmly before pulling me into a tight hug.

Over her shoulder, I watch the Hitlerjugend boys eye her, their glances sliding over her body like water.

I tell myself the tightness in my chest is because these boys do not look at me the same way, but that is a lie.

"Hallo," I say, and she pulls back, studying me.

"You look lovely. Where's Greta?"

"With the other girls. Let me—" I begin, but am stopped by Frau Köhler clapping her hands to bring us all in line.

"If the girls will follow me, the parents can take their seats in the auditorium," she begins. Her eyes rove over our entire group, and even the HJ boys snap to attention at her gaze, though they have their own group leader to follow. Once the parents have gone, she gives all of us a quick nod of her head.

"Heil Hitler," she says, her voice ringing out, and automatically our arms snap up, our voices repeating the words back to her. A unified voice for a unified Germany.

Except we aren't unified, not really. If we were, Minna and her sisters would be allowed to join. If we were, Renate wouldn't have to hide her disability. I glance around to see the pride on so many faces I have known since childhood.

God, this used to be comforting. The sameness, knowing exactly where I fit. But as we begin our march into the auditorium, our voices singing the same song about putting the flag above everything we do, all I can compare it to is the chaotic freedom of last night. The orderliness and precision with which we march rather than the enthusiastic flailing of the night before. The music, dull and monotonous, with a strict, slow rhythm rather than fast-tempo chaos. Tonight, more than usual, I can feel the watchful gaze of the Party in everything we do.

Tonight, the emblems on my uniform don't feel like a badge of belonging, but a threat.

We march into the auditorium in precise rows, like we practiced. Take our seats with our respective groups. The boys will be inducted first, then the Jungmädel, and then the older girls who will be joining our group. For this ceremony, there's nothing much for me, Renate, and Geli to do except sit and watch our siblings. I catch Greta's eye from across the rows. She's twisting her braids around her fingers, but when she notices me, she stops and sits up, her back ramrod straight.

The mayor of Kreuzberg stands and starts giving a speech, and beside me, Renate frowns slightly, tilting her right ear ever so slightly toward him. I reach over and squeeze her hand. She looks down between us, startled, but squeezes mine back.

The mayor continues talking about how our families should be proud of us, of our service to our country. Across the stage from us I see Fritz hanging on the mayor's every word, nearly identical to the boys surrounding him, so much so that if I didn't know him well, I would not be able to pick him out from the crowd. A few rows behind him sits Hans, his own face drawn.

"This is a time to be proud of our youth," the mayor repeats, thumping his chest for emphasis, his voice echoing through the auditorium. "Our youth are the future of Germany, and as the young people here today have shown us so well: there is no shame in being a German!"

He finishes speaking to a roar of applause from the crowd. I go to clap, but look over again at the boys, ready and willing for a whispered-about war that some of them hope comes to pass, at the girls by my side, preparing to be perfect mothers with no ambitions beyond that. I think again of Minna, of the other Jewish girls in my class, the way our teachers sometimes look at them, singled out on days the rest of us are allowed to wear our BDM uniforms to school, and I wonder if the mayor might be wrong.

For the rest of the ceremony, I only watch Greta, trying to distract myself from the unease building in my stomach each time one of the younger girls takes her oath. I study the pride on Greta's face as if it is a map I can memorize, and when she finally stands up to take her own oath as a Jungmädel, I have to look away. I try to think about the club, about the music, but it feels even hazier now, here in the chill of the auditorium.

It feels an entire world away.

When the ceremony ends, I immediately go to find Greta in the crowd of parents and girls gushing about how smart the boys look in their uniforms. She's one of the smaller girls, so it takes me a minute to locate her, but I finally find her standing by Geli, already at the center of a wave of chattering girls. Greta looks up at Geli with wide eyes, hanging on her every word.

Of course. Greta wants her time with Geli just as much as I do.

"Charlie, did you see me?" Greta asks as I push my way through the knot of other girls to get to them.

"Of course, Gretchen," I say. "You did great."

"Geli, did *you* see me?" Greta asks, turning now to Geli, who kneels down so she's eye level with my sister.

"Natürlich," she says. "I couldn't miss you. You were the prettiest one up there."

At Geli's praise, my sister beams, and I have to shake my head. We aren't so different when it comes to Geli, my sister and I.

Geli stands and Greta takes off running before I can admonish her not to, most likely to find our parents. Geli leans in close to me, her hair tickling my face.

"Did you get to tell the others about the club?"

"N-not yet," I say, and her face falls slightly. I hurry on, desperate for her not to be disappointed in me. "But I will—after school. Next week. Or . . . or you can."

She frowns. "I think—"

But I do not get to hear what she thinks, because then there is a hand on her shoulder, and a loud Berlin accent, so different from my father's own musical Bayrisch one.

"Fräulein Kraus," the man says, and it's Geli's father. He's dressed in the black uniform of a high-ranking SS officer, his blond hair combed back. He has the same blue eyes as Geli, but where hers are a summer sky, his are ice. "I don't believe I've had the pleasure of seeing you around our house lately."

"No, sir," I say, inclining my head a little. "I've been—busy. With school."

"Ah, yes," he says. "You're finishing Gymnasium next year with Angelika, I assume?"

Heat floods my face. "I'm not . . . I'm not in a Gymnasium, sir."

Herr Haas's brow furrows, just for a second, so quickly I almost miss it. "Of course," he continues smoothly. "I assume you'll be looking for an apprenticeship, then, Fräulein Kraus?"

"Yes, sir," I say. "I . . . in sewing," I add, because this is the type of activity that would please a man like Herr Haas. I say nothing about art.

"Sewing," he repeats. "But certainly you will be learning from a good German tailor, yes?"

I swallow, surprised at the small rush of anger I feel, but will myself not to show it. I know what he means, but I cannot talk back to a man like Herr Haas. I cannot tell him that the best German tailors I know are also Jewish, so I just bite my tongue. What I say wouldn't matter, anyway.

"Your seamstress work will serve you well as a wife, Fräulein Kraus," he continues, "once your apprenticeship is finished. My daughter should be more like you, instead of wasting my money at that Gymnasium."

"Charlotte would do well in a Gymnasium, though," Geli says quickly. "She's smarter than I am."

"Smarter than an officer's daughter?" Herr Haas says, his voice dripping sarcasm, and Geli quickly turns her head away.

"N-natürlich nicht," I say. "Angelika's just—just being

modest, sir. She's a much better student than I am." I will my voice not to crack with jealousy as I say it. I cannot look at Geli.

"Of course," Herr Haas agrees. "Or she would be, if she didn't spend her time chasing after boys."

"Papa," Geli hisses, and his fingers tighten on her shoulder. She gives me a wan smile, but it doesn't reach her eyes. I smile back.

My father would never have said such a thing about me, even if I did speak to boys. Geli's attention shifts to something over my shoulder before landing back on me.

"Well," she says, her voice high, falsely bright. "I'll see you tomorrow, then, Charlotte?" She squeezes my hand, and before I can react she turns on her heel; her father follows, perfect-looking Germans in their uniforms, the both of them.

I feel a hand brush my arm, and I turn. Renate stands next to me.

"What did Herr Haas want?" she asks.

"I don't know," I say. She nods, and I continue. "Geli's father, he's just—he makes me feel—" I begin, and then stop myself. She's turned her head, and I realize—I'm on her left side.

She didn't realize I was still talking.

The Hoffmanns and my family walk out of the BDM building soon after, calling goodbyes over our shoulders to the other families. I pretend not to notice as Renate's father grips the rail

44

of the stairs on his way down, his limp more pronounced than usual. Renate says he refuses to carry a cane out in public, that he's too stubborn.

"We are taking the U-Bahn to Aschinger, yes?" Frau Hoffmann says loudly, looking pointedly at her husband. "And the Kochs are meeting us there."

"Yes," Renate says, at the same time Fritz exclaims, "I can walk," equally as loud as his mother. "Hans and I can walk."

Renate glances at me, rolls her eyes. Whatever awkwardness was between us before the ceremony, it's gone now.

"*You* can walk," Hans says, which earns a laugh from the parents. "I'm taking the U-Bahn. My feet are sore enough from marching."

The nine of us make our way down into the station before crowding into a train car, and I look away as Frau Hoffmann makes sure her husband gets a seat. Renate and I find ourselves crammed in together, Renate at the window and Greta squished standing next to me.

"Thank goodness it's a short ride," I say.

"I don't like being underground," Renate responds, her mouth turned down. "I wish we'd just taken the S-Bahn; it's better than this."

"There's no direct S-Bahn line to Alexanderplatz from here," I say.

Renate smiles. "You would know that, you and your maps."

"I like to know where I'm going," I respond. "Is that wrong?"

"No," she says. "No, it isn't. Have you finished Greta's present yet?"

"Present?" Greta says, because of course she heard us.

"Yes, Greta—here," I say, and pull the completed map out of my bag. "You can look at it now, but let me keep it until we get home, all right? I want to make sure the charcoal doesn't smudge."

Greta takes the paper from my hands and frowns down at it. Her face lights up in recognition once she realizes what it is.

"It's a map!" she says. "Oh, from our house to the BDM meetings—thank you, Charlie," she says, genuine excitement in her voice.

"So you don't get lost." I say.

"I won't get lost. I'll follow you and Geli," she states.

"Yes, but just in case—" I gently take the map from her, trace the route with my finger as she watches. "You see? You see clearly where it's going, don't you?"

"Yes," she says. "I do. I'll take it tomorrow after school and walk the route. It's a nice present, thank you," she says, and I tuck the map back into my bag.

"I don't understand how you keep all of that in your head," Renate says, and I'm about to answer her when a voice crackles through the subway car announcing that we've reached our stop.

But here is what I do not get to say: I do not have all of the city in my head, not the whole vast expanse of Berlin. Only the parts that are important to me.

Only the ones that matter.

We emerge from underground blinking in the glare of the streetlights; the noise of the streets and people startling after the mechanical clanking of the subway car.

"There it is," Greta calls, and runs ahead of us, acting like she's never seen the restaurant before, even though we go to the one in Kreuzberg regularly. We hardly ever venture out to this part of Berlin, though; neither of my parents want to ride the U-Bahn in the evenings after my father gets home from work; and even though the food is cheap, it's not enough to justify the cost of a trip into the city when we can walk to the one right by our house.

But tonight is a special occasion, and thank goodness Aschinger is cheap, because there are nine of us to feed.

No, ten—waiting at the entrance is Minna, her hair pulled back into two low braids, in a plain green plaid dress that might have once belonged to her mother. She hugs us when she sees us, me first, then Renate.

"Your parents didn't want to come?" Renate asks.

Minna shakes her head. "No, Mama said if it was just me, I'd—I'd draw less attention." She smiles tightly. "Which is a shame. I know she loves the food here."

Draw less attention?

But I don't have time to ask Minna what she means, because Greta begins waving us all down, having already gone in and found a table near the back large enough for all of us to be able to sit and talk with each other. I take a seat, making sure to save the outside one for Renate so her good ear is turned toward the conversation.

"Danke," she says to me as she sits. The adults order steins of beer, as do Hans, Renate, Minna, and I. Fritz tries to, insisting that he's old enough.

"I don't see why you want to. It's disgusting," Greta says to him, which sets the adults laughing.

"I'm a man now," he says, puffing out his chest, his uniform starched and crisp. His declaration causes the adults to laugh again, but a knot forms in my stomach at his words as I remember the ceremony, all those boys prepared to be soldiers, and I look away.

"You can just have some of mine, Fritz," Hans says, and slides the glass to him. Fritz drinks, then promptly makes a face, which Greta laughs at. He scowls at her.

The waiter brings our orders and we lapse into silence, mouths full of pea soup and sausages. Greta eyes my potato soup suspiciously. I pluck a piece of Wurst out of it and wave it at her, which sets her to giggling.

"Charlotte," my mother hisses, and I quickly pop the Wurst into my mouth. "Behave."

I duck my head. The table quiets down again, the chatter around us dying down as everyone focuses on eating.

Until.

There's shouting from a table behind us, and all ten of us turn instinctively, watching as two SS officers haul a man up by his elbows.

"I have a right to eat here," the man says, his voice carrying. "I am a German, I have a right to—"

A sharp crack resounds through the air, the impact of skin on skin, as the man resists being dragged out of the restaurant. The commotion grows, and Fritz and Hans push back from our table to go help the officers, Fritz almost tripping in his haste to get there.

There's a hard pressure on my hand, and I look down. Greta's squeezing it, her eyes filled with tears.

"They're hurting him," she says, her voice thick, and I turn, thinking she means Fritz, or Hans. But Fritz and Hans are fine. Fritz is right next to one of the officers, trying to insert himself into the scuffle. Hans hangs back, his expression unreadable. It's the man who's hurt, his nose now bleeding profusely, dripping down his shirt.

"They're hurting him," she cries again, and I hold her to me, bury her face in my chest so she does not have to look, so I do not have to look, my hands clutching her hair.

"Shh, Greta, it's all right, they're leading him out now," I whisper. "Everything's fine, yes? They're just going to lead him out of the restaurant, there's no need to be upset." I look around the table desperately, but the adults are all too busy staring toward the commotion. Only Minna catches my eye, her face white, her teeth working into her bottom lip. She starts to say something but stops herself, instead picking up her cutlery and turning her attention back to her plate. She looks, if possible, even more upset than Greta does, and it takes me a moment to figure out why.

The man they're forcing out of the restaurant is Jewish.

The reality of the situation then makes me shiver, and as I look at Minna, what she said earlier comes back to me, about her mother saying she'd "draw less attention" if she was the only one to join us here.

If Minna wasn't with us right now, would the same thing have happened to her? If the rest of the Kochs had joined us, would they all have been forced out of the restaurant while we watched? Would Fritz have jumped up so eagerly to help the officers?

That same anger that I felt when Herr Haas mentioned "good German tailors" comes rushing back, but this time it's mixed with helplessness because I do not know the answers to the questions swimming around in my head; I do not know how to fix this.

Hans and Fritz reappear at the table, their shirts mussed

but otherwise fine. Fritz goes to smooth back his hair and I see a smear of blood on the sleeve of his shirt.

I look away.

We make the trip home in silence, wave goodbye to the Hoffmanns at the entrance to their building. Frau Hoffmann's arm hovers protectively around Minna, who looks simultaneously grateful and annoyed.

I look at Minna. I want to say something to her to comfort her, to reassure her, but any words I could try to say feel inadequate, sticking themselves in my throat. If the situation were reversed, she'd know the exact thing to say to comfort me, and I hate that I cannot do the same for her.

But what could I say with my parents around, with Renate's parents around? Minna is my friend, but my parents have never openly talked about how they feel about the Party. I want to hope they wouldn't mind me comforting her, but I don't know for certain. I settle for hugging her and Renate to me tightly, hoping that is enough to convey how I feel.

"I'll . . . I'll see you both tomorrow?" I ask them as I pull back.

"Yes," Renate says quickly as Minna nods, and Renate kisses me on the cheek before turning back to her family. My parents are quiet as we walk back to our own building, and Greta is, too. It's only once we're behind the doors that anyone even dares to make a sound.

"Gretchen, get ready for bed," Mama says. Greta nods solemnly and runs off to her room. I stand in the kitchen, trying to make myself look useful.

I want to ask them. I want to ask my parents about what happened tonight, about what they thought, because I do not know.

It turns out I do not need to ask.

"You're still friends with Minna," Mama says, and it's not a question. I nod, unsure of where she's going. She purses her lips. "I need you on your best behavior when you go places with her. Even in a group."

"Mama, I'm not going to do anything—"

"Not for you," she says sternly. "For her. She knows this. Her parents know this, but you must not attract any attention when you are out with her, do you understand? And if you do, I want you to take her and run."

"Mama . . ."

"Listen to me, Charlotte," she says, and I glance over at Papa, who nods in agreement. "You must do what I say. What happened tonight—" She shakes her head, lowers her voice to a whisper. She grasps my hands, her nails making half-moons in my skin. "I need you to protect her. I need you to protect Greta, too, verstehst du mich? She is your sister and she looks up to you, and I know she likes to follow you and Angelika, and I know she's friends with the Koch twins, but she is younger than you and she will not understand. I need you to understand for her, and promise me that you will keep them safe."

"Yes, Mama," I say, stunned by the ferocity in her voice. "I will. I promise."

"Good," she says sharply. "If I find out you have done anything to endanger any of them, that will be the end of it for you."

"Ich weiß, Mama," I say. "But I don't understand—"

It is Papa who speaks this time, looking at me hard.

"You will," he says, and he rubs my shoulders, soothing. "Meine Charlotte, you will understand soon enough, I fear." He makes eye contact with Mama over my head. "If the Führer gets his way, I think you will understand very quickly what we are saying. But until then—"

"Until then, you must carry on as if everything is normal," Mama cuts in. "Go to school, go to your meetings, make sure Greta understands her role in the JM." She looks at me. "Sei ein perfektes deutsches Mädchen so they have no reason to think otherwise, yes?"

"Yes," I say, and Papa releases my shoulders. I hurry off to my room and shut the door. My bag thumps against my hip.

Greta's present. I'll give it to her properly in the morning, once I've treated it so it will not smudge. I pull it out, look at the map I've drawn, run my fingers over the lines of it.

If Greta follows these lines, if she follows the route I've set out, then she will be fine. If I follow this line, if I am a perfect German girl like Mama says I am, if I stay in the lines and roles that have been decided for me, then I will be fine.

If I just stay Charlotte instead of Peggy, I'll be fine.

But I think again of the freedom of last night, the music, the color, the breathless feeling of it all, and I know I won't be able to keep my promise to Mama. Not when it comes to that.

Not when it comes to following Geli back there.

I cannot stop thinking about the man in the restaurant. Every free moment over the next few days, the thoughts invade my mind, the sounds. Every time I try to picture what happened after I looked away, the images grow more terrible.

But what could I have done? Gone up there with Hans and Fritz, tried to calm the SS officers down? What could I have even done that would have made any difference?

As I walk home from school with Minna and Renate a week after the restaurant, I want to ask them about it. If they still think about it. If they looked away like I did.

But we've never talked about such things, not as a group. I have never asked Minna how she feels about not being allowed into the BDM. Her being Jewish isn't something we talk about, outside my or Renate's going over for the occasional Shabbos dinner. Geli has never told her family she is friends with Minna, and we all pretend that's fine. We talk around it the same way we talk around Linda Spielmann's bakery closing, how the Waldstein siblings stopped coming to class the summer before last. We talk around it the way we talk around the book burnings, the bright red flags hung out of every window, the signs over businesses proclaiming that their owners are Jewish, warning us not to buy from them.

We have never talked about it, and I don't know if we should, or if Minna would even want to. Certainly we don't talk about such things around Geli.

I wonder, then, if that's why Minna was even invited to dinner the other night—because Geli wouldn't be there. My mother doesn't like Geli, doesn't think I should be friends with an officer's daughter, though more than once, when they thought I couldn't hear, I've heard Papa pointing out to her that it might be good to have a friend whose father is higher up in the Party.

But good for what?

Geli and her friendship are worth it to me, always have been, but for the first time a sour taste fills my mouth as I realize that her not being with us *was* the reason Minna was allowed to join all of us at the restaurant.

We're meeting Geli today—her idea—at Café Uhland just a few blocks from our Realschule. She's going to offer to pay for us and we're all going to say no, but we'll let her anyway.

My stomach is in knots as we go to meet her. Not because it's her, but because the four of us haven't gone out in a group since the day before she took me to the club.

And I know she's going to tell both of them about it today, because I haven't. That thought just makes my stomach knot more, because I know deep down she'll be disappointed in me for not telling them, like she was at the induction ceremony.

How do I tell her that I'd wanted to hold on to the feeling of it being just *us*, just a little bit longer? I'm by her side no matter what, but being by her side feels different when it's just the two of us.

In front of me, Renate and Minna walk side by side, heads bent together, Renate laughing at something Minna has said, Minna on her good side. I hoist my satchel higher up my shoulder, wishing Geli were already here so I could walk with her like that. We all get along as a group, certainly, but it's clear that Renate and Minna have each other, in the same way Geli and I do.

"Charlie, are we picking up Greta?" Minna asks.

"Nein," I say. "She's staying after school with some of the other Jungmädeln, I think."

Renate frowns. "What?"

Minna repeats what I said, and Renate sighs. "Gott, just don't let her be like Fritz. I swear, even before he got inducted, he was hanging around Hans's HJ group all the time."

"I don't think she's going to do that, unless it's just to follow Geli around," I say, and Renate rolls her eyes.

"Of course she'll follow Geli," she says. "Why wouldn't she?"

I frown. I want to ask her what she means by that, but a voice cuts in before I get the chance.

"Why wouldn't who what?" someone asks, and then Geli's standing in front of us. She doesn't look like she just came from school; she looks like she came from a department store, her hair in perfect ringlets and her lips a bright pink. I have to remind myself not to stare.

"Nothing," Renate says, smirking. "You look nice."

"Oh, this?" Geli says, and turns so her skirt flares. Renate rolls her eyes as Geli falls into step beside us and we continue our walk to the café. By the time we arrive, the wind is blowing so hard our cheeks are flushed from the cold. A few officers stand outside the entrance to the café, giving us a once-over as we enter. I try not to shiver at their glances. Geli blows them a kiss, laughing, before Renate grabs her elbow and hauls her inside.

We order coffees and hot chocolates, Minna and I glancing between each other while Renate tries to catch the attention of the boy behind the counter—Herr Rubel's son Joachim, four years older than us at nineteen. He's polite enough to Renate when she orders, but his eyes drift to Geli.

It makes that hot feeling burn in my chest again, the one I felt at the Tanzpalast last week when I saw her dancing with Tommy.

I turn to talk to Minna, to distract myself, only to see she's already studying me. A blush crawls up my cheeks, and she smiles and nudges my knee with hers, her calm energy steadying me while Renate and Geli engage in some sort of discussion without us.

"You look like you're thinking about something," Minna says.

"I'm always thinking about something."

"What're you thinking about?"

I look around the table. I'm thinking about the other night in the restaurant, because it won't leave my head. Mama's warning. The blood on Fritz's sleeve. The man being thrown out, all because he was Jewish.

"Greta," I confess, and Minna raises an eyebrow. "She's so excited about the Jungmädel."

Minna nods, but she frowns ever so slightly.

"I'm sorry the twins can't join," I say to her quietly.

Minna shakes her head. "Mama doesn't want them to, anyway; says she's glad I'm not in it."

"Is she?"

"She doesn't want it filling their heads with ideas," Minna says, but the corners of her mouth are tight, and I want to ask her more about it, but the way she glances around the café tells me it's not the right time.

My fingers tighten on my coffee cup as I glance around the table. Geli is telling a story, her face bright and animated, Renate cutting in with questions. Their banter is reminiscent of our families at dinner the other night, and for a second, my chest tightens with that fear that something will happen again.

But we're fine. The café is small, and the SA guards are only outside, and Minna is with us. We're fine. We're safe.

I turn my attention back to Renate and Geli, fully arguing now.

"Das ist nicht wahr," Renate scoffs at something Geli says.

"Doch," Geli protests, and she laughs, which earns another scowl from Renate. "It is absolutely true. You can ask Charlie." She turns to me, that mischievous smile playing at the corners of her lips.

"Isn't it true, Charlie?" she asks, her eyes shining. "The club, the place I took you? It's true, isn't it?"

My voice falters in my throat. I knew she was going to tell them today, I knew it. I search her expression, wondering if she's disappointed with me. But if she is, she doesn't show it.

"Yes," I say. "It's true."

"So the SS just lets a room full of teens dance to verbotener Musik?" Renate asks.

"I don't think they know about it," I say, looking to Geli, who nods.

"No. They don't know about it."

Renate presses her lips together. "I still think you're lying," she says to Geli, whose eyes flash.

I place a hand on Renate's arm. "She's not lying, Renate. I went with her. It was—there was music and dancing and everyone was so—so loose and free. It was—it was fun," I say. I try to think of more, to think of something to tell them that will do the dance hall justice. "The music was so loud you could feel it, and everyone was dancing like they didn't care about anything, and it was—honestly, it was magical."

At my words, Geli catches my eye and smiles, and my face heats up.

"That does sound magical," Minna says, sighing. She rests her chin in her hands. "Renate, you have to admit it does."

"You're going to love it," I tell Renate sincerely, nudging her with my shoulder. "Wirklich. I think you'll really like the music. It's loud enough it vibrates through your whole body." She starts to smile, and I know I've won her over.

"Fine," she says, and looks at Geli. "When is it?"

"In two weeks. Friday. I know they're playing at some cellar near the Zoo."

Minna frowns. "Geli, I can't do Fridays. . . ."

"Just this once, Minna," Geli insists. "I don't always know where or when they're going to meet, so we have to do this one."

Minna sighs, but I know she'll give in. None of us say no to Geli—why would we? When she's the one with the ideas, the plans, the one who will take us to exciting, forbidden places?

"Please, you'll love it," Geli adds, then she leans in even farther. "Don't you want to be somewhere where there isn't a target on your back?"

"Geli," Renate hisses, and Minna's eyes dart around the café. "Not here, bitte."

Geli huffs, but even she knows Renate's right. "Of course," she says. She takes another sip of her coffee and sets it down, her bright red lipstick marking the rim. "So that's settled. Friday, two weeks from now. Charlie and I can get ready together, right, Charlie?" she asks, and relief runs through me as I nod, because she's found a way for it to just be the two of us for a little while still. "And then we can meet the two of you at your building. Wear something fun," she adds, and Renate and I look down at our clothes and sigh, before making eye contact with each other and bursting into laughter.

Mai 1938

THE TWO weeks before we go to the club crawl along like ants. We sit through exams, quizzing each other on English and math when we can. By the time Friday night finally rolls around, we're all desperate for the break. I tell Mama we are all going to the cinema together.

"On a Friday?" she asks. "Is Minna coming?"

I pause, but only for a second, her warning from two weeks ago still fresh in my mind. "No," I say. "It's just me and Renate and Geli." Guilt twists in my stomach at the lie, but I let it go. If she thought Minna was coming with us, I'd get another lecture.

And if she knew where we were *actually* going . . .

"Can Geli stay after?" I ask Mama, and she sighs, but relents. Perhaps she knows I need to be with my friends, though maybe she's just too tired to argue with me.

Geli and I are supposed to meet Minna and Renate at their building at half eight, late enough that the party should be in full swing by the time we arrive.

Geli told me she would be at mine around six. But by half seven, she still hasn't shown up, and I pace around nervously. When there's finally a knock on the door, I rush to open it before Mama or Papa does.

"You're late," I admonish Geli, but one look at her face tells me not to press it. Her eyes are red-rimmed, as if she's been crying. I quickly pull her to my room.

"What happened?" I ask as I shut my bedroom door. She shakes her head, sits down on the edge of my bed. It's only then that I notice she's lacking her usual makeup, a bird without plumage. "Geli?"

She pulls a handkerchief out of her pocket and blows her nose into it. I wait until she is finished before I ask her again.

"Geli, what's wrong?"

"Nothing's wrong," she says, falsely bright. "Gar nichts, Charlie."

She almost sounds convincing.

Almost.

"What did he say?" I ask, and her face darkens, just for a moment. Only a few times before has Geli come crying to me, usually because of something her father has said.

"Charlie, it's not—"

But I grip her hand, look her in the eyes.

"You said you wouldn't lie to me," I say. "Remember? You

said, the first time you told me, that you were never going to lie to me. And Geli, if—if you don't want to go out tonight, we can just stay in, just me and you, whatever you want, but don't—don't lie to me, bitte," I say.

She nods. "He saw I was getting ready to go out. Asked if I would leave looking like—wie eine *Hure* aus," she says, her voice tight. "And he took my lipsticks—well, Mathilde's lipsticks—and hid them I don't know where, and I spent an hour looking for them after he left and I couldn't find them and—"

Her voice breaks.

"It's stupid, crying over lipstick," she says. "Charlie, you must think I'm dreadfully silly."

"No," I say. "No, Geli, I would never think that."

Her hands are cold, and without thinking I rub them between mine to warm them up. It's been so long since I've seen Geli alone, just the two of us without the other girls or the BDM or a crowd of people around. I study her, this girl I want to follow, and for the first time she just seems . . . like a girl.

Geli swallows, sniffs, then looks at me. "Oh," she says. "While I was—while I was looking for my lipsticks, I found this. Will you keep it for me?" She pulls something small out of her satchel, and it takes me a minute to register what it is. When I realize it, I can hardly believe it.

The cover is worn, the pages yellowed and faded, but the name on the front is unmistakable. It's a copy of Heinrich

Heine's collected poems. My mother's favorite poet—she used to recite "Die Loreley," to me when I was a child, about a woman whose beautiful singing lures men to their deaths—and a Jewish poet whose books have been banned in Germany since 1933.

I do not know if Mama still has her own copy of his works. I never thought to ask, assuming she'd burned them just like everyone else did back then.

"Geli," I breathe. "Where . . ."

"Open the cover," she says, her voice tight as she passes the book to me. In light, spidery handwriting on the first page, I can make out—

Für Ursula. Alles Liebe, Oma.

Ursula. Geli's mother, who died when she was seven. Geli rarely talks about her; her father does even less, considering he remarried less than a year later to Geli's stepmother, Mathilde.

I only knew Ursula briefly, when I was a child. My memories of her must be fainter than Geli's, though I remember she had a beautiful laugh, a strong Viennese accent; that she always smelled like lavender.

"Oh," I whisper. "Where did you find it?"

"Tucked in the back of Mathilde's closet," Geli says. "I don't know why *she* had it, but—can you keep it? Keep it safe for me, Charlie, please? If Papa finds it, he'll burn it for sure, and I don't—I don't want that."

"Of course," I say. "I'll keep it for you Geli, natürlich. Don't worry."

"Maybe I can read you some of my favorites," she says. "Tonight. When we—when we come back from the party."

"Oh," I say.

"Or not—it's a ridiculous thought—" she begins, but I stop her.

"No, no, it isn't. I'd—I'd love to hear them, really."

The smile she gives me could light me up from the inside. I will do anything to have her look at me that way, like I'm special, like I'm someone important.

This is the Geli I love, this side no one else gets to see. The shy, thoughtful girl who reads romantic poetry, who isn't above showing enthusiasm about things she likes.

"There's one in here," she says, taking the book and flipping through it, "that I think I remember Mama reading—or maybe I just wish she did, but it's my name, look." She runs her finger down the text until I see it—*Angélique*.

"Not exactly my name," she says quickly, "but the prettier version, I think."

"I think your name is lovely," I say, the words falling out of my mouth before I can stop them. Geli looks at me, smiling softly.

"Thanks, Charlie," she says, and bends her head close to mine, her soft voice reading out Heine's words.

Ich sag ihr nicht, weshalb ich's tu
Weiß selber nicht den Grund—
Ich halte ihr die Augen zu
Und küß sie auf den Mund.
I don't tell her the reason why
I hardly know myself—
Yet still I cover up her eyes
And kiss her on the mouth.

She finishes the rest of the stanza and I find myself blushing, my face hot. Does she know? What she's reading to me? A poem about love, about someone kissing a woman without fully knowing why—and worse, a poem that almost uses her name. Does she think about the implications of such things?

Does she know how I feel about her?

"It's—it's beautiful," I stammer, my heart racing. She presses the book into my hands and for a moment I'm afraid to take it, afraid that if I do, she'll suddenly realize how I feel, and I don't know if I want her to know just yet or if I want whatever is between us to stay in that hopeful space of almost-possible.

But I clutch the book to my chest and she leans back, and when her eyes meet mine, there's no hint of knowing, nothing that would suggest she has any idea how I feel, and I cannot tell if I'm relieved or disappointed.

"Learn it for me, Charlie, bitte," she says. "The whole thing, memorized."

"Memorized?"

"Mutti used to say you should always carry some poetry around in your head," Geli says. "To pull out for difficult times. And I want *you*"—she points at me, her finger pressing into my chest—"to memorize that entire poem for me."

"The entire poem," I repeat. I flip through it. It's long, eight or nine parts with at least two or three stanzas each.

"I already carry maps in my head," I say, trying to joke. "Poetry won't fit. . . ."

"Charlotte," Geli says, and she looks at me again, in that serious way I so rarely see, the way that shows me she wants me to listen to her, really *listen* to her. "I wouldn't ask if it wasn't important." She reaches out and, before I can move, presses her palm to my cheek.

I stop breathing.

"Okay," I finally say, and she smiles. "Okay."

Half an hour later we are ready for the club. Geli has borrowed one of my lipsticks, a brick color more subtle than her normal bright red, and looks more beautiful than I ever have wearing it. Mama glances at us on the way out, one eyebrow raised, her warning from the other week to be careful still burning in my thoughts.

I will try, I think, but it is hard to think of being careful when all I want to do is be brave for Geli. It's hard to think of being careful when Minna, of all of us, has been the most excited about this week, talking about what she thinks the dance hall will be like in between studying for our exams.

If she's excited, that means I don't need to worry. Even if I did lie to Mama that she wasn't coming with us—it was more to stop Mama worrying than me.

We meet up with Minna and Renate at the street corner by their flat. Minna looks graceful and elegant in a dark plaid skirt with her shirt untucked, loose on her willowy frame. Renate, to my surprise, is wearing a pair of Hans's pants and suspenders.

"I can dance fine in this," she snaps when Geli opens her mouth to say something. But instead, Geli beams at her.

"No, it's wonderful. They'll like it—you should see some of the boys there, hair longer than mine!"

"I don't know how I'll see the boys if they're all talking to you," Renate grumbles, but Geli pretends not to hear her.

The four of us walk down the street, our arms linked. Again I remember what Mama said about Minna, about watching out for her, and instinctively pull her closer to me. Her hip bumps my waist; she is that much taller than I am.

"Are you excited?" I ask her quietly as we make our way down the sidewalk.

"Yes," she says. "It's been so long since I've been out somewhere like this, I can't wait." She squeezes my hand. "You'll have to show me how to dance, Charlie."

"I think you'll be better at it than I am," I say, and she laughs.

We crowd down into the U-Bahn so we can ride to Kurfürstendamm. Geli hasn't told me the exact place, saying she wants it to be a secret, but as we ride in darkness, I'm already picturing the turns and twists of the street, the way I will map this out to give to her.

The night air is cold in our lungs when we exit at our stop. We walk for only a few minutes before Geli stops at a building and opens a door leading down to a cellar, a far cry from the glitzy Delphi Tanzpalast she brought me to last time, which sits just across the street. Music swells up the stairs. "Do you hear it?" she asks excitedly.

Renate scrunches up her nose in concentration. "Barely," she says. "Geli . . ."

"Oh," Geli cuts in. "That's right, I forgot—we need English names here. Well. You two need English names. Charlie and I already picked ours," she says, and squeezes my hand.

"But why—"

"Just pick one, Renate," Geli says, already sighing in exasperation. "Come on, it's fun. Get into the spirit of it. Or I'll pick one for you," she threatens, and Renate sighs.

"Fine. June," she says after a moment. "Like the month."

"June," Geli says, nodding her head approvingly. "What about you, Minna?"

"Shirley," Minna says. "Like Shirley Temple."

"Oh, that's perfect for you," Renate gushes, and Minna

beams. Shirley Temple's movies made their way over here last year, and while we'd scoffed at the naïveté and childishness of them, we'd all gone to the cinema to see them at least twice, if only to say we'd seen something all the way from Hollywood.

"Okay," Geli says, facing us, her eyes wide and bright. "Are you ready?"

We look at her. It hits me then, the true feeling of freedom in what we are about to do, the excitement on my friends' faces mirrored, I'm sure, on my own. There is no hesitancy, not from me, not tonight. I will follow Geli down into this basement, music and freedom filling my body, and dance and laugh until my feet are sore and try not to think about what it means that I am finding this freedom secretly and underground and cannot carry it back up into the real world with me.

I look at her, that music filling my ears, and I know I will follow her anywhere.

The cellar is already full by the time we enter, and we toss our coats onto the heap by the door. Minna and Renate clutch my hands, and I watch them take it in, the expressions on their faces as awe-filled as mine was at the Delphi, even though this room is far less grand.

Truth be told, I am still awestruck, by all of it. By the noise, the smoke, the whirl of skirts and bodies and Geli, always Geli.

"Swing Heil!" a boy shouts at us, and I shout it back, fearless, raising my arm in that mocking salute. Renate stares at me for a moment like she cannot believe what she sees, but Minna looks at me with immediate delight.

"Swing Heil!" she shouts into the room and is greeted by a chorus of cheers back. As Geli disappears into the crowd, Minna sways a little to the music before her attention focuses on someone nearby.

"Oh!" she exclaims. "I know him! That's Werner Hirsch. He goes to my synagogue." She smiles and waves, and her cheeks redden as she does so.

Werner saunters over to us, easy, and a moment later Geli reappears with Tommy on her arm.

"Hi," Werner says, reaching out and shaking Minna's hand. "Minna, right?"

"Shirley, here," Minna says softly, and Werner laughs.

"Got it. I think they named me Bobby, though I swear my name changes every time I'm in here." He grins, pulls a drag on a cigarette I didn't see him take out. "First time?"

"Yes," Minna says, and Werner—Bobby—nods.

"Great. I'll introduce you to the band once they're done with this number, though I think you already know Lizzie, our singer."

Minna cranes her head to look. "Lizzie—oh! Elisabeth Schumacher. Yes, I know her." At a glance from me and Renate, she adds, "Her family owns the grocery next to our shop. But I didn't know she—she'd be here in the band."

"The band?" Renate repeats, and now all our heads turn.

There's a makeshift stage up at the front, much smaller than the real one at the Tanzpalast, where a tall, lanky boy with dark skin stands behind an enormous bass; a pale, shorter boy next to him holds a trumpet. An abandoned drum set—Werner's, presumably—sits behind them, as well as an untouched piano. In front of them, an older girl, her dark hair curled into ringlets like Geli's, clutches a microphone stand.

"Oh, Werner, nein," Minna begins to protest, "I know what you're doing, I see that piano—"

"Come on," Werner insists, talking over her. "I know you can play, we've all seen it."

"This is so different from classical," Minna protests, but she is laughing and Werner is pulling her along into the crowd. Renate and I watch her go, and I catch something on Renate's face I don't think I've seen there before.

Jealousy.

"Aren't you two going to dance?" Geli says to us, and we both turn our attention to her. She's still hanging on Tommy's arm. When Renate and I don't move, Geli huffs, and in an instant, grabs my hand.

"Dance with June!" she calls over her shoulder to the boy, and before either Renate or I can protest, she is whisking me out onto the dance floor as the band strikes up an even faster song.

"And we've got Shirley on the keys!" Lizzie calls, and from the stage, Minna gives us a shy wave, smiling when she spots us in the crowd. She resumes playing the fast-paced song, one so different from what I have heard out of her before.

"Night, and stars shine above so bright," Lizzie begins to sing. It's a song I've heard before, and I only barely recognize the words, the English still so foreign in my ears.

"You are so inviting," Geli sings along to the song in English, and she makes eye contact with me as she says it. She laughs at the look on my face.

"Was?" I shout so she hears me over the music. "Was ist?"

"You!" she says, and twirls me before I can object. "You look so happy, Charlie," she says. Her hand finds my waist, and she pulls me closer to her as the music swells around us. We're pressed together, other people swarming behind us, and when I turn, I can see boys dancing with boys and girls with girls and Renate and that boy, their outfits nearly the same, her head thrown back in a laugh. One of the boys kisses another on the lips, and I look away, wishing *I* were brave enough to do such a thing. I've heard there used to be places that were just for—for that sort of thing, but I don't know if they exist anymore. If such a place *could* even exist now.

Which just makes what Geli is showing me now even more special. I want to draw this moment, capture it forever, map out this room and the curves of bodies, the notes from the music in the air. Geli's hands on my waist, her face so close to mine.

The song finally ends and we pull back from each other, laughing.

Geli mock bows. "Save another dance for me later, Peggy," she says, winking, and Tommy deftly sweeps her away, leaving me and Renate on the sidelines.

"What do you think?" I ask her, but she doesn't register what I've said. We push our way through the crowd, away from the stage, until we're on one of the walls, standing near a boy who offers us a flask. Renate shakes her head, and I move so I'm on her good side.

"What do you think?" I ask again, leaning close to her. She takes a breath.

"It's a lot," she says, then turns to me. "It's—it's exhilarating. You were right. Though it's a little—a little painful," she says, frowning. "The band is so loud it hurts my ear. But I do like it, even though I can't understand the words."

"They're in English, so I'm sure that doesn't help," I say, and she shakes her head, her gaze on something far from me. I follow her eyes. The band has taken a break, and the boy, Werner, is leaning over the piano talking to Minna.

Without thinking, I reach over and squeeze Renate's hand. She looks at me in surprise, but she squeezes it back. Before I can do anything else, she turns to the boy with the flask.

"May I?" she asks, and he nods, passing it to her. She presses it to her lips and tips her head back, wipes her mouth with the back of her hand before turning to me and grinning.

"Do you want some?" she asks, and I take the flask from her

before I can think to say nein, the alcohol burning its way down my throat.

The band strikes up another tune, and Lizzie's voice rings out high and clear above our heads, the song somewhat familiar. Before I can react, Renate grabs my hand, hard, and pulls me out onto the dance floor.

She is not as loose as Geli; the rhythm isn't as easy. But my hand slides around her waist as easily as Geli held that boy earlier, and when I let her lead, it feels natural. We dance for two, three, four more songs, until both of us are sweaty and panting and our heads are full of the alcohol and the music, and that jealous look I saw on Renate's face, the one I have felt on my own so many times, is gone.

After the fourth song we make our way back to the wall, clutching our sides. My hair sticks to my neck, and I look around for the boy with the flask, but he isn't there. The band is taking a longer break, so Minna comes over to join us, her face bright red, looking happier than I've seen her in a while.

"You were *magnificent*," I tell her, and she beams.

"Danke, Charlie," she says.

Renate nods at her. "What was that one song, the—the second one you played?"

"Oh!" Minna says. "It's Yiddish. 'Bei Mir Bistu Shein.'"

"'To me you're beautiful'?" Renate says, and Minna ducks her head.

"Yes. That's what it means."

"It's a beautiful song," I say. "And you were fantastic."

"Werner said he wants me to play with them again," Minna says. "So I guess—we'll be coming back here, won't we?"

"We will," Renate says, but I notice how she flinches at the mention of Werner.

"I'm going to go look for Geli," I say. I look down at my watch. "We should—oh Gott, we should definitely leave soon, maybe after another song?"

"Sure," Renate says. "Minna?"

"Fine with me. I'm going to go see if they need me for the last one—go find Geli so we can dance, and then we'll go," Minna says, and squeezes my shoulder before running off.

I do not see Geli in the crowd of the room. She is not dancing with one of the boys, not sneaking a sip of vodka. I leave behind the brightness of the main cellar and wander down the hallway toward the exit. Perhaps she's gone outside to steal a cigarette, something she likes to do to annoy her father.

And that's when I hear it. From one of the empty rooms.

Laughter. And something else.

The tightness in my chest grows, but I make myself go down the hallway anyway, make myself look, because maybe I'm wrong, maybe it isn't her—

But when I push the door open and my eyes adjust, I know it is. It's Geli and Tommy, her back against a wall, his hands sliding up her skirt, her head tipped back and his name on her lips in a way I have only ever dreamed about her saying my name.

I do not know what to do, so I don't do anything, her name still frozen in my mouth as I watch Tommy's hands slide higher up.

But I must make a sound because they turn to look at me, Geli's lipstick smeared and her face flushed.

"Charlie," she says, breathless. "I was just—"

"Wir gehen," I say, my voice as cold as I can make it. "Find uns, wenn du—when you're done here," I say, and turn on my heel without saying anything else so she can't hear the catch in my voice or see my tears.

I am such a fool.

"Where's Geli?" Minna asks as I come back into the main room. She and Renate are waiting by the wall. Our coats are piled over their arms, shoes dangling from their hands.

I shake my head. "Busy," I say, my voice venomous. "She'll meet us later."

"Charlie . . . ," Minna says quietly, her hand stretching toward my arm, but I pull away from her, grabbing my coat from Renate as I do so.

"I'm going to wait outside," I say, and push my way out of the room before either of them can stop me.

The night air is frigid on my burning face. Without thinking, I press a palm to my mouth to stifle my sobs; tears running hot down my cheeks before I furiously wipe at them with the heel of my hand.

"Charlie?"

It's her. My shoulders immediately stiffen, and I don't turn around. But the palm on my shoulder is warm and soft, and it's her touch that breaks me.

"Lass mich, Geli," I snap, wrenching my shoulder away. "Go away."

"Charlie, look at me, please," she says, and I wait a long moment before I finally turn. There's no sign of the boy on her. Her hair is immaculate, her lipstick—*my* lipstick—precisely reapplied. She doesn't even smell like him, just Mathilde's perfume.

"What?" I say.

"You're angry with me."

"I'm not."

"You are," she says, and takes my hand in hers. "Don't lie to me, please."

An echo of my earlier words. I shake my head.

"Why are you angry with me?" she asks quietly.

"Don't ask me that, please," I say, the words out of my mouth before I can stop them. "Please, I don't know. It doesn't matter."

"Yes, it does," she argues. Then, before I can do anything, she pulls me into a tight hug, her arms around my waist, my nose suddenly buried in the crook of her neck. Her breath is hot on my shoulder.

"I'll never leave you, you know that?" she whispers to me. "Not—not for a boy, not for any of them. Please, Charlie. Please forgive me."

I still under her touch. She thinks I'm angry because she left me, but how do I tell her it is more than that—that she can leave me as many times as she wants, over and over again, as long as she comes back? That it is not the fact that she left but that she was with *him*, when I wish she could have been with me?

How do I say that?

I don't. I can't. What I say instead, what she wants to hear, is *I forgive you.* I clutch her to me and whisper it. "I forgive you. Ich verzeihe dir."

And I do. I do forgive her.

But as Minna and Renate join us, I know—I may forgive her, but I will not forget.

I forgive her, but that jealousy has burrowed its way into my heart and settled there, no map to lead it out.

The four of us walk back in relative silence, our shoes loud on the cobblestones. We pass partygoers and people spilling out of bars and movie theaters, a few women holding cigarettes and the men who glance at them. Once we cross back into Kreuzberg, the scenery changes: fathers getting off factory shifts and quietly heading home, some HJ boys standing beside their bikes in front of a block of flats, smoking. We duck our heads as we pass them, even Geli.

"So? What did you think?" Geli asks once we're near Minna and Renate's building, well out of earshot of the HJ boys. Renate gives her a tired smile, as does Minna.

"Loved it," Minna says enthusiastically. "Geli, I don't know if Charlie told you, but they want me to come back and play with them—so I'll know early where all the meetings are." She nudges me with her hip. "Charlie, you should draw a map so I can mark all the locations."

"Okay," I agree, warmed a little by her enthusiasm. "Yes, I'll do that."

"Draw one for me too," Geli says, but when I glance at her, she looks away, no longer the bravado-filled Geli she usually is. "Tommy doesn't . . . I'm sure they meet more often than he tells me they do."

"How'd you meet him?" Minna asks, and I want to glare at her, but I can't because she doesn't know and because it's Minna, and I can never be angry with her.

Geli shrugs, but she looks down at her shoes. "The boys' Gymnasium near mine," she says. "We just—met up one day."

"Do you even know what his real name is?" Renate asks, and I shoot a look at her, which she completely ignores.

I half expect Geli to fight back like she normally does with Renate, but she just shakes her head. "No. Not like it matters, we don't really talk outside the club, anyway."

Renate sighs. "Well. Save some of them for the rest of us, will you?" she says. But it sounds forced, and not for the first time I find myself thinking of the jealousy on her face as Minna went to go dance with Werner.

"Of course," Geli says as we stop at the entrance to Renate and Minna's building. "And maybe we can all get together and listen to music sometime."

This time, it's my turn to glance at Renate and Minna. Geli knows the three of us hang out without her, but I find myself reluctant to tell her we've already discussed doing the same thing.

"Sure," Renate says smoothly. "Fritz has some jazz records I think we can borrow."

"I didn't think he'd like that kind of music," I say carefully.

"Technically, they were Hans's first, though I don't know if he gave them to Fritz or if Fritz took them," Renate says. "I don't know if he actually even listens to them or just wants to keep them from Hans."

"Do you think he'll let us borrow them?" Geli asks.

"If you're the one asking, he will," Renate says sourly, and the four of us laugh in unison before hugging and parting ways.

And then it's just me and Geli, walking back to my flat. If the four of us were silent, it's nothing compared to the silence that stretches between the two of us now.

We walk down the alleys to my house. Instead of talking to

her, in my head I trace our route the way I would draw it: the straight lines of the streets, the curling and winding of the Spree.

We don't talk until we reach my flat. We're standing outside the building when Geli abruptly turns to me.

"Do you still want me to stay?" she asks, and I frown.

"Geli . . ."

"Do you?"

"Yes," I say. "Natürlich."

"Because I thought"—and here her voice is tight, her lips a thin line—"I thought you'd be angry with me. That you were angry with me." She shakes her head. "You must—you must think I'm a whore for going off with that boy, don't you?"

Her malice catches me off guard.

"Nein, Geli, nein—" I say, rushing to reassure her, to comfort her, because I cannot bear to see her hurt. Because out of the two of us, she is always the strong one, and if she's in pain, then I have to fix it, no matter how I feel about her going off with Tommy.

She turns, and I grab her hand before I can think, pull her back to me. A strange dance, the two of us, her palm suddenly flat against my chest.

"I don't think that," I say. "I don't. I'm sorry I was angry with you, but it wasn't—I would never think that about you," I say fiercely, and she blinks at me, almost stunned.

"Never?"

"Niemals," I say. My eyes search her face, the openness of it, the brick-red slash of her mouth a border I cannot bring myself to cross.

"I want you to stay," I say. "Please. Stay with me."

She nods, and we walk up into my flat, careful to stay quiet, careful not to wake Greta or my parents. We dress for bed in silence, and I turn the light off and curl up next to her, my hands tucked up to my own chest.

I'm almost asleep when she speaks. "Charlie?"

"Mm?"

"Thank you."

"For what?"

Silence. Then: "For coming with me that first night. For just—being with me. Thank you."

I don't know how to answer her, so I don't. Instead, I carefully slide my arm over her waist and close my eyes.

"You're welcome," I say after a moment. She sighs, and I tense, not daring to move. "I . . . good night, Geli."

"Good night, Charlie," she says, and as soon as I close my eyes, I hear her whisper—more poetry to fall asleep to, something she must have memorized. Another of Heine's, if I can tell from the sound.

Fürchte nichts, geliebte Seele
Übersicher bist du hier;
Fürchte nicht, daß man uns stehle,
Ich verriegle schon die Tür.

Do not fear, beloved darling
You are still protected here;
Do not fear, that we'll be taken,
I already locked the door.

Juli 1938

MAY BECOMES June, July, the time marked by the end of our exams and a rotating selection of dance halls we find ourselves in at night. We dance until we can't feel our feet, laughing and falling over each other with every song. True to her word, Geli always makes time to dance with me for at least one song before going off with Tommy, and I try to pretend it is enough, because at least she's dancing with me. Some nights she stays over, reciting those poems to me as we fall asleep, flipping through the book and pointing out her favorite ones, and every night I try to memorize at least two lines. By the last week in July, I've almost mastered two sections of it.

Some small part of me believes that as long as I keep working at it, as long as I try to memorize that poem, it will keep her tethered to me. Keep her by my side.

We go to the dance halls at least once a week, sometimes with a band playing, sometimes just meeting in a cellar where one of the boys has put a record on. I've learned to recognize some of the musicians on the records just by sound—Benny Goodman, Louis Armstrong, Duke Ellington, Teddy Stauffer. When there aren't records playing, there's always the band, and between Minna's music and Geli being Geli, we've become somewhat popular.

At least, the two of them have. More often than not, Renate and I are relegated to the sidelines, left to dance with the other boys or, on occasion, with each other. But at the end of the night I'm still sweaty and tired, my hair sticking to my neck and my thoughts filled with nothing but the sounds of drums and singing.

I draw the four of us maps like I promised Minna, using old newspaper painted over with white paint I stole from the art room on the last day of school. I use charcoal to map out four identical maps of Berlin-Charlottenburg with stars on the locations we've already been to. Whenever Minna or Geli tell us about a new place, I mark it on my own map in red ink. I don't know if the other girls mark theirs at all, or if they even use them, but it doesn't matter. Even just the act of drawing out where we've been feels like a small act of rebellion, a thrill running through me at each new spot of red.

I've begun to recognize the other club members on the street: the way the boys walk with their long coats and umbrellas even in the heat of summer, whistling songs I've heard in that club so many times now, songs I find myself humming as I make my way down Friedrichstraße. It isn't particularly hot now, and a breeze ruffles my hair as I walk, humming one of those songs to myself as I make my way up the stairs of our building. Minna told the rest of us earlier that there is a meeting planned for tonight, and if I hurry, I have enough time to get ready before we are supposed to meet at Café Uhland.

But when I enter the flat, Mama is there, her arms crossed. My heart speeds up because for a second I think, *Something is wrong*. She's found the book of Heine's poetry, she's found out where I go at night, a million other possibilities I don't want to think about.

And God, I don't want her to have found the poems, even if I know she loves Heine, too.

Mama adjusts her apron strings and motions me into the kitchen. Greta's sitting at the table in her JM uniform, her hair braided into two neat plaits. It's always braided, lately; I haven't seen her wear it down even to bed.

"I didn't know you had a meeting today," I say, looking between her and Mama. "We didn't."

"Greta was asked to help organize a hike as part of her test," Mama says, and I nod. Greta was inducted in April but won't become a full-fledged JM member until she passes her test in the fall. It's mostly physical activity; or at least, mine was. Frau Köhler may be stricter.

"I'm sure it'll be a good hike if you're the one organizing it, Greta," I say. I hoist my satchel higher up my shoulder. "Mama, I'm going to go out with Minna and Renate tonight."

"Is Angelika coming too?" Mama's lips purse. She's never called Geli by her nickname.

"Natürlich," I say. "Warum?"

"I don't think you should go out tonight," she says.

I frown. "Mama—"

"You've been out three times in the past week, Charlotte."

"But it's summer—"

"It's summer, and I need you to watch your sister," she says, as if the thought has just occurred to her. "Take her out to the park or to Aschinger or something. You can celebrate school being over."

"But—"

"Charlotte, please don't argue with me right now," she says, and I bite my lip.

"Go change, Greta, and then we'll go," I say, and Greta pushes back from the table, glancing between me and Mama like she's unsure who to listen to. Once Greta's footsteps have receded into her room, Mama turns the radio back on, some symphony playing.

"Is Papa working late tonight?" I ask her, taking Greta's vacant seat at the table. She nods once, stiffly; I am not forgiven so easily for arguing with her. "Can I . . . can I call Geli to let her know I'm not coming?"

"No," she says. "No, I think you've seen Angelika enough recently. You need to be focusing on more important things— like finding an apprenticeship."

"Mama, I have one year of school left—"

"Which means you already need to be looking for one."

"If it's sewing, I could just apprentice with Frau Koch—"

"You couldn't, and I think you know that," Mama says.

"But . . ."

"Ende der Diskussion, Charlotte," she says. She pinches the bridge of her nose, looks at me, and for a second I think that'll be the end of it, but it isn't.

"I hope," she says quietly, "that you listened to me about being careful when you're going out every week with Angelika and your friends."

I swallow. Careful. Going to clubs almost every week, listening to forbidden music, Minna playing in the band.

"I'm being careful," I say. "I promise."

She closes her eyes briefly. I wonder if the scene from the restaurant back in April plays over and over in her head, too.

"Ready!" Greta says. She's dressed in one of my old plaid dresses, the sleeves almost too small.

Mama presses her lips together, but doesn't continue what she was saying. "Here," she says quickly, pressing five Reichsmarks into my hand. "Go get dinner. Be home at a reasonable hour."

"Yes, Mama," Greta and I chorus, though we both know that last comment is only directed at me. I tuck the marks into the waistband of my dress and head out the door, feeling Mama watching me the entire time.

◆ ◆ ◆

Greta insists we still go to the Aschinger at Alexanderplatz rather than the one in Kreuzberg. I let her, because the weather is nice and we can walk, and because it means we're out of the house longer.

The lie I told Mama about being careful sits heavy in my stomach, and I try to wish it away. She's just overprotective, always has been. We're going out dancing. That's it. Even if the music is forbidden, what we're doing is harmless.

Isn't it?

But as I'm thinking about the music, I remember I couldn't call Geli to tell her I'm not coming, and I curse internally.

Will they be waiting for me, the three of them? Will they get worried? Or will they just shrug and go on without me because it doesn't matter if I'm there or not?

I try to tell myself it's fine. If they go without me just this one night, it's fine. It's not like I'll have missed much.

But the thought still aches, and I speed up my pace, feeling the stretch in my muscles that I get when I'm dancing, hurriedly taking my hair out of its braids. It falls almost to my shoulders, the straw-colored strands lightening now that it's summer.

We cross over the Jannowitzbrücke as we make our way toward Alexanderplatz, and the wind coming off the Spree ruffles my hair. Ahead of me, Greta's hair stays put in its braids.

"Want me to take those out for you?" I ask, catching up to

her. She shakes her head quickly, her hands flying to the ends of her braids. "You never wear your hair down anymore."

"Frau Köhler says I shouldn't. That it's not proper," Greta says. "And none of the other girls have hair as long as mine."

I'm about to ask her more when we finally reach Aschinger and go inside to find a table. For a second, as we step through the doorway, I half expect officers to be standing around waiting, watching to see who's allowed in, the memory of that night replaying in my head.

But there are no officers standing by the doors, no boys in tan HJ jackets. Just a few scattered families and couples, their faces a range of expressions.

Greta and I pick a table, a small one by the window, far from where we sat that night. Greta glances around, one hand still protectively hovering over the ends of her braids.

"Your hair's almost as long as Sisi's," I say, a remark that would normally earn me a smile but instead now just garners me a blank stare. "Oh, Gretchen, don't worry about Frau Köhler. You can wear your hair how you want."

"I can't, Charlie," she says earnestly. "We aren't supposed to."

I frown, but don't press her. Didn't I think the same thing, just recently? Seeing the girls at the club that first night with their hair loose, their faces painted with makeup we're absolutely forbidden from wearing?

The waiter comes by to take our order, and Greta sits up straighter in her chair. I let her order for herself, knowing she'll just ask for the same soup she always does. I scan the menu for something cheap.

"The Russian eggs, bitte," I say, and the waiter nods before heading off. Greta begins swinging her legs under the table. I study her.

"Are you liking the JM?" I say, and she sighs.

"Can we talk about something else Charlie? Please. All Mama wants to talk about is how I'm liking the JM, and I'm tired of it." Her tone has an edge I haven't heard from her before, and I blink at her in surprise.

"Greta . . ."

"It's *fine*," she says. "We go on hikes and sing songs and Frau Köhler teaches us a lot of things. It's fine," she repeats.

"Are you making friends?"

It's the wrong thing to ask. Greta's face sours. "I'm going to the bathroom," she says, not answering my question, and stands up abruptly before I can stop her.

I fidget with my nails while Greta's gone, the smooth lacquer of the polish foreign on my hands. I press them against the table and look around. A boy catches my eye and I realize with a start that I know him.

Tommy. The boy in the band, the one with the crooked nose. I don't want to think of him as Geli's, but the thought is there in my head immediately, and I try to ignore it. To my surprise, his hair is shorter than when I saw him last. He still doesn't sport the same shaved sides as the HJ boys, but it's short enough now that he wouldn't immediately get clocked as different like some of the other boys would.

He waves, and before I can think to say anything, he pushes back from his table and saunters over to mine. He's whistling as he does so, and I realize it's one of the songs from the club—"Flat Foot Floogie" or something like that, some nonsense word I still don't understand.

"Hey," he says, pulling a chair from a nearby table and setting it down. "Peggy, right?"

"Oh," I say. "Um. Charlotte, actually."

"Charlotte," he repeats. His voice is low, Berlin accent light. "I'm Moritz. Can I sit?"

"Yes," I say, before I can stop myself, and he does. I watch him, the ease with which he interacts with everyone, the dimples when he smiles.

It's easy to see why Geli likes him, and jealousy burns in my chest as I think this, because compared to this boy, what am I?

"How are you liking the club, Peggy?" he asks. I frown at him for the nickname, but he ignores it.

"It's fine," I say.

"Just fine?"

"No," I say. "No, it's not just fine. It's great. How did you hear about it?"

"My cousin in Hamburg showed it to me, says there are a bunch of them up there listening to the music. Apparently the

HJ even have a name for us, did you know that?"

My throat tightens. A name means being noticed, means we're drawing enough attention to get singled out.

But the HJ have names for anyone who's different from them, so maybe it's—maybe it's not so bad.

"I didn't," I say, and he smirks.

"Swingjugend. Swing youth. Or 'lottern,' sometimes."

"Lazy," I say, and laugh. "What, just because we aren't marching all the time?"

"Exactly." His face scrunches up when he smiles. "You should come listen to music with me and my friends sometime."

"Isn't that what we're already doing?"

"Ach, like I can afford a dance hall every week," he says. "No, some of us just hang out in the park and listen. You should bring the other swing dolls with you."

"*Swing dolls?*"

"Your friends," he says, winking. "Next weekend. If you can find us, you can listen to our music. We'll be near the Zoo."

I'm about to retort, but Greta chooses this moment to reappear, her braids redone where strands had been falling out.

"Hi," she says, staring at Moritz as she takes her seat. "Who are you?"

"A friend of Charlotte's," he says to her.

Greta frowns. "No, you're not."

"And why is that?"

"Because Charlie hates being called Charlotte," she says decisively. I cover my mouth with my hand and resist the urge to laugh at the look on Moritz's face.

"Tut mir leid," I tell him. "But she is right. This is my sister, Greta."

"Greta," Moritz repeats, and holds out his hand for her to shake. She eyes him warily, but does so. "You're even prettier than your sister."

A blush crawls up my face at the realization he called me pretty, at the strange compliment, words I am not used to.

"Thank you," Greta says matter-of-factly. "How do you know Charlie?"

I shoot Moritz a look, a *do not mention the club to my sister* look. He just gives me that easy grin back.

"My sister's in her music class," he says. "Talks a lot about her."

I could punch him.

"Oh," Greta says. "Well, that's all right, then. We're here celebrating that school's over."

"Me too," Moritz says. "Better than a Schultüte, right?" he asks, referring to the cone of sweets we traditionally get on our first day of school.

"Right," Greta says, smiling now. "Are you finishing your Abitur?"

"Already did," Moritz says. "I'm going to go to the University of Hamburg, if I can."

I don't know why, but this is what surprises me. Then again, if Moritz is attending a Gymnasium, certainly his English is at least good enough for him to think about attending university.

That ache that starts in my chest whenever Geli talks about university comes back then, hot and fierce. There will be no Abitur in my future, only *Kinder, Küche, Kirche*.

And not for the first time, I think, *Who is teaching us that?* The Führer, I realize, with sudden malice. That is all I am good for; it's all we're being trained for in the BDM.

My emotions must show on my face, because Moritz looks at me with sudden curiosity. "What about you, Charlie? University for you, too?"

I bite my lip. I do not know if I can say what I think, not in front of this boy, even if he is in the club. Even if he does the mock salute like the rest of us.

"I wish," I say. "But I think my path is pretty set."

"Hm," Moritz says. But he doesn't say anything more, and after a moment he looks down at his watch.

"Oh, I should be heading home. Lovely to see you again, Charlie," he says, winking at me. "We should talk again sometime about university."

"Maybe," I say. "I'll see you—I guess not as much, since *school* is out now?"

He laughs at the look on my face, at my words. "No, I'm sure you'll still see me. I'm difficult to get rid of." He waves at my sister before sauntering back over to his own table. Greta turns back to me, her face now full of her familiar curiosity. I don't know why, but the sight makes me relax, just a little.

"Okay, how *do* you know him?" she asks the second Moritz is out of earshot.

"His sister's in my class, like he said," I say.

"You didn't take music this year," Greta says matter-of-factly, and I wince. I hate how perceptive she is. "Come on, Charlie."

"I can't tell you," I say, the words falling out of my mouth automatically, and the second I see the hurt on my sister's face, I wish I could take them back. "I'm sorry, Gretchen, but it's a secret."

"You don't think I'm old enough to handle it," she says. I don't respond because she's right. "You're so mean to me, Charlie. Geli would tell me."

"Greta . . ."

"*Nein*," my sister says, and before I can stop her, she pushes back from the table. "I'm going home."

"Greta, wait for me, please—"

"No," she says. "I don't want to wait for you. I'll see you at home."

"Mama will be mad if you come back without me. . . ."

"She'll be mad at *you*," Greta says, and turns her back to me. "I'll be fine. You drew me a map, remember?"

She turns on her heel and leaves. I signal the waiter hurriedly, pay for the half-eaten food, guilt and hunger gnawing at my stomach as I do.

But by the time I leave the restaurant, it's too late. She's gone, disappeared into the crowd of people in Alexanderplatz, and fear constricts my throat because I cannot have lost my sister, I can't.

She'll be fine, I tell myself as I break into a run, praying that I will beat her home. *She knows her way. She'll be fine.*

But the knots stay in my stomach until I reach the entrance to our building, until I see Greta's small form sitting on the stoop, her eyes red, her braids undone.

"Greta!" I call, and her head snaps up. Before I can think, I reach out and pull her to me, wrapping my arms around her and smoothing my hands over her hair. "Oh, Greta, I'm sorry, I . . ."

"I almost got lost," she sniffs against my blouse, and I stroke her back. "I'm sorry, Charlie, I didn't mean it—"

"You did, but it's all right," I say. "We'll just—have to make another map and practice, yes?"

She sniffs again, and I kneel down so I'm eye level with her.

"Greta," I say. "I am sorry. I still can't tell you how I know Moritz, but I'm sorry I haven't been spending time with you."

"No, you aren't."

"I am," I say. "I really am. In fact," I begin, thinking of Moritz, of what he said about the other Swingjugend, about getting to spend time with Geli, "why don't we go to the Zoo next weekend? Me and you and the other girls—Ruth and Rebekah can even come if you want." Surely Mama can't object to me and Greta going to the Zoo. It's not like she has to know what I'll really be doing while I'm there. Or who I'll really be with.

"Do you mean that?"

"Yes," I say. "I absolutely do."

"Okay," Greta says, her voice wobbly, and I can tell she isn't entirely convinced. "And you'll stay with us, right?"

"Of course," I say. "Of course we will."

"Good," she says, and pushes herself off the stoop, wiping at her eyes with the heel of her hand. I follow her inside the building, already dreaming of next weekend, of seeing Geli.

Mama and Papa are at the kitchen table when we come in, and though they don't say anything, I can feel them watching us. Mama's warning rings in my ears again, telling me to choose safety.

But I think again about the freedom of the club. I cannot choose both, safety and freedom, but I'll be damned if I don't try. Besides, we'll be fine at the Zoo. I can ask my parents about it tomorrow, and tonight, I will memorize two more lines of Heine's verse and add another star to my map, so I do not forget where I've been.

August 1938

AS PROMISED, a week later, Greta and I find ourselves walking up the stairs to Renate's flat, where we're meeting her and Minna before the Zoo. Greta practically skips up every other stair, she's so excited, and the knot of guilt in my chest tightens at the fact I have promised her a trip to the Zoo, when I'm going to leave her as soon as we get there to go listen to music with some of the boys—if we can even find them. Tighter still at the lie I told Mama *again* about hanging out with my friends.

I didn't mention Geli would be there as well.

At least this time we really are *going to the Zoo*, I tell myself. At least Mama will know where we are. And we'll be out in the open, in daylight—what bad can happen to us out there, where everyone can see?

Herr Neumann isn't on the stairs this time, and I let out a small sigh of relief, because I won't have to deal with seeing him today. Him hanging around can only be something bad, right?

Renate opens the door after my first knock and quickly pulls me and Greta inside. She's in another shirt that looks like it was stolen from Hans, and a skirt I could have sworn used to belong to Minna.

"Mama's in a foul mood," she explains at my puzzlement as we hurry to her room. "She found out I wasn't going back to school."

"How?" I ask, but I already know the answer.

"Fritz." Renate scowls. "I *was* planning on telling her this week, but of course she doesn't believe me now, since he went ahead and tattled that I had dropped out."

"But how did he even know?"

"Ach, wer weiß," Renate says. "For all I know, he overheard me telling you and Minna."

Greta looks between us. "You aren't dropping out, right, Charlie?"

"No," I say. "Please. Mama would kill me."

"I'm surprised mine didn't," Renate says sourly, and looks at Greta. "Charlie's not going to drop out. She's too smart for that. I just didn't like school anymore." She flops down on her bed. A flush goes through me at her words that I'm smart, the compliment warming me.

"Oh," Greta says. She settles herself on the floor while I sit on the bed next to Renate. "If I didn't like school anymore, do you think Mama would let me drop out?"

"Nein," Renate and I say in unison, then burst out laughing.

Once we've calmed down, Renate props herself on her elbows, looking between me and Greta.

"What do we want to do while we wait for Minna and the twins?" she asks. "They're eating lunch and then they'll be along." She smirks. "We could go play marbles in the courtyard to pass the time."

"Mm, no thank you," I say.

"Why ever not?"

"Because you'll win."

"And?" She nudges me with her arm. "Come on, I deserve a win today."

"Maybe later," I say, heart pounding at her teasing. "We could . . . we could listen to music, though?" I suggest it hesitantly. We've never listened to music without Minna and Geli around, and that knot of guilt contracts further at daring to suggest it without them.

But really, I tell myself, what else are we supposed to do? And the joy on Renate's face almost makes that guilt go away.

Almost.

"Yes, that's perfect," Renate says. "Let me go steal a record from Fritz." She pushes off the bed, leaving me and Greta, who I almost forgot was there. Renate returns a moment later with a record, almost running into her room, Fritz close behind her.

"But they're *my* records!" he says, trying to shove his foot in the door so Renate can't close it.

"And I'll give it back. Just let me borrow it!" she snaps, and successfully throws her weight against the door to shut it. She turns back to me and Greta, a triumphant expression on her face.

"What're we listening to?" Greta asks as Renate goes to put the record on. But Renate's back is to Greta, and she doesn't turn around. Greta frowns and looks over to me.

"It's . . . it's jazz music," I say. "You remember, like Papa used to play? You might have been too young then. . . ." I falter. "But this—this is different. You have to keep this a secret, Greta."

"Why?" She frowns. "If it's the same as Papa's music?"

"Because it's not the same. It's . . . it's American." I lower my voice. "It's forbidden, so please, please don't tell Mama and Papa you listened to it with us, okay? We could all get in a lot of trouble."

"Oh," Greta says, nodding solemnly. "All right, Charlie."

"Promise?"

"I *promise*," she says shortly. "Let me listen to it."

No sooner has she finished her sentence than trumpets fill the room, the sound familiar but not totally. I turn to Renate.

"What is this?"

"Louis Armstrong," she says cheerfully. "One of the others told me about him when we went out last week, and Hans happened to have the record." She frowns. "Well, Hans had it until Fritz stole it, and now it's mine, I guess."

"So you *aren't* giving it back to Fritz."

"Not at all," she says, and grabs my hand. "Come on, come

dance. You too, Greta." She turns the music up a little more. It's not as loud as at the club, where we can feel every note through our bodies, but it's loud enough that we can hear it. We dance until the song ends, and then Renate puts the needle back at the beginning.

"Louder!" Greta says, and Renate and I share a glance. We've always played the music quietly when it was the four of us, just loud enough so that Renate can hear it, but never more than that.

"Warum nicht?" Renate says, shrugging. She turns the volume up even more, the trumpets blaring. We spin until we're dizzy. I close my eyes and try to get lost in the feeling of it, but abruptly Renate lets go of my hand.

I open my eyes. Frau Hoffmann stands at the entrance to Renate's bedroom.

"Turn that down," she says, her voice tight. "Mein Gott, Renate, turn that off!"

Renate frowns, but moves the needle off the record. Greta and I wince at the sound.

"Mama . . . ," Renate begins, but Frau Hoffmann holds up a hand. Fritz and Hans crowd behind her.

"Do you have *any* idea," Frau Hoffmann says, "of what would happen if anyone knew what you were listening to?"

"It's jazz," Renate begins. "It's—"

"It's degenerate music," her mother says.

"But it's Hans's record—"

Frau Hoffmann's hand moves quicker than Renate can react, and the rest of us flinch at the sound of skin meeting skin.

"Herr Neumann passes by our door every day, did you know that?" she hisses. "Do you want to give him a reason to report us? Do you want to give him a reason to watch all of us even closer?"

Renate shakes her head. Her face is blank.

Her mother sighs, softening slightly. "Renate, Liebling," she says. "You have to be careful."

The knot of guilt in my chest is so tight now, I feel like I can't breathe. This is my fault. All of it. Renate wouldn't have been playing the record if I hadn't asked her to.

"It's my fault, Frau Hoffmann," I say, standing. I can feel all of them looking at me: Renate and Frau Hoffmann and Greta, especially. "I asked Renate to put the music on."

But Frau Hoffmann shakes her head. "Nein, Charlotte," she says. "It wouldn't have been you. You're too good." She turns back to Renate, any trace of former softness gone. "I don't want to hear that music in my house again."

With that, she turns on her heel and leaves. Hans follows her, but Fritz hangs back, staring at his sister.

"Greta," I say quietly, "can you go play with Fritz please, just for a few minutes?"

"But Charlie—"

"*Bitte*, Greta," I say, and she pouts, but heads out of the room, taking Fritz with her and shutting the door behind her. Renate is still standing, the blank look on her face replaced with something I can't decipher, her lips pressed together. Wordlessly, she sits down on her bed, and I cautiously take a seat next to her. The left side of her face is bright red, and she presses a hand to it, briefly, before drawing it away and closing her eyes, digging her fingers into her comforter. Automatically, I take her hand and thread my fingers through hers. Her grip loosens, but only slightly.

I want to ask her if she's all right, but I cannot make myself break the silence stretching between us now like a chasm and filling the room. My palm grows sweaty, but I don't dare move it from hers. I wait for her to speak. When she finally does, her voice is low.

"I didn't think Mama believed all of that," she says. "All those things Goebbels said—about music or art or . . . or the Jews."

I run my thumb over her knuckles, at a loss for what to say, for how to comfort her. It's not like I can easily reassure her that her mother doesn't believe those things, not after what just happened.

"We'll just . . . we'll have to be careful," I finally say, hating how much I sound like my own mother in that instant. "Maybe listen to it when she isn't around?"

"I wish we didn't have to be careful at all," Renate says, an edge in her voice. She stands abruptly, pulling her hand from mine. "God, Charlie, I'm so tired of having to tiptoe around everything with her because I don't know how she feels! She won't tell me. I don't know if my own mother supports the Party because she won't talk about it—she didn't even say anything to me when she found out about school, just sent me to my room, even though I—I tried to explain that it was difficult for me there, with this—" She indicates her ear. "But she never wants to talk about that, either, it's just—'pretend everything's *fine*, Renate, like you always have.' I hate that I have to hide everything from her because the entire verdammte Party has decided that anything not German is *degenerate* and I don't know if she agrees!" Her fists clench.

"It doesn't—it doesn't always have to be like that," I say, desperate to comfort her, to fix it the way I have before with Geli. "We'll—we'll be able to listen to the music out in the open today, with the boys—"

"It's not just about the music, Charlie," Renate says. "I wish it was, but it's—it's more than that, don't you get it?"

"Renate . . ."

She shakes her head, abruptly turning so her left side is facing me. My face burns hot with embarrassment.

Why did I have to say that? Why can't I find the right words to comfort her, reassure her that everything's going to be all right?

But how can I reassure her of that when I don't even know myself?

"We should go," she says flatly, opening her bedroom door.

"Go get Greta. Minna and I will meet you downstairs."

My face flushes even further at the obvious dismissal. Without a word, I brush past her, get my sister, and hurry down the stairs. The two of us sit on the stoop of the building, waiting.

"Is Renate in trouble?" Greta asks after a moment.

"Probably," I say.

"Are we going to get in trouble?"

"Why would we?"

"Because of the music," she says.

"I hope not," I say. "As long as Frau Hoffmann doesn't tell Mama." I look at her. "And as long as you don't say anything, either."

"I won't," she promises solemnly. But then she frowns. "You shouldn't listen to it anymore."

"I won't, Gretchen," I say, and she nods, satisfied, and I think about all the lies I've told, tallying up higher than I want to count. I tell myself it's to keep her safe, because the last thing I need is for my sister to follow me to a club, for her to tattle to Mama about the music, for Mama to find out where we've been going.

I will lie as often as I need to, if it means I can keep the rest of them safe.

Renate is silent on the ride to the Zoo. She sits with Minna and, without prompting, leans her head on Minna's shoulder. My face flushes, not with jealousy, but with this feeling of inadequacy that Minna is able to so easily comfort Renate, comfort any of us, when I constantly feel at a loss for words. When I haven't said anything to Minna about what she and her family are surely going through.

As soon as we step out of the underground entrance to the U-Bahn stop at the Zoo, Greta, Ruth, and Rebekah run ahead, charging to the elephant gate. The six of us pay to enter but stop shortly after the gate, waiting for Geli. The twins start complaining after five minutes.

"You go on ahead," I tell Minna and Renate. "We'll meet you at the bear habitat, all right?"

Minna nods, and she and Renate each take one of the girls' hands before heading off. Greta taps her foot, impatient, but I know she won't want to leave without Geli.

Geli bursts through the gates ten minutes later, difficult to miss, her hair once again down. Her lipstick today is a bright purple, and her skirt is short. She's holding something in her hand that I don't recognize until she draws closer—a cigarette holder, like the ones we've seen in Hollywood movies.

"Hi," she says breathlessly, and hugs Greta to her side. "I'm sorry I'm late. I almost forgot which station stop this was."

"It's literally the Zoo stop," Greta says matter-of-factly, but Geli smiles down at her nonetheless.

"I should keep you around just so I don't get lost, Greta," Geli says, and Greta beams. Geli reaches over and squeezes my hand. She smells like Mathilde's perfume, the scent jolting me back to that night a few months ago when I found her with Moritz.

Moritz, who we're going to be seeing today.

I can't think about that. Right now, she's with me, and that's what matters.

The three of us walk straight back, past the primate house and the antelope house, though Greta makes us promise that we'll come back to that one so she can see a giraffe. Up ahead, a girl and boy hold hands, and I watch as he slides his arm around her waist. They are older than us, maybe at university, the girl's hair cut short.

I envy them. I want to be them. I want Geli to take my hand as we walk.

I wish we weren't meeting up with the boys. But I can't say that, can't tell her how I feel, because I should have no reason to be jealous that we're meeting up with them.

But she's your best friend, says that voice in my head. Who hides how she's feeling from her best friend?

"Are you excited about meeting up with Moritz—with Tommy today?" I ask.

"Definitely," she says, her skirt flouncing a little as she walks. She gives me a mischievous smile. "I think he likes me."

"Oh?" I say. "I thought—I thought that was obvious."

"No, I mean I think he *likes* me—he might ask me to go steady with him," she says.

"What will your father think of that?"

"He doesn't have to know," she says, and winks. "Oh, Charlie, be happy for me, please?"

"I *am* happy for you," I say automatically, and she grabs my hand and interlocks our fingers.

I bite my lip as we walk. *It doesn't matter*, I think. *If she likes him. Es ist mir egal. It doesn't matter.*

"Do you like him?"

I cannot believe the words have made their way out of my mouth.

Geli looks at me. "Ja," she says, and that one syllable is a knife in my chest. "I do."

"Oh," I say, and suddenly we stop walking, the crowd stepping around us as if we're a stone in a river. Up ahead, I spot Renate, Minna, and the twins; Greta's head bobs toward them. Renate gives me a quizzical look and I nod at her to signal we'll be a minute.

"What's wrong, Charlie?" Geli says, and I snap my attention back to her.

"Nichts. I'm happy for you," I say again, and she frowns. We haven't talked about that night at the club, the night she gave me the book of poetry, and suddenly this feels like a horrible echo of it.

"Are you?" she asks. "Are you really?"

"Yes," I say firmly.

She frowns. "Charlie . . ."

"I'm happy for you," I repeat. "I just—I miss you and I don't want you to—to abandon me for him." It's the truth, but not all of it.

I pray that it'll be enough. That she won't notice what I haven't said—*I don't want you to abandon me for him because I'd rather you were with me.*

"You know I won't," she says fiercely, and I draw in a breath when her eyes meet mine, because for a second I think—*maybe she is promising to stay like I want her to.*

But I know, deep down, she isn't.

We catch up with the other girls at the bear habitat, the younger girls standing on tiptoe to look into the enclosure, the three of them completely engrossed in watching one of the brown bears prowl around.

"When are we meeting the boys?" Minna asks while the twins and Greta are occupied. She looks over at me. "Did Tommy say where they'd be?"

"He didn't," I say. Frau Hoffmann's warning flashes through my head again, her words echoing my own mother's. I steal a glance at Renate, who meets my gaze with a look of determination. "Are we . . . are we sure we actually want to meet up with them?"

"Why wouldn't we?" Geli says brightly. I frown. I'm sure Renate told Minna about what happened with Frau Hoffmann, but once again, none of us are going to bring it up to Geli.

And if Minna's the one suggesting we go meet the boys anyway, surely it's fine, isn't it?

"No reason," Renate says. "Besides, I think I know where they are. Max told me they sometimes listen to the music under bridges so they won't be spotted; I bet they're somewhere near the Lichtensteinbrücke."

Geli frowns. "Who's Max?"

"Just some boy from one of the bands," Renate says, and Minna looks at her curiously. Renate ducks her head. "Not like *that*, I'm pretty sure he's . . . anyway, we should try there," she says quickly.

Geli glances between all of us. "It's as good a place to start as any," she says.

"What is?" Greta asks as the three younger girls rejoin us.

"Well," Renate says quickly, "we were thinking you're actually old enough to wander around on your own for an hour. How does that sound?"

Greta narrows her eyes. "I thought you weren't leaving us," she says to me.

"I . . ." I falter.

"Charlie doesn't want to, she doesn't think you're brave enough to go to the predator house by yourselves," Renate says. "Isn't that right, Charlie?"

Greta's scowl deepens. "I am *too* brave." She takes Ruth's and Rebekah's hands. "We're brave, right?"

"Yes," Ruth says instantly. Rebekah hesitates but nods all the same.

"You're very brave," Geli says to them, and Greta blushes before turning back to me.

"We can do it by ourselves," she says.

"Of course you can," I say. "We'll meet you at the elephant gate in an hour, all right?"

"All right," Greta says, and the three girls head off in the direction of the predator house. None of them look back at us.

Renate, Minna, Geli, and I walk to the Lichtensteinbrücke, arms linked. A few older women glare at us as we pass, and we pull our arms tighter together. Geli rolls the hem of her skirt up and swipes on another coat of lipstick, lighting another cigarette as we head down the stairs to the water. Sure enough, some of the swing boys are leaning against the brick wall, long coats on even though the day has warmed up. I spot Moritz in the crowd, and to my surprise, he waves and winks at me before he even acknowledges Geli. One of them turns up the volume on a Koffergrammophon, and Renate glances at me and Minna, her teeth sinking into her lower lip. I reach over and squeeze her hand.

"It'll be fine," I say, and as if to prove my point, I unlink arms with Minna and Geli and pull Renate into a dance, spinning her once before pulling her back to me. Minna laughs. Geli glances back at the two of us, her brow furrowed, then shrugs and saunters over to Moritz.

"See?" I say to Renate as one of the boys starts up another song. "We're fine."

She nods, but the frown lines on her forehead don't soften, and without thinking, I reach up and run my thumb over them. She blinks as if coming out of a trance, then smiles at me and pulls me into a clumsy foxtrot.

"You're right," she says in between steps, "we're fine. Mama—Mama doesn't know what she's talking about." She presses a hand to her cheek just once, briefly, as if she can still feel her mother's palm there.

Halfway through the song, Minna comes over and joins us, taking my hand so the three of us are moving in tandem. She doesn't look worried the way Renate does, and that reassures me, if only a little. Renate smiles at her, too, and I let go so they can dance together for a moment before the song winds down.

When the music ends, we rejoin the others; the boys are passing a cigarette around, already marked by Geli's telltale lipstick. I take a drag of it when offered, but Renate shakes her head. Minna takes it from me, pulling off it before passing it back to a boy—Werner, I realize. The one who invited her to play with the band that night. When he goes to pass it back to Minna, though, Renate leans in and takes it, her eyes not leaving him.

Another song starts up and all of us stand and dance, pairing off—Geli with Moritz, Minna with Werner, and Renate and

I with some of the other boys whose names I don't know, our shoes loud on the cobblestones. The atmosphere is loose, more relaxed than the club, though whether that's because we're out in the open during the day or because there are fewer of us, it's hard to tell.

Suddenly there's shouting from above us, and we all look up to see four HJ boys racing down the stairs toward us.

"Ach Scheiße, brownshirts," one of the boys says, but they make no move to leave. In fact, they begin rolling up their sleeves, spoiling for a fight.

Renate clutches my hand. "Charlie," she says. "We should leave. We need to leave." She glances at Minna, who returns her worried look with one of her own, all joy from the previous moments gone. "*Now.*"

I look between Renate and Geli. She's right, I know she is, but Geli isn't moving.

"*Charlie,*" Renate hisses, but it's too late; the HJ boys have arrived. The youngest one looks barely older than Fritz, with his dark hair combed back in that same style they all wear, and my stomach turns at the sight. They glance over at us with some interest, gazes that make me squirm. My face feels hot when their eyes linger on Geli, and then on Minna.

"And what are you girls doing with scum like this?" a blond one asks, picking up the record off the player. Moritz steps toward him, but the other three HJ boys just laugh.

"Just listening to the music," Geli says, twirling a strand of hair around her finger. She doesn't look afraid, not in the slightest. She looks like she's having fun.

Renate squeezes my hand so hard my fingers hurt. She angles her body slightly so she can hear better, pulling Minna closer to her at the same time.

"Girls like you shouldn't be listening to this filth," the tallest one says. "Or hanging around with these *Weicheier*." He jerks a thumb at the swing boys before pulling a notepad out of the pocket of his shorts. "I'll have to get your names."

"I'm Nancy," Geli says sweetly, and the tall boy frowns. Without a word he signals to the blond boy, who takes the record and breaks it cleanly over his knee before tossing the shards into the river. Minna gasps, and the boy turns to her, but before he can do anything, Moritz aims a punch at him. The other swing boys seem roused out of their fear and join him, and this time I do not ignore the sharp sting of Renate's hand squeezing mine before I break into a run.

We run all the way back to the Zoo, ignoring the strange looks we're getting, until we're back by the entrance where we said we'd meet Greta and the twins. The clock by the elephant gate says we're five minutes early, so thankfully we can catch our breath before they show up, adrenaline still coursing through our veins.

To my surprise, Geli starts laughing, running her fingers through her curls before shaking her head and looking at us.

I know that look. I know it well. It's the one she has when she's gotten away with something.

"Can you *believe* that?" she says. "I didn't know those boys could fight! I—"

"You're *laughing*?" Renate snaps. "Geli, we could have—we could have been *arrested*, or worse, and you're *laughing*?"

"Calm down, Renate," Geli says. "We weren't caught."

Renate's jaw clenches. "We weren't caught *this* time, but didn't you see the way they were looking at us? They aren't going to forget that, and you—you didn't run, you just *stood* there, you *flirted* with them—"

"Running would've made them instantly suspicious," Geli says. "But look, we got out, didn't we?"

"I can't believe you!" Renate says, her voice growing even louder. Minna and I share a glance. We're both used to Renate and Geli arguing, but this feels so much worse than normal. Neither of us makes a move to step in. Not this time.

"This is just some game to you, isn't it?" Renate hisses. "Just some fun to get back at Daddy—not all of us have officer fathers who will bail us out if we get into trouble!"

Geli stops laughing immediately, leveling a glare at Renate that could cut through stone.

Renate folds her arms across her chest. "You really don't get how dangerous this is, do you?" she says. She juts her chin out. "I'm not going to do it anymore. I'm not going to keep putting myself in danger—putting *Minna* in danger—just to listen to music." She glares at Geli, daring her to say something.

Geli turns to Minna. "Is that how you feel too?"

Minna looks down. But to my surprise, she nods.

"I don't want to," she says. Her voice comes out choked, and she takes a breath before continuing. My nails dig into my palms when she does. "I don't want to give it up, but Geli, we could've—we could've been arrested, or worse, and it . . . it would be *so much worse* for me than it would be for you, don't you get that? I want to stay, I really do, but I can't. I'm sorry," she adds, and quickly turns away from us. Renate hurries to her and puts an arm around her shoulders, and again that feeling courses through me, of desperately wanting to fix this, of how *unfair* it is that Minna should have to give this up because of some bullies in HJ uniforms.

But I don't know how to say that, not here. Minna wipes her eyes and all I can do is give her a sympathetic smile. Renate reaches down and takes her hand.

After a moment, Geli speaks again.

"So that's it," she says. "Both of you—you're just not going to come anymore."

Minna shakes her head. "Maybe just once more," she says, ignoring the look Renate gives her. "Just to . . . just to tell the band goodbye. But beyond that, I can't. I'm sorry," she says again.

"You don't need to apologize," Renate says. She juts her chin toward Geli. "I won't go if Minna won't."

Geli turns to me, and my stomach twists.

"Is that how you feel too, Charlie?" she asks. "That it's too dangerous?"

"Geli, I . . ." I draw in a breath. I can feel Renate looking at me, Geli looking at me, my mother's warning in my head, the sound of Renate's mother hitting her, Herr Neumann outside the Kochs' door.

The sound of Minna's hands dancing over the piano keys, Geli paying attention to me like I'm the only girl in the room.

I know what I should say. What would be the smart, safe thing to say. To do.

But Minna is going back, if only one more time, and I don't have as much to lose as she does.

"I'm sorry," I say, and I don't know if I'm saying it to Minna or Renate. "I . . . I want to keep going. We can be more careful, but I—I'm not ready to give it up just yet."

I'm not ready to let go of Geli just yet.

Renate shakes her head in disappointment, like she somehow expected I was going to say that, and that cuts through me more than anything.

"Renate, Minna, I . . ."

"Vergiss es, Charlie," Renate says. She looks like she wants to say more, but Ruth, Rebekah, and Greta come flying up to us, all talking over each other about the predator house, about how one of the lions growled at them but they didn't run away. Renate leans in closer to Minna, turning her good side toward her as the younger girls continue talking. "Minna, we should go."

Minna nods and takes the twins by the hand, letting them briefly say goodbye to Greta before the four of them head off, walking quickly to the U-Bahn entrance. Geli looks between me and Greta.

"Thank you," she says, reaching over and grabbing my hand. "For not leaving me."

I nod, but my chest constricts at her words. I know I won't leave her, not ever, but as our other friends walk away, I worry that this time, I've made the wrong choice.

On the U-Bahn ride back to Kreuzberg, Greta leans her head on my shoulder, shutting her eyes. I envy how she's able to do that, how she feels secure enough with me to sleep on our way home, trusting that I'll wake her when we need to leave.

The scene with Minna and Renate plays over and over in my mind, guilt gnawing at me a little more each time it does. To distract myself, I repeat the names of the stops on our route home. Zoo to Wittenbergplatz. Change at Wittenbergplatz. Stay on for seven stops until Kottbusser Tor. I repeat the name of every stop in my head until they've settled into a rhythm, until they're the only thing in my head, no room for music or fear or disappointment at all.

Mama has dinner ready by the time we arrive home, Kartoffel-klöße with a side of red cabbage—normally my favorite. But tonight I can barely eat, pushing the dumplings around on my plate. All I can think about is the music, Frau Hoffmann, the HJ boys. The fear on Minna's face. The way Renate looked at me when I said I wanted to go back.

My parents sit across the table, and I wish I could ask them about it—about all of it. How they feel about the Party. Would they actually give me an answer, or would they brush it off like Frau Hoffmann? I know Papa is a Party member, but as a civil servant, he has to be.

Mostly, I want to ask my father about the music, about his old jazz records. About why he doesn't listen to them anymore.

Have he and Mama both fallen for the Party's lies? About Papa's beloved music now being degenerate? Mama's favorite Jewish poet?

Do I want to know the answer to that?

"Was ist los?" Mama asks. Greta also looks at me, cheeks stuffed with potato.

"Nothing's wrong," I say. "I'm just . . . tired from the Zoo, that's all."

"Did you have fun?"

"Yes!" Greta chimes in. "We went to the predator house and saw the antelope and Geli said I was brave."

Mama's fork stops halfway to her mouth, and she sets it down. "You didn't tell me Angelika was going to be there."

"We . . . decided last minute," I say, and her eyes narrow.

"Not like I got to see her much," Greta pouts.

"And why is that?" Mama asks, and I grip my fork tighter in my hands.

"She and Charlie went off without us," Greta says. "Charlie didn't think we'd be brave enough to go to the predator house alone. Rebekah was scared but we still did it."

"You let Greta and the Koch twins wander around the Zoo *alone*?" Mama's voice rises. "Charlotte, what were you thinking?"

"I—I just—"

"And what were you and Angelika doing while your sister and her friends were alone?"

"It wasn't just me and Geli. Renate and Minna were there, too—"

It was the wrong thing to say.

"Greta, go to your room," Mama says. "You can take your dinner with you, but your father and I need to have a discussion with your sister."

"But Mama . . ."

"Geh," she snaps, and Greta throws me a dirty look before picking up her plate and stomping off to her room. I study the worn wood of the table, smooth under my fingers.

"Charlotte," Mama says. "What were you and Angelika doing? What was *so* important that you sent your sister off alone?"

I finally make eye contact with my mother, stare into hazel eyes the same shape and color as my own. A mirror image, with more lines of disappointment. I wish she were like Renate's mother in this instant, unwilling to admit that her daughter is doing anything wrong.

But she isn't.

"We . . . we were listening to music," I say. I look at Papa now. "Jazz music, like we—like we used to listen to, remember—"

"Mein *Gott*, Charlotte," Mama says, slamming her hand down on the table. "Does *nothing* I say get through to you? Do you think it's just some game, that I am joking when I tell you to *be careful*, that it's nothing serious?"

It's not her voice I hear now, but Minna's.

It would be so much worse *for me than it would be for you, don't you get that?*

"Mama, I'm sorry, I—I'll be better, I promise—"

"I don't want to hear it right now," she says. She pinches the bridge of her nose. "I'm sorry, but I cannot do this, not any-more. From now on, you're staying home. No more going out."

"Mama—"

"Do *not* argue with me, Charlotte," she says. "You may see Angelika at your BDM meetings, but that's it."

I bite my tongue so hard I taste blood.

"For how long?"

"Until I am not mad at you anymore," she says, and I want to laugh, but it's not funny. I try to look at Papa, silently beg-ging him to help, but he just gives me a sad shake of his head.

"Believe me, Lottchen," he says. "We wish it didn't have to be this way, either. But your mother's right—it's for your own good."

"All right," I say, and tears prick at the back of my eyes, and before either of them can stop me, I push back from the table and run to my room, shutting my door so I don't have to see any of them, think about any of them, about anything at all that happened today.

At least, I tell myself, *Mama didn't say the music was degenerate. At least there's that.*

But it doesn't give me as much hope as I thought it would.

November 1938

I DO what Mama said. I keep my head down, I go to school. I concentrate on my exams. I walk home with Minna, trading our skirts and blouses for heavy coats as fall fades into the chill of winter. I do not ask her what her last visit to the club was like, and we do not talk about what happened at the Zoo.

In November, Mama lifts her ban on me going anywhere but straight home after school, if only slightly, so Minna and I meet Renate for coffee when she isn't looking for jobs. Sometimes Geli joins us, but we're more subdued when we meet, sticking to safe topics like school, or our siblings. I do not get a chance to see Geli alone at all, not even after our BDM meetings. I want to ask her about the clubs, if she's still going, but I don't dare ask out in the open. It's not like I can ask Minna where they meet; every time I think about that day at the Zoo, I remember the fear on her face.

But the entire time it feels like there's this itch under my skin

I can't quite get to. I want to go back, *need* to go back. Need to feel some sense of freedom that isn't the oppressive routine of being Charlotte. I want to be Peggy again.

I pull out my map, the one I made copies of for the four of us, run my finger over the spots I've marked where all of us have met. Smudging them. I wish I knew where the rest of the Swingjugend have been meeting; it's not like I know in advance, and I'm not close enough with any of the boys for them to tell me their plans.

Maybe Mama wouldn't be as angry if I tried to call Geli now. It's been three months since the Zoo, after all. Maybe she'll let me call, and I can ask Geli if the clubs are still meeting.

Ask if I can see her.

One day in November, I do not meet Minna for coffee after school; Renate and her family are in Köln, so it would just be the two of us, and I want to get home early enough to help Mama with dinner tonight, hoping that if I placate her with this, she won't mind my going out.

But when I arrive, the smell of meat hits me as soon as I open the door. It's not Mama in the kitchen, but Papa. My father only cooks every so often, usually when Mama is too tired to do so herself or when one of us has done well in school. Secretly I think he's the better cook, but I can't say that—as a proper Hausfrau, Mama is supposed to be the better one.

"Papa?"

He turns, smile almost hidden by his graying mustache.

"Lottchen. You're just in time to help with the Fleisch-pflanzerln."

"They're called Buletten, Papa," I say, but I'm already shucking my coat and rolling up my sleeves.

"We may live in Berlin, Lottchen, but if you call them Buletten again, you don't get to eat any," he says, and I shake my head. He passes me the bowl and I set to work mixing the onions and egg and bread crumbs into the meat, wrinkling my nose at the texture of the egg. When everything is incorporated, I pass the bowl back to Papa, watch as his hands form the meat into patties at least twice the size of an egg.

I glance at him out of the corner of my eye. We don't talk much, Papa and I, though when I was younger, I used to wait for him to come home from his shifts at the post office, craving that one hour with him in the afternoon before he went back to work. He'd bring me envelopes and extra paper to draw my maps on.

He doesn't do that anymore, and I don't know if it's because he's forgotten, or if because he works with so many Party members, he can't be seen taking supplies out of the office.

But I want to know how he feels about the Party, about the jazz music, have wanted to know since that night after the Zoo, and right now, with Mama out, I might actually get a chance to ask him.

"What's weighing on you, Charlotte?" he asks as he carefully places the last Fleischpflanzerl into the pan.

I don't know how to ask him, though. "Nichts." I shrug. "Wo ist Greta?"

"She wanted to spend the night with Klara."

"Who's Klara?"

Papa raises an eyebrow. "Even I know who Klara is, Lottchen."

"I can't keep up with all of Greta's friends, *Papa*," I say.

"She's Frau Köhler's daughter. They live over in Friedrichshain."

"You let Greta—" I stop myself. What I want to say, what I almost *did* say, was *you let Greta go have a sleepover with* Frau Köhler's *daughter?*

But I should have nothing against Frau Köhler. I quickly change my sentence. "You let her take the U-Bahn by herself?"

"She has all of your maps," my father says. "She won't get lost."

My maps. He does remember.

I could ask him, here—I could ask him about the jazz music and the Party and what I'm supposed to do because I don't *know*, but I don't. He turns his back to me and rotates some of the Fleischpflanzerln, and I want to reach out but Mama arrives home then and I can't bring myself to.

We eat an early dinner, the three of us. Over the last bites of Kartoffelsalat I ask, "Since Greta's out with Klara, may I call Geli and see if I can stay with her tonight?"

Mama sighs. "Charlotte . . ."

"*Please*," I say. "I've been good, I've only been to school and the BDM, I've watched after Greta. I haven't seen Geli in months."

Her lips purse. "And you couldn't have asked earlier?"

Hope fills my body. It's not a direct *no*, not yet.

"You weren't home."

"Will Angelika's father be all right with this?"

"I don't know. I'm sure he will be."

"Charlotte . . ."

"Bitte," I say. "We're just going to stay in, maybe go to the cinema."

"Going to the cinema is not staying in."

"We're going to the cinema, then," I say. "Please, Mama? We'll be careful. It'll just be the two of us."

I hold my breath while she deliberates, realizing I'm not even sure what answer I want her to give. If she says yes, I get to go out dancing like I haven't in months, I get to be with Geli.

If she says no, I'm saved from lying to her again, from feeling guilt over the fact that I'm going out dancing when Minna can't and Renate won't.

"Let her go, Anika," my father says, surprising both of us. He winks at me. "She did a fine enough job with the Fleisch-pflanzerln. We can let her out for one night."

"The Buletten, you mean," Mama says, but she's smiling. "Go call and ask if it's all right first, then you can go."

Someone picks up on the first ring, and I send a silent prayer that it's Geli and not her father. Luckily, it's her voice I hear over the line.

"Of course you can come over, Charlie," she says. She lowers her voice and I press the phone harder to my ear. "Did you want to go dancing?"

"Yes," I say, because of course I do, because my body has been aching for that kind of movement for months. I do not ask her about inviting the others. Like so many other things we talk around, it's better not to bring it up.

"Wonderful," Geli says. "A few of the boys told me about another dance hall—Femina. It's supposed to be this big ballroom, Charlie. I've been wanting to go—to take you there, for a while."

Her words send a thrill through me.

"Do you want me to meet you there?"

"Yes," she says. "Meet me at the Kurfürstendamm U stop."

"Half an hour," I say, and hang up. I go to my room and grab my coat off the back of my chair, glance at the book of Heine's poetry sitting on my dresser, open to the last stanza I was trying to memorize. Every night for the last two months I've reread the Heine poem before I fall asleep, whispering the words out loud to myself until they've started to invade my dreams, trying to perfect them for whenever I got the chance to see Geli again.

I murmur a section to myself as I get ready for the dance hall, as I take my hair out of its braids and fluff it around my shoulders. I have about half the poem memorized by now; maybe I'll be able to tell her about it tonight. Maybe she'll say she's proud of me.

I shut the book and tuck it in a drawer so Greta won't find it, then check the pockets of my coat for the Reichsmarks I sometimes keep there, hoping I have enough for the U-Bahn and whatever entrance fee this place has.

"See you later," I call to my parents, and wave to them as I head out the door.

I exit the U-Bahn stop at Kurfürstendamm and immediately spot Geli. Her hair shines under the streetlight, that cigarette holder in her hands, smoke curling from it like the punctuation to a question I have not asked yet. Her lipstick is bright red, and when she sees me, her mouth breaks into a smile.

"Charlie," she says, and hugs me close. She did not steal Mathilde's perfume tonight. "I'm so glad you called. I needed—" She shakes her head. "It doesn't matter. Let's just go dance. It's not far."

"Is it expensive?"

"Don't worry about that," she says, waving my concerns away. She crushes her cigarette under her heel and begins to walk briskly down Tauentzienstraße. We stop in front of a massive building; a sign on it reads *Femina, das Ballhaus*

Berlins, in large cursive script.

"Tommy's band is going to play here tonight," Geli says, and the knot of jealousy in my stomach loosens a little, because if he's playing in the band, he's not going to be dancing with her. "But he said he'd save me a dance or two," she says, winking, and laughs.

My stomach clenches. "Will you save me one?" I ask as we step inside the building and Geli hands over five marks for the both of us. It's a question I've asked before, but tonight there's desperation behind it.

"Don't I always?" she says immediately, though I can tell she's just saying it, and disappointment settles bitter on my tongue.

That first night she took me, where she promised to save me a dance, where she *did* dance with me, feels so far away now. I don't know why I thought tonight would be different, don't know why I got my hopes up that tonight would be special because I haven't been able to go dancing with her in months.

We take an elevator crowded with people up to the top floor, and I hug my arms closer to me. I don't see any of the other Swingjugend, not immediately, and as I scan the faces in the crowd I realize we're some of the youngest people here.

"Geli . . ."

"Relax, Charlie," Geli says. "You wanted to come dance, didn't you? You'll love this place, and we don't have to stay too long. I just want to hear a few songs." She smiles at me and, before I can respond, heads onto the dance floor. The drums are so loud I can't hear myself think.

I want to follow her, but my feet won't move.

But then I glance through the crowd, through the press of bodies, and see her greeting Moritz with a kiss. My palms clench and I push myself into the mass of people, determined to dance, determined to get lost in the music without her.

I dance by myself for two, three songs, not caring how ridiculous I look, flailing my arms wildly until I'm out of breath and sweating. Once or twice an older boy comes up and spins me a few times, and I let him, his fingers on my waist.

Someone is watching me, though, I can feel it. The song changes to something brass-heavy and as the boy swings me again, I catch the eye of a girl standing by one of the tables, a drink in her hand. She raises her drink at me, a clear invitation to come join her, and my heart beats faster.

She could just be friendly, but something in my gut tells me that's not it. I remember our second club night, the two boys I saw kissing, remember not feeling brave enough to do such a thing myself. Secretly worried what my friends would think. What *Geli* would think.

But no one knows me here, and the crowd is so large and the music is so loud and Geli's off with Tommy, and I—

I break off from the boy, giving him a quick "Sorry" before

making my way over to the girl, who smiles a sharp smile at me. Up close I can see she's a few centimeters taller than I am, with dark brown eyes and hair that contrast with her pale skin, a smattering of freckles across the bridge of her nose. She puts down her drink, and it's so noisy I have to lean in to hear her when she introduces herself.

"Ingrid," she says, her eyes meeting mine. "Du?"

"Peg—Charlotte," I say. I frown at her accent. "You're not from Berlin."

"Hamburg," she says. "My cousin brought me."

"Do you . . . do you like the music?" I ask.

"I'm the one who showed it to him," she says, and winks at me. My face heats up, and I'm grateful for the dark so she can't see me blush.

"Tanz mit mir?" I ask, and she nods, like she's been waiting for my invitation. I take her hand and pull her out onto the dance floor just as another song is starting.

I glance toward the stage. I can't help it. Tommy isn't up there anymore, which means he's somewhere in the crowd, dancing that dance he promised Geli.

My head feels hot at the thought, my heart beating faster, and I turn back toward Ingrid, who's looking at me expectantly. She takes my arm and spins me once, twice, three times, until I'm dizzy and can imagine that's why my head is pounding so much.

She spins me out again and this time I'm the one pulling

her in, pulling her close, my fingers catching on her waist. She lets out a gasp, her dark eyes meeting mine, and for a second, I falter. I open my mouth to say something, apologize, but suddenly there's movement and noise coming from above us, and the band quiets down.

It's only when I look up that I understand—the roof of the Femina is opening, and although I feel like one of the only people who didn't know it could do this, we all stop for a moment and look up at the sky, at the stars pouring in.

"Oh," I breathe.

And then the band starts up again and I look at Ingrid and my hand is still on her waist and I don't move it, not yet, and she smiles at me.

"Do you want to keep dancing?" she asks.

I turn my head. Tommy's onstage now, and there, leaning back in his arms, is Geli, face turned toward the sky.

"In a minute," I say. "I think I need some air."

We find a back way out, holding hands until we've made it outside onto the street.

"Hope we don't have to pay when we go back in, my coat's still in there," I say, and Ingrid laughs. It's a good laugh, low and rich.

I take us in the direction of the Zoo, hurrying until we're at the elephant gate, the pair of elephants staring down at us. Ingrid threads her fingers through mine and the two of us look up. The sky is just as majestic out here, perhaps even more so, and the sight of it leaves me breathless because it's something I could never map.

Papa tried, once, to teach me the constellations, said they were maps for the stars; but I could never grasp them, unable to form pictures from the millions of pinpricks of light I was seeing.

After a moment, Ingrid slides her hand around my waist, and I turn. Her face is so close to mine, and I'm reminded again of those two boys at the club, kissing.

We almost would have been safer in the anonymity of Femina, in the chaos of the dance hall. But there's no one around right now, nothing except the shouts of partygoers and the haze of smoke from someone's fire off in the distance, rising up to meet the sky.

I don't let myself think about it anymore. About Geli, about the club, the music, the poems, any of it. I close my eyes and I lean forward and I hope that Ingrid's mouth meets mine, that I haven't misread this, that I won't end up looking like a fool.

I hope, and that's the most terrifying thing of all.

But she kisses me, and her lips are soft and she tastes like the wine she was drinking, dark and floral, and I am as breathless and dizzy as when I have danced for too long.

"Charlotte," she gasps, and I like the way my name sounds in her mouth.

And then. And then. All I can think of is Moritz saying

Geli's name like that, and the hurt of this girl not being Geli cuts through me sharp.

I pull back. Ingrid notices.

"Bin ich nicht gut?" she asks, and I shake my head.

"Doch," I say. "No, you're—you're fantastic, it's just . . . I wish you were someone else."

"Oh," Ingrid says, and gives a soft sigh. She pulls away from me, leaning back on one of the elephants.

"Tell me about her," she says.

"What makes you think . . ."

"Because you're out here with me," Ingrid says. "Because if you were jealous over a boy, you would have found another boy. Komm schon, Charlotte." She nudges my shoulder with her own. "Who is she?"

I sigh. "Her name's Angelika. Geli. And she's my best friend and sometimes I think there's something more there, but I don't—I don't know. She invited me here tonight but she's off with one of the boys who's playing in the band—"

"Which boy?" Ingrid says suddenly.

"Moritz, though he calls himself Tommy," I say. To my surprise, she starts laughing.

"Moritz is my cousin," she says, grinning. "He's the reason I came up here tonight, said there was good jazz music and more swings and I should come. But *Tommy*, seriously? I'll have to tease him for that."

"Oh," I say. "I—I didn't know you were one of us."

Ingrid nods. "We can get a lot of records imported since we're near the port." She bumps her hip against mine. "Let me know if you ever want any, Lotte. I can usually get copies."

Lotte. I blush. "My friends actually call me Charlie."

Ingrid raises an eyebrow. "Are we friends?"

"Perhaps," I say, and she smiles. She leans in and kisses me on the cheek and I turn, kiss her once before pulling back.

"We should go back in," I say, pushing off from the stone elephant. Ingrid follows me, our arms brushing as we turn the corner and head back into the building.

"You'll have to point her out to me," she says, once we're in the elevator. "Your girl."

"She's not *my* girl," I say.

"The girl who's with my cousin, then," Ingrid says. "I can't believe he said his name was Tommy."

"Do they not use English names up in Hamburg?"

"They do," Ingrid says. "We do. I just think he could have picked better." She laughs.

A new band is playing when we reenter the ballroom. The ceiling has been closed, shutting off the stars once more, disappearing them from view. Geli is still hanging off Tommy's arm, magnetic even in this crowd of women all older and more sophisticated than us.

"Shall I introduce myself?" Ingrid asks. I look at her questioningly. "To your friend. A little jealousy never hurts," she says.

"She doesn't know I like girls," I say. "So it wouldn't . . . it wouldn't even matter."

Ingrid shrugs. "Doesn't mean she can't still be jealous of you spending your time with someone else, now, does it?"

"No, I suppose not."

"Then come on," she says, and pulls me across the dance floor. And I let her, because maybe she's right, maybe this will make Geli jealous.

Is that what I want?

If it means Geli will pay attention to me, then yes. It is what I want. She told me she wanted to come here with *me*; she brings me to this magnificent place and then ignores me the entire night.

So yes. This is what I want.

We make our way over to them, Ingrid's arm looped through mine. My skin feels hot where it touches hers. Moritz is leaning against the stage, Geli standing beside him. As we make our way toward them, I notice Geli holding a glass of wine that someone must have given her. It's the same color as her lipstick, and she breaks into a wine-red smile when she sees me.

"Peggy!" she exclaims, and to my surprise she pulls me in and kisses me on the cheek. My face flushes as dark as her wine. "And you remember Tommy."

"Of course," I say.

Beside me, Ingrid laughs. "You didn't tell me your name was

Tommy," she says to Moritz, who now has his arm around Geli's waist. It's his turn to blush, and Geli looks between the two of them and then between me and Ingrid, confusion blooming on her face.

"Who are you?" she asks Ingrid, not kindly. I frown, but Ingrid doesn't recoil at Geli's tone.

"Moritz—*Tommy's*—cousin," she says. "I came down from Hamburg to see him play." She bumps me with her hip. "Ran into your friend here, who bought me a drink."

I didn't buy Ingrid a drink, and start to say so, but at her look I close my mouth. If the plan is to make Geli jealous, then it's working. She's chewing on her bottom lip the way she does when presented with a problem she feels she needs to solve.

"Oh," she finally says, and smiles, but it doesn't reach her eyes. "Well. If you're friends with Peggy, then you must be all right. We were just thinking of leaving, though."

"Were you?" Ingrid asks.

"Yes—isn't that right?" Geli says, looking at me. I blink, caught off guard by her intensity.

"I thought you were going to save me a dance," I say.

Geli purses her lips. "Of course, Peggy," she says, but then Moritz cuts in, talking over me.

"Come on, doll, just one more," he says, taking Geli's hand. I shoot him a look, but he doesn't seem to notice.

Geli does, though, and I watch as she throws her arms around his neck, giggling. Before I can say anything else to her, she lets Moritz whisk her away. I pick up her glass of wine and down it in one gulp. Ingrid watches me.

"You wanted her jealous," she says, and I nod, before taking her outstretched hand and heading out onto the dance floor with her.

It's like the band is matching my mood, the drums immediately picking up the tempo and the horns blasting so loud they hurt my ears. Ingrid spins me wildly, her arms loose, laughing as I nearly bump into Moritz. Geli frowns at her, at us, but I ignore her and keep moving with Ingrid, whose body has now drawn dangerously close to mine.

I kiss her, briefly, just the corner of her mouth, fast enough someone could've missed it if they weren't looking closely enough at us.

But somehow, I know Geli was looking. And sure enough, when I pull back from Ingrid, Geli's staring at me with that same puzzled, haughty expression.

I don't care. I don't care. I don't.

I do.

The band finally slows down after two more songs, and Ingrid and Moritz walk out with us, the four of us collecting our coats and heading back out into the freezing night air. I catch Ingrid looking up at the stars, and she smirks at me.

"Will we see you again at one of the other clubs?" Geli asks her, her tone suggesting that she would very much *not* like that.

Ingrid gives her a smile as fake as the one I've seen Geli give to other girls, practiced and full of malice.

"No, I'm taking the train back up to Hamburg in the morning. Though you should write me sometime, Charlie. *Tommy* can give you my address," she says. Moritz looks between his cousin and Geli, confusion on his face.

"S-sure. I'll do that," he says. "Next meeting."

"Sure," I say. The four of us stand at the corner of Tauentzienstraße. "Well, we—we're going this way."

"We're headed to Friedrichshain," Moritz says. "So . . . gute Nacht, then." He nods at me and then pulls Geli in for a kiss; she turns her face so his mouth catches her cheek instead. Embarrassed, he ducks his head and hurries to the other street. Ingrid tosses one last look over her shoulder at us before following him.

I reach for Geli's hand, but she pulls away. "Geli . . ."

"Let's go home. We've been out late enough," she says, and begins the walk back to her house. I pull my coat tighter against the chill. That smell of smoke from earlier is even worse now, hanging heavy in the air.

Geli walks ahead of me, hurrying so I almost have to jog to keep up with her. There are shouts coming from what sounds like a few blocks over.

"Geli, slow down—"

She doesn't. If anything, she walks faster so that now I am running to keep up with her.

She leads.

I follow.

In desperation, I hurry and grab her elbow, spinning her around to face me.

"What?" she snaps, and to my surprise her eyes are bright. "What do you want, Charlie?"

"I . . . are you all right?" I ask.

"Oh, like you care," she says. My heart hammers in my chest. I wanted her to be jealous, I did. But what is she *really* jealous of? Jealous that I was spending time with someone who wasn't her?

Or jealous of something more?

"Geli, if this is about Ingrid . . ."

"Why would it be about Ingrid?" she snaps. Around us the noise grows louder, and I instinctively grip her elbow tighter. She tries to pull away, but I won't let her. "What could I *possibly* have to be jealous over with you and *Ingrid*?" She says Ingrid's name like it's a curse.

"You're not . . . you're not mad that I kissed her, are you?"

The words come out in a whisper, but I swear they're the loudest thing I've ever said, loud enough to be heard over the shouts in the distance, over the loudest jazz music. Louder than my heartbeat, which thunders in my ears.

"Why would I be mad about that, Charlie?" Geli says bitterly.

I let go of her hand. But she doesn't turn away from me; instead, she just looks at me with that same superior expression, and suddenly I can't stand it.

"What was I supposed to do?" I ask. "*You* left *me*. You're the one who wanted to bring me to this club and then you go off and spend the whole night with Tommy, and I—" I shake my head. "You can't hate me for this, Geli, for wanting—"

"Wanting *what*? Pining after the first—the first *girl* to give you the time of day?" she hisses. I step back from her.

"Geli, don't hate me for that, bitte—you can be mad at me for leaving you but don't—don't hate me for being with her, please—"

My heart feels like it's in my throat. I've read it wrong. Read *her* wrong. She's not mad at me because she's jealous—she's mad because I kissed a girl in the first place. Because of what I did. Because it is not what good German girls—girls like us—do.

"*Hate* you?" she says, and before I can respond she reaches out and pulls me to her, her mouth hot on mine. I gasp, but don't pull away.

"I don't hate you," she whispers, her fingers digging into my coat, and I'm about to say more, to ask her what does she mean, does she mean it, when the sound of glass breaking reaches us, too close, boots marching on cobblestone.

I take her hand and we run down the street. I've long held the map to her place in my head, so I quickly steer us through alleys and around corners until we've finally reached her house.

She unlocks the door and pulls me inside. The house is completely silent, and she reaches behind me and shuts the door before pushing me against it, kissing me again, and again, until my mouth is swollen.

"I don't hate you," she says between kisses. "There's nothing to hate. There's nothing wrong with you, Charlie. If there is, there's something wrong with me, too."

"Geli . . . ," I breathe, but she shakes her head, her mind made up about something, and all I can think, even with my mouth still sore from hers, is—

Does she mean it? Or is this just jealousy?

Does she mean it, or is this her making sure I will never, ever leave her?

Does she even know?

Ich sag ihr nicht, weshalb ich's tu
Weiß selber nicht den Grund—
Ich halte ihr die Augen zu
Und küß sie auf den Mund.
I don't tell her the reason why
I hardly know myself—
Yet still I cover up her eyes
And kiss her on the mouth.

I follow her up to her bedroom, get dressed for bed with her in silence, borrowing one of her nightgowns. We use Mathilde's cold cream to wipe off our makeup. Without it, Geli looks impossibly young, and I watch myself wipe off the illusion that

I am anything other than her plain best friend.

"Geli . . ."

"We can talk about it in the morning, Charlie," she says.

"Promise?"

"Promise."

She doesn't try to kiss me again.

We get ready for bed the same way we always have when one of us has slept over, and by the time we crawl into bed, I have almost convinced myself that none of it happened. That kissing Ingrid, Geli's mouth against mine, none of it was real. It happened to Peggy. Not Charlie.

But I can't shake the feeling that it meant something. That it had to mean—something.

As she reaches over to turn out the light I ask again, just to be sure.

"You don't hate me?"

"I could never," she says. "Niemals, Charlie," and I fall asleep clutching her hand, only thinking of her promise of tomorrow. Tomorrow. We'll talk about it tomorrow.

But we don't. We won't.

When we wake up, Berlin is burning.

Geli and I are silent as we walk back to my house the next morning. The air is smoky, still faintly glowing. All around us, shops are destroyed, glass littering the cobblestones.

The shouts I heard last night, the smell of smoke. The glass under my feet.

It gets worse the longer we walk, people clutching each other, sobbing, and for a second I fear that the whispers we've been hearing for half a year are true—that we are finally at war.

But as I look harder, I know it isn't true. Only a few shops have broken glass, the damage done not by bombs but by bricks. Paint mars the edges of some of the shards, and if they were whole, I know what they would say.

Kauft nicht bei Juden.

All the shops that were damaged are owned by Jews.

"Geli . . ."

She squeezes my hand as we turn another corner, and I stop.

"We should—we should go check on Minna," I say, and she nods. We pick up our pace now, and with each step, that ever-persistent knot of guilt in my chest tightens.

How did I go so long without noticing, *really* noticing, how dangerous it is here now for the Jews?

Maybe I didn't want to notice. Maybe it was easier.

With a jolt I think of the fear on Minna's face when the HJ boys raided our dance, months ago now.

I should have noticed then.

I should have noticed even earlier than that. Earlier than the incident at the restaurant, even. I should have noticed when Linda Spielmann's bakery closed, or when the Waldstein siblings stopped coming to school.

I should have, and I didn't.

We step inside Renate and Minna's building. Herr Neumann is nowhere to be seen.

Was he one of the ones participating last night? Was his voice one of the shouts I heard?

I knock on the Kochs' door, hoping they can tell it's me, it's us. Does that fear go through them every time someone knocks on their door?

I remember Herr Neumann again, the intent way he was listening outside the door so many months ago. I could have said something then, couldn't I? I could have done something to stop him.

"It's Charlie," I call, just to reassure whoever is behind the door. "And—and Geli."

Minna opens the door. Her face is pale and drawn, and when she sees it's us, she nearly bursts into tears. I immediately reach for her, pulling her into my arms as if I can provide any comfort.

"Are you all right?" I ask her, feeling ridiculous as soon as the question leaves my mouth.

"We're all right, Charlie," Minna says, but her voice isn't convincing. "The twins slept through it—the shop got looted but Mama and Papa are there cleaning it up now."

"We'll help," I say fiercely. "Let me go get Mama and Papa, I know they'll want to—"

"Charlie, nein," Minna says firmly, her hand settling lightly on my arm. "You can't. If they see you helping us—especially your father—" She passes a hand over her face. "At least Renate's family was in Köln; if Fritz had been here—" Her voice chokes off, and I pull her to me again. Geli is strangely quiet.

After a moment, Minna speaks again, her voice lowered to a whisper. "I spoke with Lizzie—the singer from the club. And Max, that boy Renate's friends with. Max has family in Paris; he said—he said they could get us out," Minna says. "Myself and the twins, at least, so I—" She sniffs. "We're going to go. Before it's too late."

"You can't leave," Geli says suddenly, and I turn to her. "If—if you come back to the club, you're the only one who can play piano—"

"That's what you're worried about right now?" I cry, and both Minna and Geli flinch away from me. "They're destroying shops and you're worried about—about den blöden Club?" I stare at her, unwilling to believe what she's just said, that she could be so unfeeling. My nails dig into my palms, my breath quickening.

"You didn't think it was so stupid last night with Ingrid," Geli hisses, and Minna looks back and forth between us. Before I can stop Geli, she turns on her heel and storms out, nearly slamming the door behind her.

Minna turns to me, her eyes wide.

"You should follow her," she says gently. But I don't want

to follow Geli, not now, not when she's angry and Minna is in front of me, hurting.

"I just—I can't believe she'd say something like that when—when you—"

"Geli's always been like this, Charlie," Minna says. "Why do you think we never talk about any of it around her?"

I falter. She's right, but in this moment I'm torn between my anger at Geli and that need, even now, to defend her.

"You should go talk to her," Minna says. "I just . . . I want to be alone right now, I think. I have a lot to think about," she adds, and reaches out and hugs me tightly. "Love you."

"Are you—are you *sure* you don't want me to stay?" I ask, that desperation creeping into my tone, that need to fix whatever is wrong.

But this isn't something I'll be able to fix, and we both know it.

"I'm sure," she says, and I let her guide me out of the flat. She closes the door firmly behind me.

Geli is not waiting for me. I leave the building, almost running down the stairs, and still I do not see her. It isn't until I step out into the street that I catch a flash of her blond curls as she walks away from me.

"Geli!"

She runs then. I follow her across the Spree, running for ages until I catch up with her.

She finally turns down Krausnickstraße, her back still to me as she slowly walks down the street. Glass crunches under her shoes, but I don't think she notices. Instead, she tips her head back, staring up at the Neue Synagogue.

It's intact. That's my first thought. How, how is it still standing after all that destruction, when so many Jewish businesses and other synagogues around us are now just burning shells?

"Geli . . . ," I say quietly.

"What, Charlie?"

"You . . ." I take a deep breath, my heart still hammering fast in my chest. I am never the one challenging her. I am the one by her side, no matter what. "You shouldn't have said that—to Minna. You're not . . . you're not at school with us, you haven't seen how bad it is for her some days, how much she was risking to just come to the club—"

"You think I don't know how *bad* it is?" she snaps, whirling around to face me. "You think—you think I'm so insulated from all of this?" She spreads her arms wide. "Did you forget who I live with? Where do you think my father was last night, Charlie? Why do you think he wasn't home when we got there?" Her voice wobbles but she squares her shoulders. "I hate him. I hate every last one of them, but what am I supposed to *do*?"

"I don't *know*!" I snap. "I don't know, but you—you can't just pretend like everything's fine, like the worst thing in the world is if you don't get to go out to some expensive dance hall while—while Minna and her family have to leave the country because of people like your father!"

As soon as I say it, I know I've gone too far. Two bright pink splotches appear on her cheeks as if I've slapped her.

"Geli, I . . . I'm sorry . . ."

"Don't," she snaps. "Just don't." She turns away, arms crossed tightly over her chest, and as I make myself walk away, I turn to look back at her, only once, but she never looks at me.

This, then, is how it begins to end. Us helping Minna and her family pack up their things, moving them in the early hours of the morning, all of us going to the train station together. Renate, face crumpling as she hugs Minna goodbye. Greta asking me the next day where they've all gone.

I do not tell her, and it breaks my heart.

A postcard from Paris to Renate, confirming that they've arrived, which she reads over and over until it's worn.

Geli and I see each other less and less. In April I go over to her house to celebrate her birthday, but I don't know the girls from her Gymnasium, and she's frosty to me the entire time. After that I only see her at our BDM meetings. We rarely talk. If Renate notices the silence between us, she doesn't say anything, not even when Moritz starts coming to pick Geli up from the meetings every week, her arm looped through his as they walk away.

Once or twice Renate and I go back to the clubs together, but without Geli's laugh echoing through the room, without the sound of Minna playing the piano, it doesn't hold the same appeal. When we go, Renate never asks why Geli isn't joining us, and I never mention the fact that the music doesn't sound the same without Minna.

I have never told Renate about Ingrid. About Geli kissing me. About what Geli said to Minna about her needing to stay at the club. About what I said to Geli about her father. I have wanted to so many times before, but after Minna left, I never wanted to be the one to bring her up, not to Renate; never wanted to be the one to cause that look of pain to flash across her face.

As for not telling her about Ingrid or Geli, there are some things I'd rather keep to myself. If I never mention it, if I never speak of it out loud, it's that much easier to convince myself that it meant nothing.

That it means—nothing.

I do not mention Minna, and she does not mention Geli, and the two of us pretend that we're fine.

But sometimes at night when I can't fall asleep I catch myself reciting the parts of the Heine poem before the ache of it hurts too much. I don't try to memorize it anymore; the book shoved at the back of my vanity drawer since my fight with Geli, along with my feelings for her.

Renate finds a job in a textile factory, of all places. She tried to work as a conductor at the Ostbahnhof but was turned away, not because of her lack of experience but because they realized she had difficulty hearing the announcements. When I mention this to Mama, she says that a factory would not be a bad place for me to work, either, that we may need the extra money. Any talk of finding an apprenticeship was abandoned when the Kochs left; most of the tailors we know are Jewish and are now gone to who knows where.

I ask Mama about why we may need the money, and she just shakes her head. It is Papa who explains that with things moving the way Hitler wants them to, those rumors about war may be true sooner than we think.

So the week after I finish school, Mittlere Reife in hand, I get a job at the same factory as Renate. I try to tell myself it's fine, that I am helping my family, but every stitch I make reminds me of the lines I drew on my maps, maps I haven't touched since we stopped going to the clubs.

A new family moves into the Kochs' flat, their sons our age. We watch them move in, take note of the boys in their Hitler-jugend uniforms with the proud badges and insignias that show they're leaders. Fritz is drawn to them immediately. Renate and I stay away. Hans does, too, and when we ask him about it he just shrugs, says he knows too many boys like that.

We settle into an odd routine, and all the time, pressure builds like gas trapped in a jar, the voices on the radio becoming angrier, louder, until they are all we can hear, until what's worse is that they fade into the background so we hardly notice them anymore except to glance at each other across the dinner table and think, *My God, is this really happening?*

But pressure builds, and builds, and builds, until it cannot be contained.

This is how it ends, and this is how it begins.

On 31. August 1939, Greta and I fall asleep, her curled up in my bed. She has changed the most out of all of us over the past year, has gotten almost as tall as me, and the two of us are almost too big for the cramped corners of my bed.

It is the last time we will fall asleep peacefully.

When we wake up, we will be at war.

Part II

SEPTEMBER 1939–MAI 1941

September 1939

WE HAVE invaded Poland.

Greta and I wake up drowsily and tiptoe into the living room, where our parents are huddled by the radio, Hitler's voice crackling through the speakers. I hug Greta to my side.

Mama's hand is at her mouth and Papa stares blankly out the window, and I want to ask how they are feeling, what they are thinking, but all I can think about is the last glimpse I had of Minna from the train window as she left, the tops of the twins' heads barely visible, the tears she wasn't even trying to hide streaming down her face.

"You're not going to work today," Mama says once the broadcast has finished.

I stand. "Then I'm going to Renate's."

Mama looks at me darkly. "No."

"Why not?"

"Charlotte, we—we don't know what might happen, if

Poland might retaliate—they said there were dead guards at the border—"

"But we invaded them—"

"You're not going," Mama says, and the look on her face is so stern I back down at once.

We are at war.

This then, is what it means to be at war. It means sitting on Renate's bed, worriedly talking; Mama finally relented when I pointed out the cellar in Renate's building can house more people than ours.

"Did you think this would happen?" I ask.

"You saw the planes," she says softly, referring to the warplanes we saw flying over Berlin a few months before. She blows out air. "I hoped it wouldn't, but when Minna left . . ."

I squeeze Renate's hand. "She's safe," I say.

"Is she? There are hardly any Jews left," Renate says. "A few of the swings, maybe, but now that we're at war . . ."

I swallow. The word *war* just feels so heavy in our mouths, tastes like smoke on our tongues.

"Do you think they'll draft your brothers?" I ask, and Renate bites her lip.

"I hope not," she says softly. "But Hans could be called up any minute. Thank God Fritz is too young."

Voices float in from her living room at that moment, her father's tone sharp.

"How is your father doing?" I ask her, and she shakes her head.

"He just wants to pretend everything's fine. Mama, too. It's not like they'll make him go back, he's too old." She sighs. "Try telling him that, though."

"How is Hans taking it?"

"He doesn't want to go," Renate says miserably. "He's almost done with his labor service, but after that . . . he wants to go to university, he was supposed to start in the spring at Humboldt."

I want to tell her it will be okay, but I don't know that it will. It's not like I have to worry about any of our family being drafted, anyway.

"Let's put on some music," I say, just to distract her, to distract me, both of us, from thoughts of her brothers in trenches, bombs going off around them. "Do you still have the Louis Armstrong record?"

She nods her head toward the player. "I put it on sometimes when . . . when Mama's at work." She shrugs. "Why should I worry if she or Herr Neumann hear it now?"

Minna's face flashes through my mind again. I shove the thought away as I start up the record player, applause and trumpets blaring out of the tiny speakers. Not a minute later, Fritz pokes his head in.

"Mama's going to yell at you if she knows you're playing that again," he says. "But if you let me listen, I won't tell."

"Go away, Fritz," Renate says sourly.

"It's not like you can really hear it anyway—"

"Go *away*, Fritz!" Renate snaps, her voice trembling. Her brother finally backs out of her room, a smirk on his face as he shuts her door. Renate rakes her fingers through her short hair, takes a breath.

"He's been hanging out with those boys in the Hitlerjugend who live downstairs," she says darkly. "Follows them around almost every day."

I look back and forth from the record to her. "Then why does he—why does he still want to listen to the music?"

"Because it belonged to Hans," Renate says. She flops down on her stomach and eyes me. "I wouldn't get your hopes up—it doesn't mean he doesn't think it's degenerate any more than Mama does. But Gott sei Dank that he's still more obsessed with Hans than with the boys from downstairs, at least for now."

"Does he know what's going on?" I ask her, and her face darkens as she wipes at her eyes.

"He's *happy* about it," she says bitterly. "Says it's what Poland gets, for attacking us. What everyone deserves, for 'underestimating the Fatherland.'"

"Renate . . ."

"I want him out of the Jungvolk," she says. "But Mama says it's not up to me. Says it's safer for all of us if he stays. But it's— it's poisoning him, Charlie, day by day. Before we know it he'll wind up like—like Geli's father."

Shame floods my face, though I can't say why. Geli's father isn't my father.

"Have you spoken with Geli?" Renate asks. She goes to turn the record down. "Her father must be ecstatic." There is so much bitterness in her voice.

I falter. This is the first time either of us has mentioned Geli in months. "I . . . I don't really see Geli anymore," I say. "Not since last week's BDM meeting. We don't . . . we don't see each other outside of that."

I could tell her, now, what happened between us. Since she's the one who brought it up. But it feels so trivial compared to being at war.

Besides. Countries at war have no time for girls with crushes. And the Party has no patience for girls who kiss other girls.

If anyone knew before, it would have been dangerous enough. But now it feels akin to suicide.

Louis Armstrong continues playing in the background. With a sigh, Renate lies back on her bed, and I join her. She props herself up on her elbow and faces me so she can hear me better.

"Do you miss it?" she asks me. "The clubs?"

"Sometimes," I say. "I miss . . . I miss dancing. I miss going somewhere we weren't watched."

She nods. "I miss it too," she says. "I was . . . I've been thinking, since we—since we don't have to worry as much anymore, maybe we could go back? I don't know, now that there's a war, we should find some release where we can, right? And maybe . . ." She licks her lips. "I don't know, that sort of resistance seems more important now, don't you think?"

I stare at her. Resistance? Is what we're doing resistance? It's music. It's dancing.

But I think back to that feeling I felt every time we went to one of the clubs. That undercurrent of danger, that feeling of belonging to something bigger than myself. That joy at hearing Minna play a song, that exhilaration at dancing with Ingrid.

"I'd like that," I say. "But how will we know where to go? Usually . . . usually Minna or Geli told us."

Renate pushes herself up on her elbows. "I still have the map you made," she says. "I marked everywhere we went, maybe we could start by checking those? Or you could—you could ask Geli." She doesn't meet my eyes as she suggests this.

"You still have my map?"

"Of course," she says. She blushes. "I marked everywhere we went on it—look." She reaches under her bed and pulls out a rolled-up piece of paper, the edges curling in on themselves. She flattens it out with her hands and I look at it. Little stars mark most of the locations we went, though a few have exclamation points on them.

"What are those?" I ask her, pointing.

"Just—places I enjoyed," she says. I stare at the map. Renate's handwriting is far messier than my own—in some places you can barely make out the names of the clubs.

"I still think you should ask Geli," she says. "She'll know better than we would, and it'll be easier than going to every single place ourselves and hoping there are other swings there."

"You must really miss it if you're trying to get me to ask Geli," I joke, but it falls flat. Renate laughs anyway before rolling up her map and placing it back under her bed.

I stand. "I should . . . you're right, I should go talk to her," I say. Renate frowns, and I repeat myself.

"I heard you," she says sadly. She sighs. "I'll see you at work, then?"

"Yes," I say, and as I leave, I hear her turn the music up just a little louder.

The walk to Geli's is cold, the atmosphere charged. I don't know what I expect—perhaps the flashiness that I am so used to with the Party. The bright red of the flags, the officers in their polished boots marching down the streets.

But no. Windows are shuttered, families drawn close, as if any second Polish soldiers will storm our streets, even though we are the ones who have declared war on them.

I pull my jacket tighter and knock on the door, hoping Geli's father will not answer. Perhaps he is away today, doing—doing something.

Thankfully it is Mathilde, Geli's stepmother, who answers the door. On her lips is that same shade of lipstick Geli always steals, that dark red.

"Charlotte," she says, having never given in to calling me Charlie the way Renate's mother sometimes does. "You're here for Angelika, I assume."

"Yes," I say. "Is she—is she in?"

"She's upstairs," Mathilde says, looking me over. "You've grown taller."

"I—danke," I say, because what else do I say? The last time she saw me was in April, for Geli's birthday. And even that had been like now, a cursory once-over at her door.

I want to ask her what she thinks of the news that we are at war. She is younger than my parents, but old enough still to remember—she would have been about my age when the first war started. Younger, even. Greta's age.

I want to know what she thinks, but then I remember Herr Haas, the sharp creases of his uniform like something you could cut yourself on, and I do not want to know what she thinks at all.

Like Mathilde said, Geli is in her room. I marvel at it when I step in, so unchanged from my last time here. It brings me some comfort, that despite everything that's changed this past year between me and her, her room hasn't. Her vanity shoved against a wall with pictures of actresses fixed to it, the worn carpet at the entrance to her room, her dirty clothes always tossed over a chair. Everything neatly mapped out, unlike how I still feel about her.

I remember the Heine book I haven't touched since the morning of our fight and close my eyes.

"Geli," I say, and she looks up from her vanity at me. "How . . . how are you doing?" I ask, and wince at how formal I sound, like she didn't used to be my best friend.

"Fine," she says.

"You heard the news, then," I say.

"Who didn't?" She turns back to her mirror, and I sit on her bed.

"How's . . . how's your father taking it?" I ask. "Is he going to fight?"

"Who knows," she says. This time she does look at me, eyes burning into mine from her reflection in the mirror. "I didn't think you'd care."

"Geli, I—" I stiffen, my hands curled in my lap. She waits. I know what she wants—an apology, for what I said about her father nearly an entire year ago.

But why should I have to apologize for something that's true?

"I do care," I say. "I know . . . I know how you feel about living with him, and you're right, I don't know what that's like for you, not really, and I . . . I'm sorry."

She finally softens then, standing and crossing the room to me and hugging me so fiercely it steals the breath from me, as if it is just that easy for her to forgive me, as if the year of distance between us never happened.

As if this entire time, the responsibility for our friendship has been resting on *my* shoulders.

She takes a seat on the bed next to me before jumping up again to riffle through her closet.

"How are you doing?" she asks. "With everything?"

"Scared," I say. I swing my legs. "I . . . it's not like I have to worry about any of my family being drafted, not like Renate, but I'm still . . . scared."

"I'm sure it won't be all that bad," she says, but she doesn't sound convincing. She finally decides on a dress, a short-sleeved light pink one I've never seen her wear.

I turn away while she puts it on, desperate to keep her talking to me, to find something to fill the silence. "Will it affect getting your Abitur?" I ask her.

"I don't know," she says.

I could hit myself for that question. It's a war, it'll affect everything. Won't it?

"Renate . . . ," I say, and my mouth is suddenly dry at her name, though I don't know why. "Renate said we should go back to the club. That—I don't know, that it's a form of resistance, that we should keep listening to the music." I shrug. "I don't know, but we—"

"No," Geli says fiercely, and for a second I think she's saying no, we shouldn't go back, that she's done with the club. "Resistance. You said it, right?" She smiles. "Why don't we have a club meeting here? A little Tanztee next Monday? Papa's never home and it's not like the HJ will ever look for us here. Especially with the war happening."

"Geli, I don't think . . ." But her eyes are already shining, and for a moment I let myself get fully caught up in it, the magic of Geli and her wild plans, her schemes. Besides, she's right: it could be fun.

"Will Tommy be coming?" I don't know what makes me ask. We haven't spoken about him since he started showing up to the BDM meetings. Maybe it's this proximity to her again, being in her room, so close to where we kissed.

"Probably," she says. "If I invite him. Why?"

"No reason," I say, my mouth dry again.

"Do you want me to invite him?"

"It doesn't matter, Geli," I say, and she crosses over to me.

"It does matter," she says. She takes a lock of my hair, twirls it between her fingers. "Everything you have to say matters, Charlie."

I hold my breath. But she doesn't lean in, doesn't try to kiss me, as badly as I want her to. What I have to say matters, she just said so. But if I told her not to invite him, would she even listen? She kissed me, once, and we haven't spoken about it since, I've barely *seen* her since, and now—

171

"You can invite him," I hear myself saying, and she nods, and I know then that she had already made up her mind to do so, no matter what I said.

The next day, Greta and I walk together to the building where our BDM and JM meetings are held. Greta has been promoted to a leader in her small JM group, overseeing the new girls who came in last year. Her face is serious, dark eyes taking in everything around us. I wonder if she likes the responsibility.

I wonder what our meeting will be like now that there's a war. Over the past year, my disenchantment with the BDM has only grown—I don't mind the songs or the sewing; I like going hiking with the other girls and might actually consider some of them my friends. But there is a war now. Are we supposed to just keep hiking, singing, now that there is a war?

Maybe we won't. Maybe our meetings will be canceled and I will stop having to give up my Wednesdays and Saturdays to be here.

"I'll pick you up after," I say to Greta as we walk up to the building. "I'll have Renate and Geli with me. Do you want to see if the four of us can go get a drink together?"

"I think Frau Köhler wants me to help her with something," Greta says quietly.

"You'd rather help Frau Köhler than get a hot chocolate with your sister and Geli?" I tease. But I feel uneasy as I say it.

"*No*," Greta says, frowning. "I—can't you just wait for me? It'll be five minutes, promise."

"We can do that, Gretchen," I say, and reach out to fix her braids.

She swats my hand away. "Not now, Charlie, they look fine. Mama did them," she says, and before I can respond, she runs up into the building ahead of me.

Renate and Geli are already seated when I enter the small room for our Heimatabend. The first thing I notice is that the other girls except for Geli are clustered together, their eyes raking over Renate and me, noses turned up. I take a seat next to Renate, intent on telling her about the Tanztee the second the meeting is over.

Liesl's face is drawn when she enters the room, and she gives us all a tired smile.

"Heil Hitler," she says, and raises her arm as the rest of us copy her. She looks at us and takes a seat on one of the desks, very unladylike and certainly not behavior befitting a Mädelschaftsführerin. Trudl and Sanne, two of the girls who snubbed me and Renate, giggle behind their hands as Liesl sits.

"You've all heard by now that we're at war," Liesl says simply, and our heads snap back to pay attention to her. "This means our efforts are—are even more important now," she says, and to my surprise her voice breaks. "We must be good women for the Führer, support our men, while they're out there fighting for us. For our Fatherland." She straightens her spine. "We'll be collecting clothing and metal and such, anything we can to help with the war effort. All of you are important, and all of you must be perfect women for the Führer, so our boys will have someone to come home to. So that when they come back, you can help them build a new generation," she finishes, and at her words my heart sinks.

Perfect women. Perfect brides, perfect mothers. *Kinder, Küche, Kirche.* This is a speech I would have expected from Frau Köhler. Certainly not from Liesl.

I hate that I am surprised.

To my right, Renate's lips are set in a thin line. Geli looks down at her shoes.

My hand shoots into the air before I can think to stop it. "Liesl—Fräulein Schröder?" My voice quavers but I try to steady it. "I—I don't know if I'll have time to go out collecting, between work and . . ." I trail off.

"You can still help out, Charlotte," Liesl says, her voice more passionate than I've heard it before. "You don't want to let any of our boys down, do you?"

What boys? Hans, who is terrified of his number coming up for the draft? Our fathers, too old and injured to fight? The boys from the club, who almost certainly will not sign up to go to war on behalf of a country they openly mock, a war none of us asked for?

"Nein," I say, and fold my hands in my lap, but how am I

supposed to help when I have work from morning until night? The precious little free time I have, I don't want to spend collecting things for the war.

Liesl nods, almost distractedly. We spend the rest of the evening figuring out ways we can help. I listen less and less as the meeting continues, and when Liesl tells us we can pack up our things, that she'll see us again next week, I don't notice until Geli taps me on the shoulder.

"I don't believe that," Renate says as we walk out of the building and stop on the steps to wait for Greta. "What do they expect us to do, wed a soldier just so he'll have a reason to come back?"

"I think Liesl's upset because her boyfriend was drafted," Trudl says, catching wind of our conversation. "Though she is right, we all need to do our part."

Renate quickly cuts her eyes at me. "What should our part be, then?" she asks the other girls.

"You heard Fräulein Schröder," says Sanne righteously. "We can run collection drives and help out with the effort. Well. Most of us can," she says, and glances at me.

"I don't have time," I say, and Sanne sniffs.

"Do you want us to lose the war?"

"We aren't going to lose just because Charlie has to work—" Renate begins, and Sanne giggles behind her hand. "And even if we do lose—"

"We won't," Sanne says. "No thanks to you two."

"Sanne," Geli snaps, and this time Sanne does drop it, her mouth set in a line at Geli's reprimand. Geli is still the leader. Is always the leader. Other girls listen to her.

I am the one who is lucky enough to get to follow her, though, to be her shadow, her right hand.

Aren't I lucky?

We're saved from having to say anything else by Greta and the other Jungmädel spilling out of the building. Greta bounds over to Geli and hugs her.

"What did Frau Köhler say?" I ask Greta, but she just shakes her head at me.

"Later," she says, and the four of us set off for Café Uhland. Greta takes Geli's hand and the two of them hurry past us. Renate falls back until she's next to me, and I switch to make sure I'm on her good side.

"All that Scheiße about helping the boys," Renate says. "What do you think?"

"You know what I think," I say. "And I did mean it—I really don't have time. I don't see how you do, considering we work at the same place."

"I don't," she says. "God. Remember when we used to do actual aid with the BDM? Helping the homeless or taking clothes to the church for them to distribute? And now it's just lie back and make good little soldiers for the Führer." Renate spits on the ground, and we keep walking. "We should quit."

"You're not serious," I say, but something in my chest thrills at the idea.

"Aren't I?" she asks. "Liesl's so preoccupied with her boyfriend, do you think she'll even notice if you and I aren't there? Like you said, we already have jobs, so it's not like we have the time. And I am technically 'medically unfit,'" she says, rolling her eyes.

I think about it. Quitting the BDM. Not being involved anymore. Liesl suddenly sounding like Frau Köhler, the extra weight of responsibility that now, more than ever, we must support the Party and fulfill the Führer's expectations for girls like us.

I look at Geli's retreating back, her blond curls falling past her shoulders. "Only if Geli quits, too."

Renate turns to me. "Do you think she will?"

"I—yes," I say, though the answer falters in my throat and I know she hears it. "If we do, she will."

"Since when has Geli followed our lead?"

"I think she's as disenchanted with it as we are," I say. Renate nods, reaches down, and squeezes my hand.

"But you will even if she doesn't, right?" she asks.

"Renate . . ."

"Charlie," she says. "You can't tell me you're going to stay in the BDM just because Geli's in it."

I remember, suddenly, the look on her face a year ago at the

Zoo, when I told her I wasn't going to quit going to the clubs. The look like she'd expected me to say that and was disappointed I hadn't changed my mind.

"No," I say. "I . . . I won't. I'll quit."

"Good," she says. She bumps me with her shoulder.

"So what do we do? Should we tell Liesl?"

"No," Renate says. "I think we can just stop showing up, to be honest. What's she going to do about it? I shouldn't be in there to begin with, and it's not like you can quit your new job to be in the BDM." She smiles. "So it's settled. We're quitting."

"We're quitting," I echo, and the smile on Renate's face grows. "How are we going to convince Geli to join us?" I glance ahead to where Geli walks arm in arm with my sister. "We certainly can't do it now, not with Greta here."

Renate shrugs. "You're closer with her than I am."

Mentioning Geli makes me remember the Tanztee, and for a moment a little of the excitement that had been bubbling up in my chest before Liesl's speech comes back.

"That reminds me," I say. "Geli's throwing a Tanztee at her house next week. Her father and Mathilde have tickets to some opera and the house will be empty."

"That's perfect," Renate says. "I bet some of the boys at Geli's party will know where the regular swing meetings are and we can start going back more often."

"I'd like that," I say, even though I know she doesn't mean to include Geli in that *we*. Just the prospect of dancing again is exciting. "God, I don't know if I even have anything to wear."

"I'm sure you'll find something good, you always do," Renate says, and my face heats up at her words. "Now. Let's catch up with Geli and your sister before they abandon us completely."

Sunday night at dinner, Greta and I crowd around the radio with Mama and Papa to listen to the news about the war, both my parents' faces drawn and tired. Herr Lang, our Hausmeister, knocked on the door last week to tell us to expect air-raid drills soon, and that our cellar will have to do, since there is no Luftschutzbunker near us, that we should be prepared to pack our things and leave if we have to. Our bags sit by the door just in case, ghosts waiting to be summoned.

"I have to work late Monday," I say to my parents over red cabbage. I don't let myself look at Greta as the lie trips off my tongue. "I'll just catch the U-Bahn back, and if it's too late I'll stay with Renate, since their flat is closer."

Mama shakes her head. "I'm not sure about this factory job, Charlie."

"You're the one who suggested I get a job," I say. "Besides, what else am I supposed to do now that the—now that the war is starting? I can't do university with just a Mittlere Reife."

"As long as you still have time for the BDM. And to help around here," she adds. "Though I'm sure Greta can take some of your chores now that she's older."

Greta makes a face. "I'm not sure about this factory job, either," she parrots, and I have to laugh at that.

Monday night I find myself on the U-Bahn heading toward Charlottenburg, clutching my sketchbook in my hands, my bag on the seat next to me saving a spot for Renate. When she gets on, I move it and turn my attention back to my sketches, a map of the route from the factory back to my parents' flat. Later I will change it to include Renate's flat, Geli's house, but the paper isn't big enough right now.

We hurry off the train at Geli's stop. I let my braids down, hoping we're early enough that I can still borrow some of Geli's things to get ready. There's already music playing from behind her door when we knock, but thankfully when Geli answers it's clear we're still early. She isn't dressed yet, but that lipstick is already precisely drawn on her lips, her eyelashes dark, her face older.

"Charlie," she exclaims, and hugs me, then pulls Renate in as well. We hurry up the stairs to Geli's bedroom, where a few dresses are laid out on her bed.

"Renate, you're welcome to pick something, but since you're so tall, I don't know how well it will fit," Geli says, and Renate shrugs.

"I'll just stay in the pants," she says. Geli purses her lips but doesn't respond.

I run my fingers over one of the dresses on Geli's bed. It feels silky, soft, a breathless nothing. It's the color of smoke.

"That one's for you, Charlie, I borrowed it from Mathilde," Geli says cheerfully. "Try it."

I turn my back to both of them and shuck off my clothes from work, smelling like the factory, then pull the silky dress over my head. When I swivel back, both Renate and Geli are looking at me. I blush.

"Well?"

"Perfekt," Geli says, and Renate nods.

"Schön, Charlie," she says quietly.

Geli takes a lipstick off her vanity and comes over to me with it. "Darf ich?"

"Ja," I say. She places a thumb under my chin to steady herself before drawing a precise line onto my lips with the waxy lipstick. Her thumb brushes the edge of my mouth as she wipes away a stray mark.

"Schön," she echoes Renate, then pulls back. I remember how to breathe, my glance flitting over to the mirror. My light brown hair hangs loose and straight to my shoulders, despite being braided up all day for work. The lipstick Geli drew on is a dark rose, but it goes well with the dress, brings out the green in my eyes.

I look beautiful. I could be Marlene Dietrich, Empress Elisabeth, any of those women stories are told about.

Geli finishes applying another coat of lipstick to her own mouth. She does not offer any to Renate before quickly changing into her own silk dress, a blazing red to match her lips. Her blond hair catches the light.

She is dazzling, brilliant.

But tonight I might be enough to keep up with her.

I watch Renate smooth her palms over her thighs before standing, pulling one of Hans's hats out of her bag, and setting it determinedly on her head. With it she could pass for one of the boys.

"Handsome," I tell her, and she grins. Geli glances between us, like I've made a joke she isn't in on.

"One last thing," she says, and picks up a pearl necklace from her vanity. I don't know if the pearls are real or not; knowing Geli, they probably are. "Charlie, will you fasten this for me?"

"S-sure," I say, and take the necklace from her. She turns around and lifts up her hair, my fingers brushing against her neck. My face flushes. This feels so painfully intimate, like she's doing it on purpose, but I can't quite put my finger on why.

I fasten the necklace as quickly as I can with my hands shaking, unable to look at Renate once I've done so. When I finally work up the courage to, she's staring between Geli and me, her lips in a flat line. When she meets my gaze, she tries to smile, but it looks forced.

"Danke, Charlie," Geli says, and I turn my attention back to her. The pearls shimmer in the light.

"Ready?" she asks, and we nod, following her down the stairs. She goes to the record player, and to my surprise, she puts on a jazz record—not Louis Armstrong or Benny Good-man, but someone else, someone I don't recognize. I didn't think she'd have been allowed to have this sort of record, not with her father, but Geli has always been good at hiding things.

"How did you get that?" Renate asks. "Hans told me they were difficult to find."

"Tommy let me borrow it. His cousin sent it to him," Geli says, looking back at me. "Ingrid, right, Charlie?"

"Yes," I say, swallowing. "Ingrid. I . . . I didn't realize she had any records." Her name feels heavy in my mouth.

"Tommy says they're easier to get in Hamburg," Geli continues, then turns the music up loud, so loud I cannot hear myself speak, let alone think—about Ingrid, or Geli, or myself in this dress.

"Let's dance," Geli says in English, and she opens the door and lets the other swings in.

The atmosphere is like nothing I've known. If I thought the music felt carefree and jaunty before the war, now, with that tension underpinning it, it's something else. The horns sound shriller, the drums pound so hard though my body they rattle my teeth.

It's like the music means something different this time, or at the very least feels more dangerous. Soon Geli's living room is filled with swings—some boys I recognize from last year, some girls, too, but mostly a lot of people I don't know. But tonight at least I look like I belong with them, and I can hold on to that feeling.

I spot Moritz hanging by some of the other boys and, feeling bold in Geli's dress, go up to him.

"Moritz," I say.

He stares at me before recognition dawns on his face. "Peggy," he says. He grins. "Not Charlotte."

"Not Charlotte," I echo. I lean in. "Geli told me you got this record from Ingrid?"

He nods. "Yeah. Why, you want one?"

"I want her address like you promised me," I say, for a minute feeling like the Charlie from that night. Moritz shakes his head but finds a spare pen and writes Ingrid's address on the back of an envelope addressed to Herr Haas, ripping it in half and giving me the side with her address on it.

"Write her," he says. "I know she'd like to hear from you."

"Really?" I ask, and a blush crawls up my face. "Thanks."

I let him go back to the other boys, Ingrid's address clutched in my hand. Renate comes up to me and tries to spin me, but stops when she sees the paper.

"What is that?" she asks.

"An address," I say. She frowns. "An address," I repeat.

"Whose?"

"Ingrid—Tommy's cousin?" My face heats up further and I find, suddenly, that I can't make eye contact with her. "I was hoping to—to maybe get some records from her."

"Geli made it sound as though you knew her," Renate says.

I shrug, then, trying to sound casual, "We met at one of the clubs last year—one Geli took me to."

Renate studies me for a long moment. "Huh," is all she says, before taking my free hand and spinning me, perfectly this time, as another song starts up.

"Speaking of Geli," she says. "Should we ask her?"

"Now?"

"What better time?" she says. The music is dying down; one of the swings has produced a flask and is passing it around. Geli is deep in conversation with a few girls in dresses that look even nicer than hers. As we walk up to them, I realize their conversation is in English. Beside me, Renate frowns.

"Geli," I say, and the girls give me a once-over. They do the same to Renate; I watch one girl's eyes rake over her the way the boys do to Geli, until she reaches Renate's face and abruptly turns her head away.

"Was ist?" Geli says, smiling and turning to us. "Charlie—Peggy—you should meet these girls. They're in Gymnasium with me."

"Hi," I say, and they smile, and I'm grateful tonight for Geli's gray dress, for the opportunity to look a little more like her. Like I fit in.

"Hi," one of them says. She's taller than Geli, with a long pale neck and eyes slightly too close together. I think of a giraffe, and have to bite my lip. "I'm Marianne. Do you speak English?"

"Ein—ein bisschen," I answer, surprised at the question, and the other girls laugh.

"You're not in Gymnasium with us. Where do you go?" another of them says.

"I . . . I finished my degree already. I'm working," I say, my face hot.

"Charlie works in a textile factory," Geli says in German, smiling at me. "I usually get her to hem my clothes."

"Your little seamstress, how cute," Marianne says, and the others burst into laughter.

My face is as red as Geli's lipstick. Beside me, Renate stiffens.

"I'm going to get a drink," I say, and before Geli can respond, I make my way into her kitchen, Renate following behind me.

"Charlie . . ."

"I'm fine," I say, and when I turn, she's frowning, not having caught what I said. I sigh. "Wirklich, Renate. I'm all right."

"Do you still want to try to convince her to leave?"

"If she still wants to talk to us," I say bitterly, and Renate squeezes my shoulder.

"You're better than they are," she says. "Besides, if the Führer has his way, we'll all just end up mothers, Abitur or no Abitur."

"I don't know if that's comforting," I say, and she laughs. "Do you want children?"

"I don't know," Renate says. "Sometimes, yes. But then I

look at—at this, and I think, who would bring a child into a world like this?" She sighs. "I'm not earning the Ehrenkreuz der Deutschen Mutter anytime soon."

"You mean you aren't going to have at least four children in the next year?" I say, and she snickers.

"What about you?" she asks, pouring herself a glass of wine. "Do you want children?" She takes a sip and makes a face before passing the glass to me.

"Someday," I say.

"Really?" she says. "I didn't think . . ."

My heart thrums in my chest. "Didn't think what?"

Renate shakes her head, and I will not get to find out what she thinks because Geli has swept into the kitchen, smile bright.

"Are you having fun?" she asks.

"Not as much fun as your friends seem to be having," Renate says coolly.

"They're harmless," Geli says. Renate raises an eyebrow but doesn't contradict her further. "Really, they're just here for the music."

"Hm," Renate says.

Geli glances over at me, but I don't say anything to agree with her. She sighs, pouting slightly. "Oh, don't be that way, Renate, bitte."

"They were rude to Charlie," Renate says simply. I fidget, running the silk of Geli's gray dress through my fingers.

"They really didn't mean anything by it," Geli says, and the look on her face tells me at least she believes it. "Besides, you two are still my best friends."

"Of course," I say, and try to smile. "Geli, actually, we—we wanted to talk to you."

"Oh? About?"

"We're quitting the BDM," I blurt. I hold my breath, waiting for her to respond, realizing as soon as the words are out of my mouth that in this past year of growing apart from her, I actually *don't* know how she'll respond to this.

"Wirklich?" she asks, and I nod. "Warum?"

"We don't . . ." I take a breath, unsure how to phrase what we're doing without making it sound so treasonous. "We don't want to be in it anymore. We don't see the value, not with the war, not with—"

"We don't want to support the Party," Renate says flatly.

"So you're going to leave?"

"We're just not going to show up," Renate says. "If they ask, well . . . I am medically unfit, and Charlie is busy with work."

"What does this have to do with me?"

"Quit with us," I say. "Please."

Geli presses her lips together, and my heart sinks.

"I can't," she says sadly. "My father would notice, and I was thinking of maybe . . . of trying to get a job next year, since—since university isn't an option right now. And they'll check to see if I'm in the BDM."

"But you'll have an Abitur," I say. "Why isn't it—"

"Papa doesn't want me to leave," she says simply. "Not with the war. University would be a 'waste of his money.'" She mimics his accent perfectly, and again I am reminded of Geli the actress, the Geli who wants to be Marlene Dietrich. The Geli who is always performing. "And the only reason he doesn't mind me looking for work is it means I'll be around to bother him less."

"But you don't believe in it, right?" Renate says.

"Natürlich nicht," Geli says. She lifts her chin. "Of course I don't, but I . . ."

"It's convenient for you."

"It's not that simple and you know it," Geli snaps, and Renate takes a step back. Geli turns to me. "Charlie, you know I would quit if I could."

I hate him. I hate every last one of them, but what am I supposed to do?

"I . . . ," I say, looking between them. I want to believe her so, so badly. "I do. Yes."

The party winds down and Renate and I stay to help Geli clean, though the three of us are silent the entire time. When we're done, we say quick goodbyes to Geli, not wanting to be caught by her father and Mathilde should they come home early.

"Do you think she meant it?" Renate asks as we walk up the stairs to her flat, where I'm staying the night. "That she would quit if she could?"

"Yes," I say fervently, and I look at her. "You don't believe her."

"I think you put too much faith in her," Renate says simply.

Did you forget who I live with?

"She wouldn't lie," I say. "Not to me. Besides, you know how her father is, Renate. It probably . . . probably would be dangerous for her to quit."

Renate gives me a long look, and for a second I think she hasn't heard me, but she only sighs.

"I hope you're right," she says, and I tuck her words into my pocket for safekeeping, because I am right, I know I am.

I hate him. I hate every last one of them, but what am I supposed to do?

I have to be.

Oktober 1939

QUITTING THE BDM is easier than I thought. I simply stop showing up, citing late work hours when Mama or Greta asks. They just need to think it's temporary. They don't need to know I've quit entirely.

It's strange. Part of me misses it, the Heimatabend, the comfort of knowing where I fit within our small group, the songs and sewing and hikes.

But there is a war going on, and I am not allowed to miss those things.

And then a notice comes in, in Liesl's handwriting, notifying my parents that I have missed too many meetings, wondering where I am.

I place it in the fireplace, strike a match, and burn it.

I want it to be that simple. And it is.

Until it isn't.

"You quit?!" Mama's voice, reaching my ears the second I come in the door and shrug my coat off. Her face is drawn, and I open my mouth to deny it, but then I catch a glimpse of a letter clutched in her hand.

Liesl must have written again, after I didn't respond to the first letter she sent.

"Yes," I say. "Yes, I . . ."

But she holds up a hand to stop me, shaking her head. "Go," she says, her voice tight, shoving a ration coupon into my hand. "Go to the store. I don't want to speak to you right now, Charlotte."

"Mama . . ."

"*Geh*," she says, and I go.

I start to take the route to Herr Jacobowitz's grocery like I always used to do, before I remember, again, that it is closed, that the Jacobowitzes disappeared in the middle of the night. A flash of anger burns hot in my chest at the thought, and I turn hard on my heel and head in the other direction.

There is already a crowd of people at the other Lebensmittel-geschäft on Ritterstraße, the prices having risen since just last week, angry people in front of me brandishing their ration books like that will change the cost back to something we can afford. I come home with less food than I thought, even more afraid now of Mama's wrath.

"Hier," I say, placing the bags on the table. "I'm sorry, the prices changed, Herr Müller said—"

"I don't care about the prices right now, Charlotte," Mama says. There is no sign of Liesl's letter, probably tucked into her apron. I don't know if she's moved from this spot since she sent me to buy groceries, but it seems she's aged years in the hour I've been gone. "I don't understand what you think you're doing. Do you know how dangerous it is, to just—to just leave the BDM? They're watching everything, they're watching your father, and you—to not be in the BDM—"

"I can't, Mama," I say. "Es tut mir leid. I know it's not safe, but what are they going to do besides send another letter?"

"They could do plenty worse things," Mama says. She passes a hand over her face. "Why? Why would you throw away such opportunity?"

"Opportunity?" I say. "A year ago you were telling me to—to protect *Minna* at all costs, and now you talk about how I have to stay in the BDM for the opportunity? I can't do both—"

"I just want you to—"

"To be *safe*, I know! That's all I hear!" I say. "But I need—I don't want to be safe if it means just sitting back and watching all of this happen without doing anything about it!"

She takes a breath like she's about to speak, but I can't let her or I will lose my nerve, and every emotion that has been boiling up inside me will vanish. "I don't want to be safe anymore, Mama. This—this is different from the Zoo, this is different from that, I can't—I can't just go along with the BDM anymore, with what they want from me. *Kinder, Küche, Kirche*, right?"

I look at her and my eyes well up with tears, but I can't stop them.

"Is that all you want from me, too?" I ask, my voice breaking at the same time my mother's face crumples. That wicked knot of guilt that's been growing in my chest is so tight it feels like I can't breathe.

"I want you to do what will keep you alive, Charlotte. Do you know what it would do to me to lose you? I would have you join the BDM a thousand times over if it meant you wouldn't disappear in the night." She wipes at her eyes, and it is this motion that breaks me, because in all this time, all the horror of the past year, I have never seen Mama cry.

"I'm sorry," I say, and I don't know what exactly I'm apologizing for, but I have to say it. Whether it's *I'm sorry for not staying safe* or *I'm sorry for not being what you want*. I want to reach for her, embrace her like I'm ten again, but I cannot bring myself to cross the distance between us. She would rather I be safe, and I would rather resist, and in this wretched, miserable war I cannot do both.

"Your sister cannot know," she finally says, and looks at me. "I won't have you influencing her to leave the Jungmädelbund."

"I don't want Greta in the Jungmädelbund, Mama, not with Frau Köhler filling her head with ideas—"

"I would rather have her filling Greta's head with ideas than have both of you disappear." She presses her lips together and does not say anything further for a long moment. "Tell your father. Tell him that if they ask why you are not in the BDM, he is to say you're working."

"I will." I take a breath, pause. "Renate quit, too."

"Renate is not my child," Mama says. "And I'm surprised she lasted that long with that ear of hers. There is an excuse they will buy. Not for you."

"I know," I say, and I want to hug her still, but I do not know how to reach for her just now.

So I don't.

Mai 1940

MY LIFE becomes work and occasional visits to cellars to listen to music with Renate, until suddenly in March, a police ordinance is issued "for the protection of the youth," stating that all of us under eighteen cannot be out after dark. When Mama finds out about it, she looks relieved, and secretly I am relieved, too, because now here is an excuse for why Geli has not invited me out with her in a while. I've been trying to memorize the poem now that she and I are talking again, but it's like the words refuse to stay in my head, disappearing as soon as I've read them. But still I try, if only to tell her I did.

And throughout it all are the air-raid-drill sirens, punctuating the air in a grotesque sort of Morse code. With each one my fear grows stronger, that someday soon it will not be a drill, but the real thing. With each one the city holds its breath a little more, waiting.

Mama and Papa purchase gas masks for Greta and me, and the first time Greta puts hers on, I cannot decide whether to laugh or cry at how she looks in it.

I focus on drawing, on avoiding the BDM. Papa raised his eyebrows when I told him I wasn't going to go anymore, but he did agree to lie about it if asked, which did nothing to ease my feelings of guilt. He did not warn me not to tell Greta, but I keep lying to her about it anyway. At this point, it's easier.

Geli has her Abitur exam in May. We celebrate her taking it, the three of us, despite the jealousy I feel that she gets a chance to take it when Renate and I do not. The three of us go to the café in the Ufa Palast near the Zoo, somewhere Renate and I can barely afford—if we couldn't before the war, we certainly can't now. We order Deutscher Kaffee, an ersatz-Kaffee since normal coffee is so scarce, and try not to grimace at the taste. Geli waves her hand when we try to pay, insisting that she wanted to take us here because it's her Abitur exam and she should be treating us.

We let her, and afterward, when we take the U-Bahn back to Renate's flat, Renate and I do not let Geli pay for our tickets and she doesn't push us to.

The flat is silent when the three of us arrive. Herr Hoffmann is asleep in his chair. The door to Hans and Fritz's room is shut; Hans is finishing his second semester at Humboldt, and I feel a sliver of relief that he hasn't been called up yet. Renate's mother is also out.

"Mama's at work," Renate explains to Geli. She does not elaborate on what her mother's job is, not to Geli, and I know why, since she confided to me when her mother first took it that she's working as a maid in an officer's house.

"At least it's *Hausfrau* work," Renate had tried to joke, but we both knew it wasn't something to laugh at—or something to tell Geli.

Still, it lifts suspicion from Renate's family, and I wonder if that's why Frau Hoffmann did it.

Geli does not ask, though, and I can't tell if I'm relieved or annoyed with her for that. "You're lucky, then, that she's never home," Geli says. "Mathilde's been accompanying Papa to more and more social events, though, so at least I don't have to see her as much." She sighs and lies back on Renate's bed.

"Lucky," Renate says dryly.

"Let's—let's put some music on," I say hastily, before Renate can say anything that will cause Geli to fight with her. I go to the record player and put on a Benny Goodman record, making sure to keep the volume low in case Herr Neumann—or Fritz—is listening again.

The music stops anything we were going to say. We let it fill our senses until it's the only thing we can pay attention to, Renate occasionally moving the needle to try to find one of our favorite songs so we can dance.

I'm so busy listening, twirling Geli, that I do not see Fritz standing in the doorway until it's too late.

We've all changed in the past year, but he's changed the

most. He's taller than both me and Renate now; almost as tall as Hans. His voice, too, is beginning to crack.

But he is still a boy. A boy too gangly for his body.

A boy in a uniform that he almost never takes off.

"You shouldn't be listening to that," Fritz says, his eyes dark. Renate's back is to him as she adjusts the record player, and without a word he hurries over to her and pushes her shoulder, causing her to yank on the needle, deeply scratching the record.

"Hey!" she cries, spinning around. "Fritz, what the hell?"

"You shouldn't be listening to that," he repeats. I stare at him. What has happened to the little boy who used to insist these records were his, who used to guard them like treasures?

I know what has happened to him.

"Calm down, Fritz," Renate says. "Herr Neumann won't hear."

"I don't care about Herr Neumann. You shouldn't be listening to degenerate music," Fritz says, his voice cracking, and it should be funny, but it isn't. He looks from his sister to me and Geli, then back again.

"It's just music," Geli says lightly, and Fritz turns his attention to her. The one thing about him that hasn't changed.

"It's not just music," he begins, but she puts a hand on his arm.

"You won't tell on us, will you?" she says, smiling that dazzling smile at him. "Please?"

He swallows. Before, this would have worked. Before, he would have bargained with us, saying that we could listen to the music if he was allowed to join us.

"Fine," he says, then turns to Renate. "But I'm still telling Mama."

"Go ahead," Renate shoots back, and Fritz leaves her bedroom, slamming the door behind him. She sighs, looking down at the record, at the deep gouge across it.

"I think it's ruined," she says quietly.

"We can just—we'll find another," I say, desperate suddenly to fix it, to make it right.

Renate looks up at me and gives me a small, sad smile. "Doubt it," she says, and sets the needle back on the record. It plays for about a minute before it starts skipping, and she puts her head in her hands.

I want to fix it. I want to reach over and touch her, comfort her and let her know it'll be okay. I almost reach out, almost stand, before I stop myself.

What would Geli think of me comforting Renate?

I turn. Geli's staring at the spot where Fritz was just a moment ago, her mouth pressed into a thin line. I want to ask her if she could ask Moritz about getting a record, but something stops me. Asking Moritz would mean bringing up Ingrid, and I don't know if I want to do that, not when Geli and I are finally talking again.

Besides, I have Ingrid's address. I could ask her myself.

Renate finally moves the needle off and we sit there in silence until Fritz throws open Renate's door again.

"*Was?*" she snaps, but stops at the look of glee on his face.

"We've bombed the Netherlands," he says, triumphant. "The Dutch finally surrendered."

August 1940

AND THEN—

One night in August, the thing we have feared the most comes to pass. Mama shakes us awake, her eyes wide.

"Get dressed," she says, but her words are drowned out by the sound of sirens up above. "Quickly."

"Mama . . ."

"Papa and I will meet you in the cellar. Charlotte, get Greta ready. Grab jackets, shoes, masks, and then hurry down to meet us."

I freeze at her voice. She has never sounded this urgent before during a drill, and my chest tightens at the realization that this probably isn't one.

"Yes, Mama," I say, and push myself out of bed, the sound of my parents shutting the door to our flat drowned out by the sirens.

"Charlie?" Greta yells, appearing in my doorway with her

braids half down, clutching a stuffed bear. Her lower lip trembles. "It's just a drill, right?"

"I—yes, Gretchen. It's just a drill. But I still need you to get your coat and shoes and mask like we practiced, all right? As quickly as you can." I try to keep any note of worry out of my voice. But she just stands there, looking at me with wide eyes.

"Go!" I snap, and she hurries back to her room. I grab my shoes and shove my feet into them, looking around for my jacket.

I'm almost out of my room when I remember. Geli's book. Heine's poems. I turn to grab it, because I don't want it to be destroyed if—if we get bombed.

But what if someone notices I have it? Isn't it safer up here than with me?

I need to memorize that damn poem.

I reach in my vanity drawer for it, my fingers closing around the cover of the book, when I hear Greta's voice behind me.

"What is that?" she says, peering over my shoulder.

"Nichts, Greta. Let's go," I say, shoving the drawer closed and taking my sister by the hand. We hurry out of the flat, past sleepy-eyed families with children younger than Greta, older brothers and sisters who look as tired as I feel. The Reichmann family rushes down the stairs, all six children in identical nightclothes.

Herr Lang, our Hausmeister, ushers everyone into the cellar.

"Nothing to worry about," I hear him tell a family ahead of us, but his voice is cut off by the sirens. "Just a drill, I'm sure." He spots me and Greta and waves us forward. "Anika and Jürgen went in a few minutes ago. I'm sure they're looking for you," he says, and Greta tugs free of my hand to run farther into the cellar to look for our parents.

It's damp in the cellar, and colder than it should be for an August night. A few people have thought to bring lamps, and their warm glow lights up the cellar but does nothing to hide the fact that it's still cold and cramped and this many people weren't meant to fit down here, surely.

"Charlotte," Mama's voice calls, and I push through the bodies until I am near her. Greta has settled herself on the floor, her stuffed bear clutched to her chest.

"Was ist?" I ask softly so Greta can't hear me. "Is it—are we—"

"We don't know," Mama says, her face taut. Beside her, Papa's eyes are closed.

They remember the raids from the first war, the constant Luftwarnungen, and though we've all grown somewhat used to the drills over the past few months, this feels different.

"I hope we don't have to go through this again," Greta grumbles from the floor, and the people around her laugh, but I can tell from the glances the adults exchange that they think it will happen again, that this is only the beginning.

I do not want them to be right, but at the same time, a

small part of me does. Is this what we deserve? Being made to huddle small and scared in our cellars like we have made so many others?

Renate would know the answer to that, I think suddenly. I should talk to her, ask her about it. It's not something I can ask my parents.

It's not something I can talk about with Geli.

Hours later, we finally hear the all-clear sound, and the four of us head back up the stairs. I want to make sure the Heine book is safe, but I make myself wait so Mama doesn't get suspicious. Greta runs back to her room while Mama and Papa hang up their jackets.

"Do we . . . do we think that was real?" I ask them once Greta is out of earshot. My mother nods, and reaches out to tuck a piece of hair behind my ear.

"I think so," she says, and Papa nods, too. "Make sure you have everything packed that you'd want, Charlotte. For—for next time," she adds.

"Can I call Geli?" I ask. "Just to—to see if she's all right."

"Be quick," Mama says, and goes to turn on the radio to see if there is any news about the damage.

Geli's line rings, and for a moment I worry no one will pick up. But after a few rings, I hear her familiar voice.

"Hallo?"

"Geli," I say, unable to stop the relief at hearing that she is okay. "Thank goodness, are you—"

"We're fine," she says. "We waited it out in the underground, with some of the other officers' families."

The underground. Certainly more spacious than our cellar, and safer, too.

"The underground," I repeat, because of course Geli's family would have somewhere better to wait out the bombs, her father being an officer.

The gap that has been growing between us inches just a little bit wider, and I find myself suddenly desperate for some way to close it.

"It was honestly so boring, Charlie. I wish you'd been there," she continues on before I can. "We could've listened to something."

"With everyone around?"

"It would've been better than just cowering in silence," she says. "Anyway, I want to see you soon. How's work?"

"It's fine," I say, glancing over my shoulder to see Mama motioning at me to hang up. "I'll see you soon, then?"

"Of course," Geli responds, and hangs up before I can respond. Mama sighs, but doesn't say anything to me, dismissing me to my room with a wave instead.

I hurry to my room and shut the door, grabbing the book of Heine's poems out of my vanity. I need to memorize them. If something happens to this book, I need to have them, so I can give them back to Geli like she wants me to.

I open the book and begin to read, whispering the words to myself, trying to get a feel for their rhythm so they stay in my head, as if they will keep me safe, as if they will keep her near me, hold her fast as she tries to slip away through my fingers like smoke.

Dezember 1940

SOMEHOW GRETA manages to talk our parents into letting us go to the Christmas market near the Berliner Dom. I don't know quite how she does it, but it's a chance for the two of us to get out of the house, to escape the ever-growing feeling of being stifled by our own fear.

Greta doesn't wear her JM uniform, instead opting for a long skirt and blouse, her long hair neatly pinned up. I'm in a skirt I hemmed and an old blouse of Mama's I tailored to fit me better, changing the sleeves to short ones and loosening the bust so it wasn't quite so formfitting. Normally I don't give as much thought to my appearance; normally I'm content to not think about it. But I get so few opportunities to dress up now that taking this chance feels more important than perhaps it actually is.

I have a little pocket money saved from work, just a few marks, and it's with this that Greta and I wander the Weihnachtsmarkt, already drawn in by the spiced smells of Glühwein and roasting chestnuts. Greta tugs my hand toward a display of colorful nut-crackers.

"Charlie?"

I turn. Renate is walking toward us, flanked by Hans and Fritz, the latter of whom is scowling. I'm relieved to see that neither of the boys are in any sort of uniform. Even Fritz is dressed down today.

"Renate!" I say, and hug her. She's dressed almost identically to her brothers, her hair even shorter than when I saw her just last week at work. "Was gibt's?"

"Same as you," she says, smiling. "We wanted to get out of the house. See the market. Not like we can really afford any-thing," she says, shrugging.

"Not like I can either," I say, and lower my voice. "Well. Maybe something for Greta, for Christmas."

Renate nods. "Of course. Odd, isn't it—this still feels the same, even with the war." She glances around. The wooden stalls are lit up with twinkling lights now that the sun is going down; everyone dressed in their warmest coats.

"It does," I agree, and turn to Renate's brothers. "How are you holding up? How's university, Hans?"

"Fine," he says.

Greta smiles shyly at him from my side. "Hallo, Hans," she says. Nice to know the years haven't dampened my sister's crush on Renate's brother.

"Greta," he says, his voice warm.

"Do you want to wander the market together?" I ask. I mainly direct the question at Renate, hesitant about spending that much time with Fritz. But Hans is here, too, and it's not like I can wander with him and Renate and leave Greta alone with Fritz. Soon the five of us are walking around the market, Greta running ahead every few minutes to check out a new stall or shop, disappearing into the crowd. Hans buys us all mugs of Glühwein and shakes his head when I try to pay him back. Greta tries to sneak a sip of my drink when I'm not looking, and I quickly snatch it back from her.

"You know Mama only lets you have that at home," I say, and she grins mischievously.

We pass a stall selling cotton candy, sugar lingering in the air, and I almost pause in front of it before Renate takes my hand and suddenly pulls me down a side street.

"What're you—"

"They'll be fine," she says. "I have something I want to show you."

We keep walking down the alley, and Renate finally knocks on the door of an old building, then opens it and pushes me inside.

"Renate, was—"

"Hush," she says, and knocks on a second door. After a moment, a voice responds.

"Who's there?"

"It's Shirley," Renate calls back, ignoring me when I glance at her, at her use of the English name Minna picked out for the club last year.

The door opens and Renate and I enter a dark room. It takes a moment for my eyes to adjust, but when they do, I see clearly—records. Crates and crates of them. Sitting at a desk in the center of them is a man—man, boy, he looks only a little older than Hans. His hair is long, and an unlit cigarette hangs out of his mouth.

"Rudolf, this is Peggy," Renate says. "She wants to look around at the records. Is that okay?"

"Fine," he says, and eyes Renate. "Didn't expect to see you back so soon. I told you you'd know if I got any shipments of what you're looking for."

"I wanted to bring Peggy," Renate says, shrugging.

"Of course," Rudolf says.

I begin digging through the records, not even sure of what I'm looking for. "You asked him about the record, then?" I whisper to Renate. She nods.

"He doesn't have it. Says he's supposed to get a shipment in from a friend in London soon but it might just be lost, especially since the SS are looking for any contraband coming in," she says, sighing.

"How did you meet this guy?"

"He's Hans's friend," she says. "But I figured . . . you like the music, too, so I thought you might—might want to look through the records. Just don't come without me; I only trust

Rudolf because Hans knows him, and even then I don't think Hans likes him very much."

"Does Hans know about the clubs, then?"

Renate shrugs. "If he does, he hasn't mentioned them to me. I've only ever asked him about his records—well. When Fritz wasn't hoarding them." We drift over to a stack of postcards, and I pause to pick one up.

"Don't touch that," Rudolf says, and I jerk my hand away, but not before catching a glimpse of the back.

Hitler's war is the worker's death!

Anti-Party sentiment. Anti-Nazi sentiment. I glance at Renate and she presses her lips together, urging me not to say anything.

I want to ask her—did she know? Is she involved? Is Hans?

Can I be involved somehow, too?

"Rudolf, do you still have that old radio?" Renate asks, her voice too loud. "The long-range one?"

"Yes, but . . ."

"Give it to Charlie," Renate says, in that tone that means she doesn't want anyone to argue with her.

"Why should I?"

"I can snitch on you easily," Renate says, studying her nails like she can't be bothered. "We have a friend whose father is an officer. You wouldn't want him to find out about the records you're selling, would you?"

"And if I tell him you're my top client?" Rudolf sneers.

"Me?" Renate says, making her voice high and light like the other girls we know. "A girl with a busted ear, your biggest client? Yes, I'm sure he'll believe that."

Rudolf scowls, but he hands the radio over to Renate, who passes it to me.

"What am I supposed to do with this?" I ask.

"You'll see, Charlie," she says.

"Okay," I say to her, and she smiles, and something flutters in my stomach.

Renate? I think, then brush it off. It's because Geli hasn't talked to me lately and I'm lonely; it's because Renate looks as handsome as her brothers and is giving me the time of day and showing me all these records.

I miss *Geli*.

"Did you want to buy any records before we leave?" Renate asks, and I look around the shop again.

"Not at the moment, but—thank you. For showing me this place. I definitely want to come back." I stumble over my words a bit, but if she notices, she doesn't say anything.

"Anytime you want me to take you, I will," she says, smiling. "Let's go catch up with the boys before they totally corrupt your sister."

Greta is laughing. Over all the shouts and sounds of the market I can hear it. There is Greta, on one of the carousel horses, her long hair whipping around her face, Hans on another horse not far behind hers. Fritz stands to the side with his back to us, his shoulders hunched.

"Charlie!" Greta cries when she sees me. "Look, I look like Sisi!"

"You do," I call back, cupping my hands around my mouth. I turn to Fritz. "Where did she get the money?"

"Hans paid for her," Fritz says sourly.

"And you didn't want to ride?" Renate asks, teasing.

"I'm too old," Fritz says.

"You're Greta's age," Renate says.

"She's a girl. Girls can do stuff like that," Fritz says, tugging down the hem of his shirt, his Adam's apple bobbing. I forget, sometimes, that he *is* Greta's age. That he is still a boy, not even thirteen.

"If you want to ride, Fritz, Charlie and I will go with you," Renate says.

Fritz shakes his head. "No."

"Do you want to ride, then?" Renate asks, turning to me. I glance down at my skirt, shorter than Greta's.

"It'll have to be sidesaddle," I say, and she laughs.

"Let's go, then. Fritz, don't wander off, we're leaving after this," she says, and goes up to pay as the carousel winds down. I walk over to the horse Greta is on.

"My turn," I say, as she jumps down and beams. "Go wait with Hans and Fritz."

"I want to ride again, Charlie," she says.

"Tut mir leid, Greta, I don't . . ."

But the look on her face stops me, and before I can think, I climb onto the horse and pull her back up with me. She swings her legs around and grips the pole, and I wrap my arms around her to keep her from falling, craning my neck to look back at Renate, who's laughing at us.

"Hey—" the attendant calls, but it's too late, the ride has started up, and we move around and around until both of us are dizzy and I cannot hear Greta's laughter over the sound of my own.

But of course, it can't last. It never lasts.

No matter how much I want it to.

Januar 1941

SOMETHING TERRIBLE is coming.

We ring in the new year at home, subdued, crowded around the radio together. Mama and Papa somehow get me a new sketchbook for Christmas; for Greta, a small piece of chocolate, which we haven't had since nearly a year ago. She cups it in her hands like it's something precious. Maybe it is. I spend the rest of the evening in my room drawing, not maps for once, but outfits. Things I would wear if I had more money, if I were a girl like Geli, like Marlene Dietrich. The package from Ingrid that arrived a few days before Christmas is hidden under my bed, waiting for the right time to be opened.

I fiddle with the radio Renate gave me, which I haven't really touched since we went to the Weihnachtsmarkt. I turn the volume down and scan the stations, trying to find a station that isn't propaganda or Hitler's voice.

I give up after ten minutes and pull out the book of Heine's poetry. I still only have half the poem memorized.

Geli's birthday is in April. Maybe I can finally finish it by then, present it to her.

Use it to bring her back to me.

Renate calls a week later, in the evening once we're both off work, never mind that we saw each other at the factory an hour ago.

"Do you still have that radio?" she asks, her voice quiet.

"Of course."

"Bring it to mine tonight. There's something I want to show you."

"Okay," I say, and my heart beats slightly faster at the thought.

Greta stands in the hallway next to me, her feet in socks, her hair in long braids almost to her waist. Now twelve, she is almost taller than I am.

"You're going to Renate's?" she asks.

"Yes," I say.

"What about dinner?"

"Frau Hoffmann will cook, I'm sure," I say. Renate's family gets slightly more rations than we do because they have more children, but Mama is better at stretching a meal than Frau Hoffmann is. "If it's pea soup, I'll save some for you."

"Yuck, don't bother," Greta says. "You'll be back in time to help tomorrow, won't you?"

"Tomorrow?"

"The BDM drive? I'm surprised Liesl hasn't put you in charge," Greta says. "Frau Köhler told me to watch the younger girls, and you said you'd help me. Remember?"

"Of course I remember, Greta," I say. "I'll be back in the morning in time to help with that."

"Good," Greta says. She looks down at her feet, then back at me. For a second, she looks so young. "Can you tell me a story before you go?"

I grab my coat from the hook, shrug it on. "It's barely evening. You're going to bed so soon?"

"I'm tired," Greta says. "So, yes. Please, Charlie?"

"A quick one," I say, and Greta nods as I follow her into her room. I've barely finished the Grimms' Märchen—this time, "Schneewittchen"—before she's asleep.

"I'm staying with Renate," I call to my parents, slipping out the door before they can respond, knowing my mother will have something to say to me about it later.

I make sure the radio is tucked securely into my coat pocket before heading out onto the street, the gift from Ingrid in my bag. Herr Neumann lets me into the building with a nod, having grown used to seeing me over the past three years. I pass the floor below Renate's where the new family lives, the one that took over the Kochs' flat—well. I guess they aren't new anymore.

Renate opens the door, smiling, and steps out of the flat into the hallway. "Mama's out at work and Papa's asleep, Fritz is doing God knows what with some of the HJ, and Hans is back at university," she says breathlessly. "Come on, I want to show you something."

I keep my coat on as she grabs my wrist and pulls me along up several more flights of stairs.

"You brought the radio, right?" she says.

"Yes."

She pushes open the door to the rooftop garden, which we hardly ever visit when I come over. There's some grass, a few plants someone has tried to keep alive. I shiver. I feel exposed up here. The air raids have become more and more frequent lately, and most of us now cram ourselves into the underground stations rather than our cellars just so we can be safe as more bunkers are built. The underground feels safer than the cellar, but those moments when we are rushing to the station do not. Luckily no one we know has been harmed yet, but on the occasions Greta wants to go near Alexanderplatz, I try not to look at the damage done to the Brandenburger Tor.

"What are we doing up here?" I ask, but Renate has her back to me. I tap her shoulder and she turns, and we are suddenly, startlingly, very close to one another.

"Oh," I say, and step back, my face growing hot. "What . . . what did you want to show me?"

"This," she says, and reaches for the radio, her hand brushing mine. She fiddles with the dials for a while, her good ear turned toward it, until she looks at me, triumphant. "Can you hear it?"

I frown and lean down closer to her. There's music in what must be English coming out of the speaker, and what's better, the rhythm—or lack thereof—is familiar.

"It's jazz!" I say, incredulous, and Renate beams. "How did you—"

"I heard Rudolf talking about it; figured we could try it. And"—she takes a breath, smiles—"I volunteered for lookout duty. For the air raids. So now we'll have an excuse to be up here and listen to the music."

"'We'?" I ask, and she ducks her head.

"I figured you'd want to listen with me—it's not like I was going to ask Geli," she says.

"I . . . I actually got something for you, too," I say. "Not a Christmas gift or anything, and it's too early for your birthday, but—here." I grab the package from Ingrid out of my bag and thrust it toward her. She gingerly unwraps it, pulling a plain record out of its sleeve.

"It's—it's the Benny Goodman record," I stammer, looking up at her. "I asked Ingrid if she had it, if she could get a copy, since yours . . . yours got destroyed."

Without warning, Renate throws her arms around me and pulls me to her.

"Danke, danke, danke," she whispers. "Charlie, this is—this is honestly more than I could have asked for, you didn't have to do this, really—"

"I wanted to," I say. "We should listen to it—later. For now, show me how the radio works."

She nods, and the two of us lie down facing each other, the radio between us. Renate fiddles again with the volume, and a minute later, jazz is pouring out of the speakers, tinny and full of static, but more than we've been used to hearing the past few months.

"I wonder if we can get other broadcasts," Renate says thoughtfully. "News that isn't just Goebbels's propaganda. I've heard the BBC is broadcasting news for us."

"I didn't realize you understood English that well."

"They've started broadcasting messages in German, too. They know we're listening, they know Goebbels controls every message that floats over those damn airwaves." She smirks. "Of course, I'll still learn some English."

"How?" I ask, and she laughs, closes her eyes.

"The clubs. I practice. I listen." She opens her eyes, nudges me with her shoulder. "Just because *you're* not going out places doesn't mean I'm not. Besides, do you remember me telling you about Max?"

"No, sorry."

"He was one of—one of the boys in the band with Minna sometimes," Renate says. "We got back in touch and he's been showing me places." She looks down, tracing a finger over the ground. The static jazz from the radio stretches out behind us, but it isn't uncomfortable.

"Can I . . . can I ask you something?" Renate says, finally, when the song has ended.

"Na klar."

"You and Ingrid . . ." Renate bites her lip. My heart thuds louder in my chest. "Did anything ever . . . happen with the two of you?"

"Why would you ask that?"

She shrugs. "The way you've talked about her, sometimes. Like how you talk about Geli." She looks at me. "Like you've got a crush."

I feel like I can't breathe.

"Why does it matter?" I ask, defensive, my hands clenching into fists. Already I am pushing myself up, already I am planning my escape from this roof, from this conversation, from the truths about myself.

"Charlie . . ." Renate sighs and pushes herself up on her elbows, makes sure I'm looking at her before continuing. "It matters because—because—" She runs her fingers through her short hair. "Oh Scheiße, Charlie, it doesn't matter, I just thought—ach, es macht nichts."

I sit back down, closer to her now, my guard dropping because the way she's acting, the way she asked—she couldn't . . .

Could she?

"Doch," I say. "It does matter." I close my eyes for a brief moment. "I liked Ingrid. We . . . we kissed, once or twice. But it—she wasn't . . . wasn't who I wanted to be kissing, so . . ."

"Who did you want to kiss?" Renate asks, and I open my eyes. Her face is suddenly nearer. I swallow as her gaze flicks down to my lips, tell myself she's only looking at them like that so she can understand me.

"Geli," I say, and Renate exhales like she's been waiting for that answer, leaning back from me slightly.

I suddenly, desperately don't want her to be leaning away from me. "But now—"

I don't finish my sentence. She doesn't let me. She grabs the collar of my shirt and pulls me to her, her mouth hot against mine. My hands shake as I place them on her waist, kiss her back fiercely. When we break apart, we're both breathing hard, my shirt collar still clutched in her hands. "I—was that—" she begins, but I don't let her finish before I kiss her again.

"Yes," I say, and then we're both laughing, the moment before just so *serious* that we find ourselves doubling over, unable to catch our breath.

We lie back down, and Renate twines her fingers through mine.

"So what girls have *you* kissed?" I ask, and she laughs again softly. "I never saw you go off with girls at the club."

"Who says I only go to the same clubs you and Geli did?" she says. "Do you know how many Swingjugend there are in Berlin? How many clubs?" She smiles. "I've been to a few of them. I'll take you sometime."

"Is that a promise?"

"It can be," she says. "If you want that."

"I do," I say, and squeeze her hand.

"Some of them are different," she says. "A lot wilder than the ones you've gone to before. Boys with boys and girls with boys and girls with girls and some people I can't tell—sometimes I wear Hans's clothes and go. You'd love it, Charlie, I really think you would." She smiles. "But yes, a few girls. A boy or two as well."

"Minna?"

"No," Renate says, her voice firm. "I . . . I loved Minna. I love her. I might have been in love with her, once, but she didn't feel the same way."

"Did you ever tell her?"

"I wish I had," Renate says. She closes her eyes. "And you? And . . . Geli?"

"She kissed me once," I say, thinking back to that night, more than two years ago. "But she's never—I don't think . . . I don't know." I close my eyes. "I know the two of you don't always get along, and I don't—I don't want to compare her to you, I just . . . I can't explain it, Renate, I just . . . like her. There's something about her. She . . . she makes me feel special."

"You are," Renate says fiercely. "Gott, Charlie, why can't you see that?"

"I . . ." I'm so stunned I can't speak.

"You are. You're quiet, but you've got this great laugh when you want, and you just—you care so much about all of us, about everything, sometimes so much I can see how much it hurts you. It's one of the things I've always liked about you."

"I didn't . . ." I swallow. "I didn't think you noticed. That anyone . . . noticed."

"I always notice you, Charlie," Renate says.

I kiss her this time. Softly. She wraps her arms around me and I lay with my head on her chest, her hand absentmindedly drawing patterns on my shoulder.

"What now?" I ask her, afraid of the answer to the question.

"Do you mean tonight, or generally?"

"Both," I say.

"Well, tonight, mother won't be back until later. . . ."

"Renate!" I say, and she laughs.

"We don't have to if you don't want. I just thought I would offer," she says, and I can feel my face growing hot. "Have you ever?"

"No," I say. "Have you?"

"Yes," she says. Her hand stills on my shoulder. "Do you want me to tell you?"

"Not right now," I say, my face still burning. "Someday— later, maybe. For now . . ."

"For now," she echoes. "I don't know, Charlie. We can't . . . It's not like we can let anyone find out. Not with the way things are." I feel her exhale. "This city used to be such—such a haven, for people like us. And now . . . now just being the way we are is a crime."

"What can we do?"

"We can change it," she says. "Come to—come to one of the clubs with me some night. I'll show you."

"You'll show me?" I ask, and she laughs again, and I realize how much I like the sound of her laugh.

"Yes," she says. "What some of us are doing." She presses her lips to the top of my head. "It's cold up here. Should we go in?"

"Yes," I say, and we both stand, brushing grass off our clothing, looking awkwardly at each other, as if we're both just now seeing one another for the first time. Renate smiles at me and picks up the radio, turning it off. I follow her taller form back down to her flat.

When her mother and Fritz come home, we eat a late meal, leftover cabbage and rolls. I find myself looking at Renate all throughout dinner, watching the way she laughs at something her mother says, trying to figure out if anything's different about her now that we've kissed, if anyone can tell what happened between us.

"How's work, Charlie?" Frau Hoffmann asks.

"Fine," I say. "Busy, but—it's nice to have something to think about that isn't . . . ." I bite my tongue. "How's Hans? Any word from him since Christmas?"

"He says university is fine," Frau Hoffmann says, nodding.

"I should think when this is all over you should follow him."

"I don't have an Abitur," I say.

But Frau Hoffmann just shakes her head. "Then when this ridiculous war is ended, you should get one."

"The war isn't *ridiculous*," Fritz says, before I can reply, and I take a bite of my roll to keep from responding, my gaze flitting back and forth between the four Hoffmanns.

"You can't say it's ridiculous," Fritz says again. "Is the Führer ridiculous?"

Frau Hoffmann's knuckles turn white around her fork.

"Your mother didn't say that," Herr Hoffmann says, and it's the first time I've ever really heard him speak. His voice is softer than I expected, gentler. An awful lot like my own father's. "We just meant . . ."

"I know what you meant," Fritz says sourly, pushing back from the table. "You're just a coward because you can't fight anymore."

"Friedrich!"

"It's true!" Fritz says, turning red as he faces his parents, Renate and I just sitting there silently. "You're weak, a coward—I bet you're *glad* you can't fight!"

"Friedrich, that's enough!" Frau Hoffmann snaps, but Fritz hasn't heard her. He's still standing, shaking his head at his parents.

"Forget it," he says, and goes to grab his Jungvolk jacket, shrugging it over his shoulders and grabbing his bicycle by the door. "I don't want to be a coward like you," he says, and before anyone can say anything else, he's gone.

Renate looks at her parents, their faces pale, fear-stricken.

"Do you think . . . ," Renate starts, swallows. "He's not going to—to report us . . ."

Frau Hoffmann's face grows even paler. Renate's father reaches across the table and grabs his wife's hand and Renate's.

"If he does, we lie, Liebchen," he says. "We say we support the Party, that you were a member of the BDM, that our other son was an HJ leader. We act like we still support them, and we lie, because it is safer."

Renate nods, but I see the way her brows knit together.

Her mother turns to me. "I'm sorry you had to see that, Charlie," she says. "Just please don't—don't think worse of my Fritz because of this. He's just a boy, he . . ."

"He's old enough to know what he's doing, Roberta," Herr Hoffmann says quietly.

"He's been brainwashed just like the rest of them," she snaps. "That's not my son, Ulrich." Frau Hoffmann stands, wipes her eyes with the heel of her hand, and begins clearing our plates, though she clears Fritz's last. "Charlie, you're welcome to stay the night. I'm . . . I'm sorry," she says again, and I don't understand fully what she's apologizing for. She turns and studies me thoughtfully. "Is Greta still in the JM?"

"Yes," I say, and she nods, but doesn't say anything further. Fear settles in my stomach like a stone.

◆ ◆ ◆

Renate and I get ready for bed in silence, occasionally shyly glancing at each other, though I know she's still listening for Fritz, her good side turned toward the door.

"He's just been getting worse," she says quietly. "Ever since Hans left and the war started, the HJ boys are the only ones he follows around. I worry . . . I worry sometimes that he'll report us, I really do." She sighs. "Mama's been making excuses for him like she always does, but tonight—she can't ignore what he's becoming any longer. She can't ignore any of it any longer." She gives a laugh. "Is it bad that I feel relieved at what she said about him being brainwashed? This whole time I thought . . . I thought she believed what the Party said, but now . . ."

"It's not bad. I'm relieved, too," I say, and she gives me a grateful smile. "Mama's not—not in denial, I don't think, but for the longest time all she would say to me was 'be careful, be safe.'" I sigh. "When I quit the BDM, I told her I couldn't do that anymore."

"And?"

"And she believed me, but it still feels like—like there's this wall between us," I say.

Without a word she reaches and brushes her knuckles against mine, pulling me closer, pressing her lips against my forehead. Impulsively I stand on tiptoe, try to kiss her, and she laughs.

"He'll come back," I say, and I hope I'm right. I hear the sound of her parents' bedroom door shutting, and Renate finally shuts her own door.

We curl up in her bed, close together for warmth. I tuck myself under her chin, and she absentmindedly runs her fingers through my hair, down my shoulders.

And for the first time in this wretched, miserable war, I don't feel so alone.

I wake early, say goodbye to Renate and her parents before shrugging my coat on and hurrying out of their flat. Herr Neumann is outside smoking when I leave; he looks me over, then says, "Heil Hitler." I just nod, pull my coat tighter, hurry away as quickly as I can.

By the time I get home, Greta is already dressed for her meeting, satchel over her arm.

"Ready?" she asks me.

"Just—just let me change," I say breathlessly, hurrying to my room and shutting the door, shucking my clothes off and rooting around for my old BDM blouse and skirt, hoping they still fit. There's a mark just by my collarbone where Renate's mouth was last night, and I brush my fingers over it as I change, still hardly daring to believe any of it was real.

"Charlie! We're going to be late!"

"Coming!" I yell back at Greta, and hurriedly tuck my blouse in, straighten my skirt and stockings. Greta gives me a once-over before we leave, then, apparently satisfied, heads out the door, leaving me to follow her.

"Frau Köhler wants us to do these three blocks," she says, pulling out the map I made her and running her finger over it. "I'm supposed to take some of the other girls from the Mädelschaft."

"It sounds like you don't need me," I say, half hoping to avoid Frau Köhler, avoid any interrogation as to why I'm not in the BDM anymore, which Greta still doesn't know.

"Doch," Greta says. "You said you'd help. And besides, you can tell the younger girls what the BDM is like." She fixes me with a look that is so like our mother, I have to laugh.

"Okay. I'll stay. Let's go."

We meet the other girls in front of the BDM building, all of them lined up outside, whispering and giggling to each other, Frau Köhler towering over them like a stern mother hen.

"I brought Charlie," Greta says, hoisting her satchel up.

Frau Köhler looks me over. "Fräulein Kraus. I didn't expect to see you. Fräulein Schröder tells me you left. I would've expected a girl like you to become a leader, maybe even go on to Glaube und Schönheit."

Glaube und Schönheit. Faith and Beauty. Further training to become the Party's perfekte Hausfrau.

I can feel Greta staring at me, and I silently beg her not to say anything.

"I'm working," I say, my mouth dry. "In a—in a clothing

factory, actually. We're making . . . we're working on the uniforms," I say. Truth be told, we aren't, just producing normal clothes, but Frau Köhler doesn't need to know that. There are several factories producing uniforms for the soldiers; who says the one I work at isn't one of them?

"But you're still a member of the Party, surely."

"Yes," I say. "Our parents, too. I just didn't have time, with my work, and I—I didn't want to do anything half-hearted. And I wanted to . . . to support my family." It's a bold thing to say, putting my family above the Party. I think of what Herr Haas said to me on induction night nearly three years ago, how sewing would serve me well as a Hausfrau. "I think supporting a family is one of the most noble things a woman can do for the Party, nicht wahr?"

I can feel Greta's eyes boring into me. Frau Köhler raises an eyebrow. "Well. We're glad to have you this morning, Fräulein Kraus," she says. "The rest of you girls, follow Greta and Charlotte, they'll show you what to do."

The girls nod, excited chatter continuing as they grab their buckets, used to collect money, and follow us down the block. Greta falls into step beside me.

"You *quit?*" she whispers. "Wann?"

"Last year," I say.

"Last *year?*" Her eyes are wide.

"We can talk about it later, Greta," I say, and she pouts but relents. But when I go to grab one of the buckets from her, she pulls her hand back.

"Maybe you shouldn't help," she says quietly.

"Gretchen . . ."

"Don't call me that," she says. "Look, I can handle this. Maybe it's just better if you go home."

My hands drop to my sides, and I take a long look at my sister. Gone is the little girl who followed me to BDM meetings, to Geli's, who wanted to be Kaiserin Elisabeth.

"I'll see you at home," I say, and she nods.

I can't get the look of Greta's face out of my mind, her telling me to go, to leave. That she doesn't need me.

God, I used to hate her following me around, and now I want nothing more than that—I want her to need me, to be my little sister again.

My feet take me to Geli's house. I shove my hands in my coat pockets and look up at it, this grand house so much nicer than anywhere I will ever live, with Geli inside, so much more charismatic than I will ever be.

Greta has outgrown me. I hope Geli hasn't done the same.

I knock on the door and make sure my uniform is straightened, only just remembering that I have it on. Herr Haas answers, and for a second it's like he doesn't recognize me, despite the fact that I've been friends with his daughter since

Grundschule, that I spent so many nights in my youth at her house, in her bed, whispering secrets back and forth to each other.

"Fräulein Kraus," he says after a moment. "How lovely to see you. Angelika is inside, though I don't think she was expecting you."

"I was in the area and thought I'd—I'd say hello," I say. "My . . . I was helping my sister's Mädelschaft with collecting for the Winter Relief."

"How very noble of you," he says. "And where are you working now?"

"A clothing factory sir," I say, my voice tight, remembering his mistaken belief that I was getting an Abitur, his disdain when he learned that I wasn't.

"Honest work," he says, and nods to me. "I must be going, Fräulein Kraus. Stay for dinner, if you'd like. Nadia is cooking. Heil Hitler."

I swallow. I did not say it to Herr Neumann this morning, but I can hardly be expected not to repeat the words back to Herr Haas. "Heil Hitler," I say, my mouth dry. Herr Haas salutes and then I'm inside that grand house, hands shoved again in my pockets.

A girl greets me, younger than I am, maybe fifteen, her eyes downcast. She motions for my coat and I clutch it to me, feeling self-conscious.

"Wo ist Geli?" I ask, and she shakes her head. I clear my throat again. "Angelika?"

The girl nods and I follow her up the stairs. Geli is sitting at her vanity and springs up when she sees me. "Charlie! Oh, you look lovely—Nadia, you can go, this is just one of my friends," she says.

Nadia gives me a once-over, like she can't quite believe I'm up to Geli's level. She doesn't say anything, though, just leaves, and Geli hugs me again, that familiar perfume of Mathilde's ever-present, sending a surge of longing through me I thought I'd forgotten.

"I've missed you," Geli says. "Sit, tell me everything."

"Who's Nadia?" I ask. "Last time she wasn't—wasn't here."

"Father insists on having a servant since he's away half the time now; I think he just wants someone to watch me. She's Polish," Geli adds, "so I don't think she understands half of what we say, anyway."

"You don't—feel weird about that?" I ask.

"I feel weird that she's here and watching all the time," Geli says.

I think about the girls who work in the factory with me, the girls from Poland, the Soviet Union, who don't speak our language, who huddle together like they're constantly afraid. Taken from their countries by us, and I know they're paid less than any of the German women.

"Oh," I say, twisting my BDM scarf around my fingers. I want then, suddenly, to tell her about Renate, about Renate and me. Because Geli is my friend, and I have told her about every boy I have ever kissed, because she knows about Ingrid. Because she kissed me.

But there is a small part of me that is still holding out hope that she will kiss me again, and if I tell her about Renate, I know that won't happen.

"How's Tommy?" I ask.

"He's good," Geli says, turning from me and drawing her lipstick on, then swiping mascara over her eyelashes. "I'm going to see if he'll take me out to the cinema on Saturday."

The cinema. I haven't been since—since years ago, since before the war. Since we went to see one of Marlene Dietrich's films—*Die große Zarin*, about Katharina the Great—when I was Greta's age. I remember staring up at Marlene like I couldn't believe she was real, my face growing hot. Geli spent weeks after we saw the film mimicking Marlene's movements, until she had them down completely.

I wonder if she remembers that, too.

I wonder if she and Moritz are still going out dancing.

"Fun," I say. We sit in silence for a moment and I find myself desperate to fill it, blurting out the first thing I can think of. "I was at Renate's last night, and Fritz—he stormed out. He left." I tell her what happened, leaving out Frau Hoffmann's indictment of the Führer in case Nadia is listening, even if I suspect her own feelings may not be dissimilar, even if she can't fully understand what I'm saying. "You haven't . . . I don't know, you haven't seen him around, have you?"

"Why would I have seen him?" Geli asks, turning back to me with a frown.

"He's in love with you—didn't you ever notice? How he looks at you, follows you around?" My mouth goes dry at the words.

"I haven't seen him," Geli says.

"Plus, he idolizes your father, so I thought . . . I don't know. He just wants to be a soldier so badly."

"If I see him, I'll let you know," Geli says, already turning away from me, already slipping from my grasp.

I want to keep her, make her stay with me a little longer. But I don't want to tell her about the radio, about the way Renate has found for us to listen to the music. About the clubs she has invited me to. Those things, I just want to be between me and Renate.

"I'm almost—I'm almost done," I say. "Memorizing that poem."

"What poem?" she asks.

My chest feels tight. It must show on my face, because Geli tries to backtrack. "Oh, Charlie, I didn't forget, I know I gave you the book, I just—couldn't remember which poem you meant—"

"Vergiss es," I say coldly, standing, my voice trembling. "Forget it. I—goodbye, Geli."

"Charlie, wait, bitte—"

But I do not turn around, do not wait for her. Not this time. For once I walk out of her house and I do not look back, not even when she calls my name.

Anger and disappointment and so many other emotions swirl in my chest as I walk home. Absurdly, I think of something one of the factory girls told me once.

"You Germans," she spat, her tone derisive, "you cannot just let something *be*, can you? No, you have to have a word for everything, every insignificant thought or feeling that crosses your head."

But I do not have words for this.

I'm jerked out of my thoughts, my anger, *Verrat* and *Wut* and *Lust* and *Sehnsucht* and all the others, by that horrible, now familiar sound of an air-raid siren.

"Scheiße," I hiss, looking around at the people clutching each other, fleeing, and follow the crowd to the nearest air-raid shelter. Fear grips my heart at the thought of Greta, out with her group but having to go wherever is safest; at the thought of our parents, who won't know where we are.

We don't go underground like I thought we would. Instead, I follow the crowd of people toward a large gray monstrosity rising out of the ground, a Flakturm I've only ever heard of, never seen before. It looks like a giant tower, like the rook in a chess set, with notches at the top where HJ boys wait with guns to shoot down any aircraft they see. The sight of it makes me shiver, but it's my only choice right now; I'm surrounded on all sides by people pressing into the shelter.

It's cold inside, the walls doing nothing to retain any heat, and I worry—we're aboveground, we're so exposed, what if something should hit us? This doesn't feel safe at all.

But as soon as we're all crowded in and the doors are shut, the atmosphere relaxes a bit; everyone here is more used to this shelter than I am.

I settle onto a bench, close my eyes. Wish desperately that I had brought my sketchbook, a book, something to pass the time.

"Charlie?"

Oh, nein.

I look up. Geli stands just a few meters away. Her father stands behind her, his back to us. I don't see Mathilde, or Nadia.

I don't want to see her. Not now, not after what she just said, what I just said.

"Geli," I say coldly, and she sighs, settling in next to me. I shift away from her and I can see the hurt on her face when I do, but I can't stop myself.

"Charlie . . ."

"I don't want to talk to you right now," I say. "Please just let me sit here."

She sighs but doesn't respond. I sneak a glance at her out of the corner of my eye. She's biting her bottom lip, a habit I know her father hates. Her nails are chipped, her stockings have a run in them. Things she did not let me get close enough to see back in her room.

"I'm sorry," she says, finally. "I did forget about the poem. You were right. Will you let me make it up to you?"

I press my fingers into the splintered wood of the bench we're sitting on. I can feel it immediately, that softening toward her I'm so inclined to have. I will forgive anything if she's the one who's done it. I always have.

"How?" I ask coldly.

She reaches for my hand, smooths her thumb over my knuckles. I don't move, but I don't pull my hand back, either. In the dark I can feel her skin on mine, cold, and I wonder if anyone is looking, if anyone can see.

But two girls holding hands, well—girls do that all the time. If we were boys, we'd have to be worried, but we aren't.

"Ich sag ihr nicht, weshalb ich's tu / Weiß selber nicht den Grund— / Ich halte ihr die Augen zu / Und küß sie auf den Mund," she whispers, her voice rhythmic and low.

I don't tell her the reason why
I hardly know myself—
Yet still I cover up her eyes
And kiss her on the mouth.

Her lips then brush across my knuckles, carefully, and I am so grateful for the dark so no one can see.

"I told you I wouldn't leave you," she says softly. "Remember? Three years ago I told you I wouldn't, and I meant it. I mean it, Charlie. I am sorry about the poem." She smiles at me. "I do expect you to have it memorized the next time you see me."

"I will," I whisper, and before I can reach out to her, before I can do anything, the all-clear siren sounds and everyone around us stands, pressing together to hurry out of the shelter, and she disappears from my sight, like she was never there to begin with.

I hurry home, nearly running along the Spree so I don't have to think about Geli or Renate or the poem or the look on Greta's face. By the time I reach our flat, I'm out of breath. When I open the door they're immediately there, all three of them, hugging me and pulling me to them.

"Gott sei Dank you're safe. We didn't know where you were when the alarm went off. Greta said you'd left the Winter Relief drive early," Mama starts, smoothing her hands over my hair.

"I went to see Geli," I say. "Don't worry, we sheltered in one of those Flaktürme."

Mama nods, but the crease between her brows doesn't go away. She shakes her head and turns away from me. "Dinner will be ready soon," she says, and I think that's going to be the end of it, but she pulls me back and gives me one quick hug. "You're safe," she repeats, as if affirming it to herself, before heading down the hall and back toward the kitchen.

I set my satchel down and turn back to Greta, who's changed out of her JM uniform.

"Greta . . ."

"The rest of it went fine," she says. "We collected a lot. When Frau Köhler asked where you were, I just said you had to leave early for work." She shrugs.

"I'm—" I swallow. "Es tut mir leid, Greta. I'm sorry I didn't tell you that I'd quit."

She frowns. "I'm not mad that you quit, Charlie. I'm mad you didn't tell me." She shakes her head. "It doesn't matter. I'm going to be a leader when I enter the BDM, so I can make up for you leaving," she says, and there's that hint of earnestness in her voice and I know she believes what she's saying.

My heart sinks.

"Greta, why do you want to be a leader?"

"Frau Köhler thinks I'd be a great leader," Greta says, and internally I curse again at Frau Köhler and her ideas, filling my sister's head. Not just my sister's, but the other girls' heads, too; not just Frau Köhler, but the whole Party and their propaganda.

"I'm sure you would, Greta, but don't you think . . . You have school, and the war, and . . ."

"I can help with the war this way," she says. She narrows her eyes at me. "You don't think I can do it."

"Doch, Greta . . ."

"You don't!" she says. "Do you—do you remember when we went to the Zoo?"

I'm so startled by the change of direction that for a moment I just gape at her before nodding.

"You didn't think I was brave enough then," she says.

"Ach, Greta, Renate was just saying that. . . ."

"But it's true!" she says. "You never trust me, even now you don't trust me!" She blinks rapidly, her eyes filling with tears. "You think I'm just going to follow everything Frau Köhler says, don't you? Well, I'm not!"

"I . . ." I falter, because she's right. Because I thought exactly that.

"I am brave, Charlie," she says, and she almost whispers it.

Without warning I pull her to me, hugging her smaller body close to mine.

"I know," I say. "I know. You're the bravest person I know, and I'm sorry—I'm sorry for not trusting you. I'm really, really sorry."

"So does that mean you'll tell me where you used to go at night sometimes?" She levels an accusing stare at me. I can't help but laugh, just slightly.

"Not yet, Greta, maybe later."

She sighs, but she hugs me back, and I can tell that—at least for now—I'm forgiven.

◆ ◆ ◆

A few nights later I find myself walking along Kurfürsten-damm with Renate, her arm casually linked through mine. I told Mama we were staying late at work.

She did not tell me to be careful this time. It's curfew, but we're old enough—well, Renate is; I will be next month, but I'm hoping that with how I look, they won't look at me twice.

I'm hoping they don't look twice at me and Renate together, either; I've got on an old dress of Mama's, lilac blue with an A-line skirt, and with Renate's short hair and Hans's suspend-ers, she looks like a boy, enough that we could just be any couple on our way to a party.

A couple. *Ein Paar.* The words thrum in my chest. Renate glances over at me and gives me a shy smile.

"You'll like this club," she says. "It's different than the ones we went to before." She bites her lip. "It's, um . . . louder. Than the other club."

"Louder how?"

"It's just—oh, you'll see what I mean when we get there. But don't get too distracted, there are a few people I want you to meet, all right?"

"All right," I say, and she leans over and presses a kiss to my cheek. My face flushes hot under her lips and she laughs.

We pass crowds of people on the street in similar clothes to ours, and for just a moment it seems like there isn't a war on, that we don't spend our waking moments cowering in fear of another air-raid siren, that half of us aren't starving, that they aren't sending the Jews to God knows where.

I feel guilty for it, for any sort of laughter or feeling of freedom on my part, because there *is* a war going on and we shouldn't be allowed to forget so easily.

"It doesn't feel right, does it?" I say, and she looks at me. "I think of Minna hiding . . . somewhere, and I think of— of being able to walk around here as much as I please, and it just—I'm tired of not doing anything about it, Renate."

She kisses me then, hard, and I let her, before my mother's warnings about being careful can come into my head again.

"Let's go in," she says. "There's someone I want you to meet."

Like always, we drop our coats at the door. But this time I immediately see what Renate meant about this place being louder. Different. It's not just the music, though it is so loud I can feel it in my teeth; the dancing is looser, and when I pause to look around, I almost blush: so close is everyone dancing together, bodies pressed tight, girls' straps falling off their shoulders, boys' shirts unbuttoned.

"Oh," I breathe, and someone spins me, and I laugh, and then there's a hand on my waist, and I turn, and there's Renate, her face barely centimeters from mine.

When I kiss her this time, it's not the same as the kisses we've shared before. There's a heat to it that has nothing to do with the packed bodies in the room, her tongue swiping across my bottom lip, then her teeth.

"Renate," I gasp, and she laughs, her voice husky. For a

second I'm not sure if she heard me, but her lips brush my ear and she whispers my name and I know she did.

Her hands slide up my waist as the music changes, and even though it's something faster, we keep dancing that close, not caring if there are other people around, if they're looking, if they care. Renate doesn't look worried and so I won't be, either.

"What're you thinking?" she asks me, laughing.

"Nichts," I say. "Nothing, I—I—"

I pull her to me and kiss her again, desperate, hard, nothing around me but her and the music, both pounding a rhythm through my body that I never want to let go of.

"Stay with me," she says. "Tonight. I know you didn't plan to, but I want you to come back to mine."

"Yes," I say immediately. "Yes."

She kisses me again just as the song is winding down, then pulls back and twirls me, my skirt flaring around my thighs. Renate laughs and heads off toward one of the walls, away from the middle of the dance floor. I follow, trying to catch my breath.

"Who did you want me to meet?" I ask, and Renate tips her head toward a boy who looks about our age, wearing lipstick drawn on even better than Geli's.

"Max," she says, tapping him on the shoulder. "Hey, I brought Charlie."

"Charlie!" Max says, and hugs me like he's known me my whole life. "Gott, Renate won't shut up about you."

246

"Hey!" Renate says, lightly hitting him on the arm, and he laughs. "Only because you won't shut up about Hans."

"Hans, your brother?" I ask, and Renate rolls her eyes.

"Max thinks he has a chance."

"I do."

"Auf keinen Fall," Renate says. "I know Hans, trust me. Sorry for you, but he doesn't like boys."

"Who says I'm a boy?" Max winks, but shakes his head. "Calm down, Renate, I'm not going to chase after your brother." He looks at me. "Charlie, however, you'll have to keep an eye on."

"Nonsense, Charlie's with me," Renate says, her arm around my waist, and presses a kiss to my cheek.

"Yes, but who says I won't leave you for Max?" I say, feeling bold. I lean over and kiss Max's cheek, making him blush. Renate laughs, and for a second I worry that I've messed up, that she's going to turn possessive, that she's angry with me. But she just shakes her head.

"Max wouldn't dare, and neither would you," she says. Max scoots over and she takes a seat next to him. I follow her, making sure I'm on her good side.

"Max?" I say, the name suddenly sparking recognition within me. "Wait, didn't you . . . didn't you help Minna and her family escape?" Saying Minna's name hurts, here in this space filled with music and dancing, which she loved so much and so dangerously. From the look on Renate's face, hearing Minna's name hurts her just as much.

"Mm," Max says. "Gave her my cousin's name in Paris. I remembered after . . . after she mentioned her parents that our families had once done a Seder together when we were small." His mouth twists. "The Nazis and their ridiculous race laws, thinking they can tell who's Jewish and who isn't simply by looking."

"But you're still here—"

"Hiding in plain sight," he says. "*Halbjuden*, like the other boys up there." He jerks a thumb at the band onstage. "Hiding in plain sight, and causing trouble to boot," he adds, grinning. But then his expression changes. "Don't think I don't know how dangerous it is, or how it was for your friend. She's lucky she got out. But I figured, since I'm staying, I could do something to mess up the Nazis while I'm at it. Do you want to tell her, Renate?"

"Tell me what?" I ask.

"I was going to wait to tell you, but what—what you said tonight—" she starts, then continues, nearly breathless, "We've been—do you remember the postcards in Rudolf's shop? The record shop we went to at the Weihnachtsmarkt?"

"Yes," I say, thinking of the treasonous words written on them. "I remember."

"Max has been slipping those into mailboxes at night," Renate says.

I turn to gape at him. "You haven't."

"I have. Me and a few others. But we need more people," he says. "I told Renate about it at the last club meeting and she was interested, but said she wanted to ask you first." He grins. "Now I know why."

My conversation with Mama about leaving the BDM resounds in my head again, that line between safety and resistance that I have, until now, never crossed.

But I am tired of only choosing safety.

"I want to," I say, and look directly at Renate when I say it so I know she understands me. She takes my hand, brushes her thumb over my knuckles.

"You do?"

"Yes," I say, then lean over and kiss her. When I pull back, she's grinning.

"See?" she says to Max, who's staring at me. "I told you she'd agree. I told you Charlie'd want to help."

Max rolls his eyes, pressing a mark into her hand. "Fine. I owe you a beer, Hoffmann."

"You do." She smiles. "Buy it for me next week when we go get postcards from Rudolf. Charlie, want to come?"

"Yes," I say again, and Renate pushes off the ground, pulling me up with her.

"Perfekt," she says. "Let's dance."

By the end of the night, my feet are sore, but I'm more elated than I have been during the whole war. Elated to be doing something. Finally doing something concrete, something that will resist Hitler and Goebbels and the whole verdammte lot of them.

Renate kisses me as we're leaving the club, both of us giddy, neither of us caring if anyone sees.

"Back to mine?" she says, and I nod, and kiss her again, and again.

We try to stifle our giggles as she opens the door to her flat, knowing her parents are asleep, that Fritz is in his room. She pulls me into her bedroom, peppering my lips with kisses, both of us breathless as she shuts the door and we fall back onto her bed.

Her hands roam over my body and I take my time unbuttoning her shirt, her suspenders, sliding them over her shoulders as she kisses my collarbone, her thighs on either side of my hips.

"Renate," I gasp, and she laughs, pushing my skirt up as I free the last button on her shirt. "Oh—"

"Charlie," she says, and she kisses me and kisses me and kisses me, her hand between my legs, and the way she says my name, the way she kisses me, makes me finally feel—

seen.

Mai 1941

THE MONTHS trip on, the noose of war ever tightening around our necks. I begin delivering postcards with Renate after work. The first few times we go my heart hammers so loud I fear it's going to alert the SS to what we are doing.

But the feeling that we are doing something *good*, the feeling that I am helping, is so much louder. Every postcard we deliver makes me—makes Renate and me—feel like there's finally something we can do to make a difference.

And then Hans is finally sent to the front. His first letter comes only two weeks after he leaves, and Renate reads it to me while she clutches my hand; stopping every few sentences so her voice doesn't break. She reads it to me because she cannot read it to her father, or her mother, because neither of them can take it. Even as censored as this letter is, it's easy enough to see that Hans is terrified.

If Mama notices all the time I'm spending with Renate, she doesn't say anything. When I'm home, she constantly studies me, like she's trying to figure something out, but every time I think she's going to say something to me, she doesn't.

More letters from Hans come in, and I envy Renate those letters, the knowledge that her brother is thinking about her. Geli never writes me. I've barely seen her except for one or two times when she invited me out for coffee with her and Marianne, and it was so obvious she was the only one who wanted me there.

I haven't heard from Ingrid since she sent me the record for Renate, but then one day I come home from a factory shift to find a letter waiting for me. I tuck it under my blouse and hurry to my room, open and smooth it out.

Liebe Charlotte,
I don't know if you'll get this letter. Truth be told, I shouldn't be writing it. I'll say it quickly, I don't have much time.
We've been raided. The Tanztee in Hamburg—they've ██████████████████ *most of us, sent the leaders* ██
██████

I don't know what to do, but bitte, Charlie, be careful.
Deine Ingrid

I press my hand to my mouth so Mama won't hear my sobs. Whatever words ended the sentence where Ingrid talked about where the leaders have been sent are blacked out.

And in Hamburg! Where there were so many of us. Maybe what we're doing—the music, the dancing—maybe it is more dangerous than I thought. Maybe it scares the Nazis more than I realized.

I call Renate, wishing desperately for the comfort of her voice. "Hallo?"

"Frau Hoffmann," I say breathlessly. "Is Renate there?"

"Einen Moment bitte, Charlotte." I hear a rustle, Fritz yelling in the background, then Renate picks up the phone.

"Ja?"

"Renate," I say, filled with relief at just the sound of her voice. "I got a letter from Ingrid. They . . ." My mouth is dry. What if someone's listening? "The . . . the Tanztee in Hamburg got . . . interrupted by the SS."

"Gott," Renate says. Then, "Scheiße." I can hear the steely resolve in her voice. "Charlie . . . do you want to go record shopping?"

"Yes," I say immediately, knowing what she's asking. "Yes, I do."

It's half nine when I decide to leave; I'm old enough now that the curfew doesn't apply to me. For my birthday this past February, Mama tried to bake me a cake with what little flour we had, but it turned out so poorly that none of us ate it, not even washed down with ersatz-Kaffee. Greta hated it most of all, but even she knew better than to complain.

I wrinkle my nose thinking about that cake now, as I try to tiptoe past Greta's room, hoping she doesn't try to follow me.

"Charlie?"

"Shh," I say. "Greta. Go back to your room."

"Where are you going?"

"Out with Renate," I say. "But you can't tell Mama, please."

"I want to go with you."

"Nein, Greta," I say, already seeing the pout forming on her face. "It's too dangerous."

"If it's so dangerous, why are you doing it?" She crosses her arms in front of her chest.

"Because I have to."

"What are you doing?"

"I promise I will tell you," I say, the lie heavy in my chest. "Greta, I promise, but only if you don't tell Mama and you go back to sleep right now." I look at her. "I told you I trust you, and I mean it this time. I do."

And I do trust her. But this is too dangerous to share, even with my brave little sister.

Greta sighs, and for a second I think she's going to waver, that she's going to yell and Mama will come running and I'll have to explain every wretched, traitorous thing I've been doing for the past few months, the past few years.

"Na gut," Greta says. "But you have to tell me when you get back."

"I will," I say, and she nods. I wait until I hear her door shut before I grab my coat from the hanger by the door and tiptoe out of the flat, shutting the door behind me.

I hurry down the street, the breeze from the river chilling me even through my coat. I could have taken the U-Bahn, but I want the walk, want the time aboveground, looking around at the names of the streets.

When I was growing up, these streets were called something different. When Hitler rose to power, he changed them. Changed the street names, and then the borders, so the lines on our maps became lies.

Maybe that was when I stopped fully trusting in what he stood for. What kind of man sees a map and decides to disregard it, to make it his own, with no thought for the people who live within its borders? How does one man decide he can redraw the lines of an entire country?

What can I trust if I can't trust those lines, the shifting, changing borders of where I belong?

This is what I have mapped out: the route from Renate's flat to mine, the route from her place to the underground bunker we hide in during air raids. These are things I know to be true, lines that Hitler cannot change.

The lines of her hands I have traced my fingers over until I have them memorized, the curves of her body under my own hands.

By the time I reach the record shop, it's freezing. I pull my coat tighter and open the door.

"We're closed," Rudolf says, not looking up. Then—"Oh. Shirley's friend. Here alone?"

"Nein," I answer, watching the way his eyes linger on me and deciding not to take my coat off. "She'll be here any second."

"Of course," Rudolf says, and just like clockwork, Renate pushes open the door.

"Hallo," she says, her eyes softening when she sees me.

"Hallo," I say, grateful that she's there, for her calm, steadying presence. "Are we ready?"

"That depends." She turns to Rudolf. "Have you finished them?"

Rudolf nods, pushing himself back from the desk, nearly tripping on a crate of records. I press my hand to my mouth to keep from laughing.

"Here," he says, his expression sour, as he brandishes a stack of postcards at Renate. "They're all ready to go."

"Perfect," she says. "Danke, Rudolf. Do you want to come help deliver them?"

He shakes his head. "Nein. The SS are already watching this place more than I'd like them to. It's bad enough I'm still getting shipments in and selling records. You and your little Freundin go have fun," he says. My face flushes at his words. He could have meant *friend*, but something tells me he didn't.

"Fine," Renate says, and I follow her out of the building,

wanting for a moment to stop and riffle through the records, see if there's anything I can take home to Greta. But Renate's long legs are already striding ahead of me, and I have to hurry to keep up with her.

"So when do we want to deliver these?" I ask.

"Now," she says. "Come on. There's a club meeting tonight; we can go before then."

"Renate, it's still early—"

"And a lot of people are probably getting ready to head out," she calls over her shoulder. "Besides. We're going to the nicer part of town; they'll all be out at the opera or whatever by the time we get there. Wars don't matter when you have money," she spits. "Let's go to Charlottenburg. Your namesake." She winks at me.

Charlottenburg. Where Geli lives.

Renate notices my hesitation. "Was ist, Charlie?"

I don't want to run into Geli. Not with Renate, not with what we're doing. About to do.

But it's Geli. I trust her.

Don't I?

"Nothing," I say. "It's just—I'm not dressed for the club. And you're too tall for me to borrow anything of yours."

"Es macht nichts," she says. "Just for tonight. We won't stay long. We can just dance a bit after we deliver the postcards, okay? I'm too tired for a full night out, anyway."

"Of course," I say, and the two of us walk down the street.

"I hope Ingrid's okay," I say as we cross over the Gotzkowsky-brücke into Charlottenburg. "And . . . and the rest of them."

"Me too," Renate says, and squeezes my hand. "Scheiße, this damned war. I hope we lose, I really do." She spits. "You see what we're doing? What this damn country is doing to its own citizens, to everyone?" Her voice is raw, and I worry that someone is going to hear her, hear us, that we'll be arrested for such talk.

"We deserve to burn for this," Renate says, her voice miserable, and then she's crying in the middle of the street and I pull her to me, smooth my hands over her back, whisper nonsense in her ear so she stills—or what I think is nonsense before realizing it's that Heine poem, the one Geli wanted me to memorize so long ago.

We're cut off by an air-raid siren. Renate swears, but doesn't turn and begin making her way to the nearest underground or Flakturm like we should.

"What?" I say. "Renate, wir müssen los."

She shakes her head. "Nein, Charlie—it's the perfect time. Everyone will be in the shelters. We can deliver the postcards now—no one will see."

"And we could get bombed in the process," I hiss, but she's already pulling away, wiping at her eyes fiercely.

"Maybe it's what we deserve," she says.

"Renate, that's suicide."

"If I think it's actually bad, I'll go hide."

"You'll go hide? I'm coming with you."

"No," she says, shaking her head, stepping away from me. "No. Like you said. It's too dangerous, and I don't want to lose you."

I reach out for her, grab her wrist, remembering suddenly that evening on the street when Geli did the same to me, pulled me in for a kiss.

"You're not leaving me," I say. "Let's go."

The streets are empty soon enough, save for the clusters of HJ boys who've been put on lookout duty. Their eyes narrow when they see us.

"We should've worn our uniforms. We could've blended in," I say.

Renate scoffs. "Mine doesn't even fit anymore," she says, laughing. "Come on, let's hurry. If anyone asks, we'll say we're with the BDM and just forgot our uniforms, that we're out here as lookouts, too." She shouts a Heil to one of the boys watching us, her face twisting in disgust as soon as he turns away.

"Which mailboxes did you want to hit this time?" I ask.

"Does it matter? As long as they end up somewhere people will see them. Komm," she says, and pulls me into a residential building much nicer than either of our own. She finds the mailboxes and begins sliding postcards in. I wring my hands, looking out for any HJ boys who might barge in and ask what we're doing.

"Are you finished?" I ask. Renate doesn't respond, and I realize I'm standing on her wrong side.

Footsteps, coming from the flat above us.

"Renate," I hiss, but she doesn't turn. I grab her elbow and she whirls around. I point upstairs, eyes wide, and panic flashes across her face before she tucks the rest of the postcards under her coat and we hurry out of the building.

"That was too close," I say.

"That's why you're my lookout. I wouldn't have heard that if I was on my own," she says. I can tell she means it as a joke, but there's frustration creeping into her tone.

"We could stop," I say, but she shakes her head, and whatever panic I glimpsed in her a moment ago is gone, replaced by anger and determination.

"Just a few more before everyone comes out, okay?" she says, already pulling me down the street. She hands me a small stack of postcards. "Here. Meet me back here in five."

"Renate—"

"Fünf Minuten," she says, holding up five fingers, then disappearing down the block before I can protest. I glance over my shoulder, looking for any Hitlerjugend, then head down the street, pausing at mailboxes to slide the postcards in, my heart beating fast.

The last house I stop at is Geli's. It's like my feet take me there before I even have time to think about what I'm doing, where I'm going; I've walked to her house so many times before.

I know her father won't read the postcard; most likely he'll tear it up and burn it before she even gets to see it.

But maybe she'll see it first. Maybe I can convince her to finally quit the BDM, join us, join *me*. Even with Renate, even as much as I love her—and I do love her, I realize—there's a small part of me that misses Geli. Misses how fearless she made me feel. How with her, with our small group, I knew exactly where I was supposed to be.

I carefully slide the postcard into her mailbox before looking up at her window. For a moment, just a moment, I think I see her curtain move.

But it was just a trick of my imagination, I'm sure.

I'm always waiting for her, following after her.

She never is for me.

True to her word, Renate meets up with me a few minutes later, back at the street where we started. Her face is flushed, and the two of us hurry toward the Flakturm just as the all-clear siren begins.

"Told you we'd be fine," Renate says. Then, "Hey. Alles gut?"

"I'm fine," I say, trying to smile at her.

Geli has moved on from me. And Renate is here, in front of me, and she sees me and she wants me and I am not her shadow. I am right beside her.

I kiss her before the siren stops, before everyone comes pouring out of the shelters and I lose my courage.

"Ich liebe dich," I say, and when I pull back from her, she's smiling.

"I love you too," she says. "Let's go dance."

As we enter the club, things feel different; the atmosphere is more subdued, the music quieter. Whether they've heard the news about what happened in Hamburg and are just trying to be cautious or the club has lost its appeal is difficult to tell right now.

But we dance anyway. There's no band tonight, just someone with a record player, and Renate goes over and asks them to turn up the volume. Soon we are not the only ones on the dance floor; soon others have joined us, that fear that held us so tightly finally loosening.

It happened in Hamburg. Who says it has to happen in Berlin? Our city is big enough that maybe they won't find us here. We are young enough to think we will never be caught.

Renate spins me and spins me and spins me until we're both breathless and dizzy, holding on to each other for support. There are more of us now, the music thrumming, and we are here and young and I—

I lean in and kiss her, hard, like my life depends on it, and maybe it does.

"Charlie?"

At first I think it's her. Renate. So I kiss her again, and I hear my name again, cutting through the noise of the club.

But no. It isn't Renate. Renate is in front of me and the voice is coming from my left. And I know it.

I turn, and time slows down, because Geli is standing in front of me, taking in how close Renate and I are and how my hand is flat against her chest and my lipstick is on her mouth.

"Geli—" I say, but she's already turned from us, from me, and is pushing her way through the crowd. "Geli, warte, bitte—just wait—"

Renate's hand is still in mine, anchoring me, and I turn back to her, hoping she sees the desperation on my face, because I have to explain to Geli, because as far as Geli has pulled away from me, I'm not ready to lose her. I can't lose her.

"Go," Renate mouths, and I squeeze her hand and she squeezes mine back before I hurry out of the room.

Geli isn't in the pack of bodies pressing against me, so I push my way out into the hallway, catching a glimpse of her blond hair as she rounds a corner.

She's always leading.

I'm always following.

"Geli!" I call, but she hurries away faster, so I break into a run, trying to catch up, to catch *her*, because if I can just explain, then—then—

She's outside, her back to me, her shoulders rising and falling, and I'm reminded of that night three years ago, of running out of the club after I caught her with Moritz, jealousy burning in my chest.

I wonder if she feels now like I did then.

"Geli . . . ," I say, and she turns.

"How could you?" she spits, blue eyes cold and staring straight at me. "*Renate?*"

"Geli, please, let me explain. . . ."

"You don't need to explain," she says. "You kissed her. You're with her, and you didn't—didn't tell me, you didn't—"

"I didn't what?" I snap, and now I'm the one who's angry. "I didn't *wait* for you? I didn't follow you around? You're the one who barely makes the effort to see me anymore. You're the one who abandoned me for your new Hautevolee friends. I know they laugh at me when I'm not around, and I bet you don't stop them. You just like having your little *seamstress* to fawn over you, don't you?" I cry. My voice breaks and I don't care, I don't care, all the resentment and anger I've felt at her over the past year just now boiling over. "So *yes*, I'm with Renate. What was I supposed to do, Geli? You—you kissed me once and we never talked about it. What was I supposed to do? Just keep waiting for you?"

Her face falls, and I realize that's exactly what she thought, that I was just going to keep waiting around for her forever.

"I told you," she says, her own voice breaking. "I told you I wouldn't leave you."

"But you did," I say. "You—you left when you wouldn't quit

the BDM with us, you left us at the party last year, you—"

"What does that have to do with us?"

"It has everything to do with us!" I say. "Geli, I want—" I reach out, desperate, grab her hand, press it between my palms, hoping she won't pull away. "I want—if you meant it, that you wouldn't leave me, then join us—resist, leave the BDM, talk to your father, please—"

She does pull away. "You," she says. "You put that postcard in my mailbox."

"Yes," I say. "I did. You know this isn't right, what the Party is doing, you *know* it isn't."

For one moment, one blissful, wild moment, I think she's going to do it. That she's going to join us, join *me*, finally leave behind her father and his ideas and the rest of the whole damned thing.

"Charlie, I can't," she says, and she's crying now. "You know I can't. I'm sorry."

I take a breath. Look at her. See the girl I loved, the girl I wanted to follow everywhere, the girl I wanted to be with. Want to be with still. The girl with such bright ideas, who showed me this club to begin with.

"I'm sorry, Geli," I say. "But I can't wait for you anymore."

And before she can respond, before I can rip my own chest open any further, I turn.

I am the one who walks away.

I am the one leaving her.

Part III

APRIL 1942

April 1942

BOMBS. BOMBS falling. We spend most of the year hiding in the cellar or the underground, so frequent are the bombs; Berlin slowly reduced to rubble and ash thanks to the Soviets. I try to keep lookout with Renate, occasionally going up to her roof and using the radio, but this ends after a few months when Mama insists I stop.

"But I want to help. . . ."

She narrows her eyes. I suspect she knows I'm not listening for air raids out of love and fear for my country. What would she do if she knew I was listening to broadcasts by the BBC that suggest our army isn't doing as well as Hitler and Goebbels want us to believe?

I do not hear from Geli. I try not to think about Geli. I didn't call her on her birthday. I still haven't memorized that damn poem, but now every time I look at that book of Heine's poetry it makes my fists clench and my chest ache, so I just slam it back into my vanity drawer.

Instead, I spend my time drawing maps—from my flat to Renate's, from Renate's to the record store, the route along Unter den Linden, along the Spree. Everything continues quietly on, the only change being fewer and fewer letters from Hans, which I know worries Renate.

Renate and I have fallen into a quiet routine, into something. At night I often find myself curled up in her bed. She kisses me on the cheek and lays her head in my lap and I stroke her hair. When her father screams from nightmares, I hold her. Sometimes she stays at our flat, just to get away from it all, and from Fritz.

Sometimes we walk along the Spree just to clear our heads, to spend time aboveground instead of hunkered down in a shelter. We rarely pass any Swingjugend we know anymore; instead, more often than not we pass the same family: a young couple and their daughter, who looks a few years younger than Greta, all with yellow stars with the word *Jude* in thick black stitching affixed to the fronts of their coats. The stars all Jews have been forced to wear since last year.

Renate and I try to wave every time we see the family, and once or twice I catch Renate slipping them a mark or two from her pocket, since we've heard their ration cards are even more limited than ours.

I can never tell if the father looks grateful or upset when we do.

"At least Minna's safe," I say one evening as we walk away

from them. "At least she doesn't . . . doesn't have to . . ."

"Is she safe, though? It feels like there are as many Nazis in Paris as there are here," Renate says, biting her bottom lip. I take her hand, knowing that I do not have the words to reassure her, or reassure the family we pass by every evening, that nothing I say will ever be enough, and I will, somehow, have to live with that.

The year ends, 1942 begins, and before we know it, it's April 19. Greta is fourteen, and Fritz is fourteen; they are supposed to be inducted into the BDM and HJ proper tomorrow.

I cannot take her going through another induction ceremony. And the sick feeling that has been growing in me since this war started finally bubbles over.

I find Mama sitting in the kitchen mending Greta's navy skirt, wishing I'd offered to do it instead. "Mama?"

"Hm?"

"I don't want Greta inducted." I close my eyes so I don't have to see the look on her face as I say it. "I don't want her in the BDM. The JM was bad enough, but now—*please*, Mama."

"*Charlotte*," she snaps, and I open my eyes. If the war has aged anyone, it has aged my mother, her hair streaked with more and more gray every month, the lines on her face deepening. "It is bad enough that *you* quit the BDM. Greta can't afford to. *We* can't afford for both of you to drop out of the Party—"

"We can't afford to keep her in it! She barely fits into that uniform anymore; we can't afford the dues, they just want her to—to become just another leader, and it's bad enough that Fritz is just following along to be a perfect little *soldier*—"

"I am not Fritz's mother," Mama says, standing. "I am Greta's. And yours, Charlotte." Her voice is tense. "I cannot have Greta following you anymore. I know what it means to you, but I won't have you putting the entire family in danger because of it."

"Charlie's putting us in danger?"

I turn. Greta stands in the doorway, one sock on, her hair loose. She is taller than I am now.

"Do you want to join the BDM?" I ask her, and she shrugs.

"What else am I going to do?"

"You could—" I begin, but Mama shoots me a look, and I shut my mouth.

"I'm not quitting," Greta says. She closes her eyes. "Mama, actually . . . Frau Köhler wants me to lead my own JM group once I'm inducted into the BDM. She says I'm good with the girls, that I've earned it."

"Nein!" I say, not believing what my sister has just said. Greta and Mama look at me. "Greta, please, if you become a leader you're just giving the Party what they want—"

"I know you quit, Charlie," she says. "But did you ever think that me being a leader might . . . might be how I can resist? I'm not Frau Köhler. I'm not going to fill my girls' heads with—with what the Party wants." She lifts her chin. "I'm going to take them hiking and teach them songs and we're not going to talk about the Party at all."

"They won't let you get away with that," I say. "They'll send someone to watch you, Gretchen. You can't—staying in the Party, in the BDM, it means—"

"It means *what*, Charlotte?" Mama says, looking at me. "It means you support the Party wholeheartedly? It means that every single person who stays is a coward who thinks what Hitler is doing is good?" She steps toward me. "Your father is in the Party because he has to be, Charlotte. Does that make him a bad man?"

"You aren't in it," I point out.

"No," she says shortly, "I'm not, and there are days I regret it. Your father has been questioned *twice* at work about it, did you know that?" She passes a hand over her face.

"Papa's been questioned? Why didn't you tell me?"

"When are you ever here for me to tell?" Mama says. She rubs at her temples. "Honestly, Charlotte, there are days I think about joining just to ease any suspicion that has fallen on this family."

The words she leaves unspoken are clear. *Any suspicion that has fallen on this family* because of you.

"Renate's parents aren't in the Party," I say, a last, desperate attempt to dissuade her.

"How many times must I tell you we are not Renate's family?" Mama snaps.

"You think you're the only one who hates the Party?" Greta

273

turns to me, her eyes wide. My stubborn sister. "Just because Mama and I aren't going out after curfew like you doesn't mean—"

"You're going out after curfew?" Mama cuts in.

"Greta!" I cry, turning toward her. She narrows her eyes. "I'm too old for the curfew," I begin, but Mama holds up her hands.

"Where are you—you know what? For once, I don't want to know. Don't tell me." She closes her eyes, briefly. "But before you think about doing it again, I am begging you—please, just think for a moment about what will happen to the rest of us if you don't come back."

Greta comes to my room as I'm getting ready for bed and stands in my doorway chewing her bottom lip. She doesn't say anything as I brush out my hair, as I wipe my makeup off with some cold cream I stole from Geli forever ago.

"Was ist, Greta?" I finally ask, when it becomes clear she isn't going to speak first.

She shifts her weight back and forth from foot to foot. "Do you . . . do you really not want me to join the BDM?"

"No," I say, and her face falls, like she was hoping I would say something different. "But you're fourteen. I can't stop you."

Greta sighs and walks into my room, sitting down on the edge of my bed.

"Where do you go?" she asks. "When you go out at night. You said you'd tell me."

I look in the mirror at her face. At fourteen, she looks so much like me, but her eyes are more like our father's, dark and serious, the lashes thick.

"Do you really want to know?"

"Yes, Charlie," she says, sighing. "I don't want you to keep secrets from me. You always keep secrets from me."

"Greta, das ist nicht wahr."

"It is true," she protests. "You snuck off somewhere with Renate at the Christmas market a year and a half ago, you didn't tell me about quitting the BDM until Frau Köhler let it slip. You want me to quit, and you didn't even tell me you did. That's not fair."

"I'm sorry," I say.

"I don't care," she says, and this time I do turn to look at her. "I don't care that you're sorry, Charlie, I just want to know. Please," she adds, and I sigh, finally getting up and crossing the narrow room to her.

"You know, I dream about them," she says when I sit down. "Ruth and Rebekah. I have dreams where they've been found out, or taken, or they're just on the other side of a fence and I can never get to them. They're always ten, in my dreams. They don't age. They just . . . stay the same."

I look at her then. Really look at her, and I know—she isn't ten anymore. Even if I think she is. I've been doing the same thing she has, picturing her frozen in glass like a girl in a Brüder Grimm Märchen. An unchanging fairy tale.

"When I go out," I tell her, "I go to Renate's. And sometimes, we go to this club and we listen to music."

"What kind of music?"

"Jazz," I say. "Verboten. And we dance, and half the people there don't belong to the HJ or the BDM, and it's honestly just—freeing, Greta. And sometimes I go to Renate's and we'll volunteer for air-raid lookout duty so we can try to find jazz on the radio, and we listen for broadcasts from the BBC so we can hear what's actually going on with the war—"

"Papa does that, too," Greta interjects, and I look at her in surprise.

"Was?"

"He does," she says. "You'd know that if you were home sometimes. After Mama's gone to bed, I'll sneak into the living room and we'll crouch down by the radio and keep it low so Herr Lang doesn't hear." She shrugs. "We learn a lot that way."

"Oh," I say, because what else can I say?

"I told you," Greta says, "that you aren't the only one who wants to resist. You aren't the only one who's upset with our friends disappearing, with never being able to question the Party." She sighs. "Mama's right, you know. I stay in the BDM because I don't want them to look at Papa any worse than they already do because of you and Mama. One of us has to not draw suspicion. That doesn't mean I like it, even if I like some of the other girls there."

"I'm . . . I'm sorry, Gretchen."

"I'm not ten anymore," she says, and I nod, because I know.

"Can I tell you something else?" I ask, because suddenly I want to tell someone, because I am tired of keeping secrets from my sister. Greta looks at me and nods. "I . . . you know I've been spending a lot of time with Renate. Just . . . well, not really as a friend. More than that."

I wait. But to my surprise, Greta just shrugs and laughs.

"What's so funny?"

"I already knew that, Charlie," she says. "I mean, about Renate, not about you, but it's pretty obvious whenever she's over—you can't stop looking at her."

"How did you know about Renate?"

"Fritz told me," she says. "One time when he was really mad at her he told me."

"And how does Fritz know?"

"He said Renate doesn't exactly keep it a secret," she says, laughing. "Though I'm sure she does with you. I don't think Fritz knows about you, if you're worried."

"I'm more worried he'll turn Renate in," I say, only now realizing that I am, in fact, worried about that as the words leave my mouth. "I don't trust him."

"I don't either," Greta agrees. "Thank goodness Mama has stopped trying to push us together."

We laugh at that.

"So, can I come to the club with you sometime?" she asks, and I shrug.

"I don't know—not that I don't want you to come, but that—I don't know how many more times they're going to get together, since the one in Hamburg got raided," I say truthfully. "But—yes, Greta, if it's safe, you can come."

"Promise?"

"Ich verspreche," I say. "Now. Let's make sure you're prepared for tomorrow."

The building has not changed since Greta's first induction ceremony; if anything, it's even more elaborate, trying to spark some spirit back into a nation that's quickly losing it; the Party's pretense, *our sons may be dying, but everything is fine.* The cellar of the building has been turned into an air-raid shelter, and I try not to look at the glowing paint indicating the way down as I make my way in to watch Greta be inducted into the BDM.

There is no group for me to sit with this time, no uniform to wear, nothing but waving to the Hoffmanns and finding myself somehow seated in the audience between Renate and my mother.

The ceremony begins and I tune it out until the mayor stands up, the same man from four years ago at Greta's last ceremony. The years have not changed him like they have the rest of us; certainly his rations have not been limited in the name of the Fatherland.

His speech, I quickly realize, hasn't changed either. The words are the same; if anything, his tone is different, more urgent, convincing a crowd of boys that their future deaths on the battlefield will be the greatest possible honor, the greatest sacrifice for their country. My fists tighten in my lap, and someone takes my hand. I assume it's Renate, but when I look down it's my mother, her thumb smoothing over my knuckles. When I look up, her face is as white and drawn as I'm sure my own is.

The mayor finishes his speech, looking out over us, and as he says his final sentence, I realize coldly that it is the exact one he spoke four years ago:

"There is no shame in being a German."

But as he takes his seat and I grip my mother's hand, I know for certain this time that he is wrong.

The inductions begin after that. The girls are first, and we watch as Greta takes her oath, her face solemn and serious.

I think about what she said. How she hasn't been listening to Frau Köhler, how she and Papa are finding other broadcasts. How she wants to come with me to the clubs.

I can't let her go to the clubs, I decide. It's too dangerous, and I don't want her there, not in this place I've carved out for myself. Maybe that's selfish, but I want to protect her. I want to keep her safe.

Safe.

I think about safety as Renate's fingers brush against mine, sending electricity through my body.

Here we are, in a building full of people, in a system that would like to see people like us destroyed, and I want to hold her hand, but I know I can't, because that isn't safe, it's the most dangerous thing of all.

The girls' ceremony ends and the boys' begins. Fritz is called up, his eyes hard, taller now than his parents. I sneak a glance at Frau Hoffmann. Her face is stone. So is her husband's.

We could live so many lifetimes and never atone for this.

I want to make Hitler pay. I want to make him pay for the fear in my own chest, in the Hoffmanns' faces, in the dreams I have of Minna. I want to make him pay for every bright yellow star I see sewn on the coats of Jewish people now, for the fact that we have so few Jewish neighbors left.

I remember, suddenly, the man in the restaurant four years ago, the one being dragged out, Greta burying her head in my chest, the blood on Fritz's shirt, that terrible, awful feeling in my gut and knowing that I had to look away.

I cannot look away anymore.

I link my fingers with Renate's and squeeze, just once, just so she knows I'm there. The ceremony ends and we all stand; having decided earlier that we'd all go to Aschinger after the induction, scraping together the money for Fritz and Greta so they can at least have something special tonight, even if most of us don't feel like celebrating.

I'm about to go find Greta, tell her how proud I am of her, when I see her. That flash of blond hair, of red lipstick.

Geli.

Geli's here.

"I'll be back," I say to my mother, and before she can stop me, I push through the crowd, still drawn to Geli, a moth to a golden-haired flame.

"Geli," I say. At first she doesn't turn, and for a second I think she's ignoring me, and I almost don't call her name again.

But something compels me to, so I do. "Geli!"

She turns, but someone else does, too—a boy beside her, a boy I don't know, in one of the HJ leadership uniforms, his dark hair slicked back. His arm is around her waist.

I step toward her, toward the boy, when I realize—I am not the only one who notices her. Fritz's eyes are narrowed at Geli, at the boy, and I watch as he stares at her for just a second too long before pressing his lips together and turning away.

I don't have time to worry about Fritz right now, though, about his petty crush. I push my way through the crowd, certain she's seen me.

"Geli," I say a third time, and then she is there in front of me, looking the same as always. "What . . . what are you doing here?"

"Johann is moving up," she says, looking up at the boy beside her. "I came to support." She smiles at him, and I hate that I find myself wondering if it's sincere or not.

"Oh," I say. "Gratuliere, Johann."

"Danke." His eyes are friendly, but the rest of his face is stoic. "Wer sind Sie?"

Who are you?

She hasn't told him about me. But why would she? It's not like we talk, not like we've seen each other in months.

Geli looks back and forth between us, briefly biting her lip. "This is Charlotte. We . . . were in the same Mädelschaft in the BDM together," she says, and each word pierces my chest.

She's never called me Charlotte before.

"Schatz, I think I see Herr Meisner over there. Would you get him for me?" she says to Johann, not meeting my eyes.

"Of course," Johann says. "Don't be too long, Angelika." He kisses her and I turn my head away, not daring to look at her until he's sauntered off.

When I finally turn my head back, Geli is staring at her shoes.

"Angelika?"

It's all I can think to say.

"Bitte, not here, Charlie," she says.

"So I'm Charlie again? Or Charlotte? Which is it? Your friend, or just a girl from the BDM?"

"What did you want me to say?" she finally snaps, her pale blue eyes boring into mine. "You're the one who left me."

I wish I hadn't, I think, so suddenly I cannot stop it. And for a split second I know she sees the regret on my face, she must, because she looks like the Geli I knew, the one I would follow anywhere.

"I miss you," I say softly.

"Charlie, don't . . . ," she says. Her gaze flits around the room, looking for Johann, before she leans in close to me, so close her breath tickles my ear.

"There's a Tanztee tonight. I haven't been in months, but—come with me. Just tonight. Please. It's in the Delphi Tanzpalast, there's supposed to be a band and everything. Ten o'clock, Fasanenstraße. Meet me outside?"

"Yes," I say, before she's even finished her sentence. "Yes, yes."

"Tonight," she repeats, and pulls back just as Johann rejoins us.

"I didn't see Herr Meisner. Are you sure it was him?"

"My mistake," Geli says. "Well. We must be off. Congratulate Greta for me."

"I will," I say.

Johann holds out his hand for me to shake. "Nice to meet you, Charlotte. I'm sure we'll see you around." He gives me a wink, and I watch as he and Geli make their way through the crowd. Ein perfektes Paar.

But tonight. Tonight. One last dance with her, I tell myself, and then I will finally rid my thoughts of her for good. One last dance. That's all.

It'll have to be enough.

Mama and Papa retire as soon as we enter the flat, though I notice Papa takes the radio into their room with him. I wonder if it's really to listen for air-raid warnings, or if he's trying to catch another broadcast from the BBC. Greta looks after them, then turns to me.

"Are you going to sleep?"

"Yes," I say. "Are you?"

She shrugs. "Vielleicht. I'm not tired."

"I can tell you a story, kleines Gretchen," I say, reaching out and messing up her hair. She swats my hand away.

"Nein. I'm not small anymore." She looks at me and grins. "You know I'm only one year younger than Kaiserin Elisabeth was when she got married."

"Don't tell that to Mama. She'll start looking for suitors."

"All of them have gone off to war," Greta says. "Good luck to her." She laughs quietly but doesn't head to her room. "Are you . . . are you sure you're going to sleep?"

Verdammt. "I'm sure, Greta."

"Oh. All right," she says. "Good night, then, Charlie."

"Gute Nacht, Greta. Schlaf gut," I say, and we head into our bedrooms, though she does so reluctantly, looking back at me every few seconds. When Greta is finally in her own room, I make sure to shut my own door firmly behind me.

I wait. Ten minutes, twenty minutes, until I'm sure Greta's asleep. Pace my room and dig through my closet for something suitable to wear. Pull out that book of Heine's, flipping through the pages, whispering the words to myself as I get dressed so I can carry them in my head to Geli. I finally settle on a short navy dress

I made two years ago, even shorter now that I've grown taller.

I set the book down, look at myself in the mirror, fish around in a drawer for an old lipstick, a dark brown color so different from Geli's red. I swipe it on, and startle when I look at myself in the mirror. Because sometimes when I look, I expect to still be fifteen, Geli leaning over my shoulders and applying my lipstick, telling me I look beautiful.

But the girl who looks back at me isn't fifteen anymore. She's not even really a girl. Her face is thin because of the war, her hair still plain, but at least tonight when I look at her, at me, I almost see what Renate sees, what Geli sees.

One last time. One last dance, then, before it's all over.

The night is warm enough that I don't need a jacket; I'm almost sweating by the time I've reached Fasanenstraße. Just as I'm about to cross Kurfürstendamm I feel it, that feeling of being watched, and I turn, thinking it's the HJ or some SS officers out on a late-night patrol.

But when I turn, there's no one there. And no sooner have I crossed in front of the Tanzpalast than I see her, waving and crossing the street toward me, heads turning as she does.

"Hi," I say, my mouth dry, as Geli approaches me.

"You came," she says.

"I did."

She nods, like she's decided something to herself, and then grabs my hand. "Shall we go in?"

I nod, and I let her lead me into the dance hall like that first time, like always, and for a moment I am fifteen again, following her anywhere.

We stop just outside the door, music pouring out, and she looks at me.

"You look stunning," she says, then, "Wait." She reaches out and runs her fingers through my hair, trying to give it more volume, making it looser. I freeze, because she is so close to me, her face barely centimeters from mine.

"Du bist schön, Peggy," she whispers, and there's a look on her face that I can't fully decipher as she pulls me into the club.

We dance. She finally dances with me like I wished she had at the beginning, her arms around my waist and our bodies close and the music so loud we wouldn't hear an air-raid siren over it but I don't care, because she's dancing with me and we are dancing like everything is fine, like our world isn't on fire, like we aren't going to burn.

"Charlie," she says at one point, leaning in, staring up at me. I swallow.

"Geli . . ."

"Kiss me," she says, and she tilts her face toward mine. This is not like the first time she kissed me, tentative and unsure. This is fire and heat and the want I have been chasing for so long, and before I can stop myself, I kiss her, I kiss her, like that night in her house, and she kisses me, her arms around my neck, and I want to ask her about Johann, about Renate, what this means, but her mouth is on mine and I cannot find the space to ask.

"Ich liebe dich," she whispers into my shoulder, over and over and over. "Ich liebe dich, ich liebe dich, ich liebe dich."

But she pulls back, and she looks at me, and I know then—this will not exist outside this room, this club, this night. Whatever this is, whatever the sudden connection between Geli and me that I have been wanting for so long, it will die as soon as we set foot outside this room.

I have followed her for so long I have finally caught up.

"Do you?" I ask, and she nods, but there's a small bit of hesitation before she does, and I know then that she knows it, too. That I may love her, care for her, but we are not in love, no matter how much we pretend to be, no matter how loud the music is and how many times we say the words over it.

"Ich liebe dich," I tell her, and it feels like a confirmation of what neither of us has said. *Es tut mir leid. Ich liebe dich, doch. Doch. Es wird nie passieren.*

It will never happen.

Ich sag ihr nicht, weshalb ich's tu
Weiß selber nicht den Grund—
Ich halte ihr die Augen zu
Und küß sie auf den Mund.

"One more dance?" Geli asks, after I've caught my breath, just as the band strikes up another song, and I nod, because I'm not ready for this feeling between us to stop existing just yet.

She pulls me close, her hand on my waist, and I close my eyes as we dance, not quite fitting together anymore.

When I open my eyes, I think I see something, some glimpse of something familiar, and that nagging feeling that's been in my gut since I left the house grows stronger. As the beat picks up, it's there again, a flash of long dark hair, a face as familiar to me as my own.

"Greta," I say, but she doesn't hear me over the noise and Geli looks up at me quizzically and I am about to just ignore her—what does it matter if she's here, she can just dance for the night—when the doors burst open. And there are screams, and not the ones I have heard so often in this club of laughter or passion, but the ones that live in an echo chamber in my ears each time a bomb falls on our city.

Fear.

I look up and there are the SS and there are the HJ boys storming their way in, and I see Fritz's eyes scanning the crowd for Geli, and beside him—

Oh God, beside him, Herr Haas.

"Charlie, we have to go," Geli says, but I pull away from her because all I can think now is *Greta Greta Greta wo ist mein Schwesterchen where is my little sister Greta—*

I'm pushed on all sides by the crowd, that jostling of bodies now turned painful, elbows in ribs and someone stepping on my feet, and I yell until my voice is hoarse, "Greta! Greta!"

"Charlie!"

I turn, and by some miracle there she is, and I'm not thinking about Geli anymore as I grab my sister, pull her to me, and the two of us push and fight through the bodies and we—

run.

We don't stop until we're well away from the Tanzpalast. Twice I think I've lost Greta, but every time I look back, she's right behind me.

I'm always leading.

She's always following.

When we're finally far enough away that I feel safe, I clutch her to me, hug her, not aware that I'm crying until I've stopped moving, until I hear her own sobs and realize she's crying, too.

"Greta what—what were you doing there?!" I say when I finally have the breath to, pulling back and looking directly at her. Her nose is running and she wipes it with her sleeve.

"I just wanted to be with you," she says, her voice raw. "I saw you talking to Geli at the meeting and I thought you might sneak out, so I followed you and wanted to see—see the club, but then I thought someone was following *me*, so I ran inside and I couldn't find you but then I did and then Fritz was there and—" She bursts into tears again and I pull her to me.

"I led him there," she sobs into my dress.

"Nein, Gretchen," I say. "You didn't. He probably—he probably followed Geli," I say, realizing when the words are out of my mouth that they're probably true.

Geli.

I left her. I let go of her hand and I left her to find Greta and oh God what if she didn't make it out—

But Greta is safe. My sister is safe. Geli is smart, cunning; Geli will be fine. She always is.

Greta's sobs gradually slow, and mine do too, until we're breathing calmly, or as calmly as we can.

"Komm," I say. "We need to go home. You can't be out after curfew."

She nods, and falls into step beside me. "Es tut mir leid, Charlie. I'm so sorry."

"Wofür?"

"I just—I just wanted to follow you."

I turn around to face her. "Don't apologize, Greta, bitte. I'm sorry for not including you." I close my eyes. "But maybe we should keep this from Mama when we get home, yes? Just so she doesn't worry." *More than she already has.*

Greta nods, and the two of us trudge on back home, because I know the way, though the entire time my mind is back in that room with Geli, with her hands on my waist.

If I could turn back, though, I don't think I would.

◆ ◆ ◆

290

I cannot sleep. Every time I close my eyes I see her, hear the screams of everyone around us, the feeling of bodies closing in as Greta and I run out of the building.

In my dreams I'm being chased, and when I look back, Greta is never behind me.

I wake up to a shrill sound and for a second I worry it's another air-raid siren. I'm already halfway out of bed to grab my bags when I realize it isn't—it's the phone.

I hurry out of my room but Mama is already there, cradling the handset against her shoulder, her face drawn and pale. I can't hear what's being said to her, but my heart sinks when she holds out the phone to me.

Geli, I think, and I take the phone.

"Charlie?"

The voice on the other end of the line isn't Geli. It's Renate.

"Ja?"

"Charlie . . . ," she says, and her voice is thick. "You need to come down. Outside the Zoo. They've—they've rounded up the other Swingjugend, they—"

"Ich weiß," I say, ignoring my mother. "I was there last night—"

"Charlie, they've arrested Geli."

I can't speak. For a second I'm sure I've misheard her. "Was? But—"

"Fritz told me," Renate says, and then she's crying. "They're

291

going to punish them publicly, as a warning to the rest of us—you have to come, bitte, I wouldn't ask if it wasn't important, please—"

"I'll be there," I say, and hang up, feeling Mama and Greta both looking at me.

"I'm coming too," Greta says decisively, and I shake my head.

"No, Greta, I don't—I don't want you to see this, please," I say. "Please, please just listen to me. Stay here, all right? I—I have to go—"

"Lottchen," my mother begins, but I can't hear what she has to say, not now, because I have to get to Geli. And I'm almost out of our flat when I remember—the book. Maybe I can give it to her, maybe I can—

I run back to my room, my mother and Greta still watching me, mirrored worried expressions on their faces.

"What's going to happen to Geli?" Greta asks, and I don't respond because I don't want to think about it, not now, nicht jetzt.

I grab the book from my drawer and tuck it under my shirt, hurry out the door before either Mama or Greta can stop me, because I have to get to her, I have to get to Geli, because if I don't—

There's already a crowd in front of the Zoo when I arrive, an audience gaping at a different kind of zoo, at the people in front of us. It takes me a minute to spot Renate's tall form near the front.

"Renate," I say, and she does not turn, and I curse again and run up to her on her good side and almost throw myself at her, the book thumping against my chest. "Renate—"

"Charlie," she says, and pulls me in close. "Gott sei Dank, I thought you—I thought you might've been—"

"Greta and I made it out, before—"

"*Greta* was with you?"

"She followed me," I say, and I pull back, wanting so desperately to kiss her, to reassure myself that she's real, but I don't. "I . . . Renate, I went out with Geli, and I . . . I'm sorry, I . . ."

A flash of pain crosses Renate's face, just for an instant, then disappears. "It's—I know, Charlie. I know. We can—we can talk about it later," she says, and then she stops talking because at that moment the crowd starts shifting, a living moving thing, and I finally turn and see what they can see.

The Swingjugend. Not all of us, but some, lined up in a row, the boys' downturned faces obscured by their long hair, and there, at the end of the row, a flash of gold—

Geli.

Her face is not down like the boys', it is turned up in defiance, her lipstick somehow still perfect, her mouth curled into a red sneer. The officers go down the line, reading out their names, and I realize with a sickening feeling that the officer at the front is Geli's father, with Fritz not far behind him. I grip Renate's hand.

With each name called, the officers jeer, one of them reaching out, and I catch a flash of silver before I realize—they have scissors. They're cutting the boys' hair.

I want to look away. The sound of scissors and laughing is so loud and I know then, that like the air-raid sirens and the bombs and the jazz music and Goebbels's voice on the radio, it is a sound I will never forget.

One by one they move down the line, yanking the boys' heads back forcefully and laughing. With a start, I see a boy who looks like the spitting image of Moritz, and I think—*it can't be, Moritz is gone, off somewhere in Russia*. This boy's face is too young to be him, and I know it has to be his brother.

Moritz, Tommy, the boy I was so jealous of. I send up a silent prayer of thanks that at least he isn't here right now to witness this.

I watch, my nails digging into Renate's hand until she gently extricates it from mine. When I look up, her face is white.

And then.

And then.

They reach Geli. Quickly force her down to her knees, laughing, and that sick feeling in my stomach just grows even more. I want to do something, and I pull away from Renate, toward her, toward Geli, but am surprised by Renate's firm hand on my arm.

"Charlie, nein," she whispers. "You . . . you can't save her."

"Das kann ich," I hiss, and try to pull away; she pulls me back even harder, a quiet struggle as I realize she's not going to let me go.

"Renate—"

"Charlie," she says firmly. "I'm not losing you, too."

"Isn't this your daughter, Ludwig?" one of the officers says loudly. Herr Haas stares down at Geli coldly, and for a moment I think he's going to hit her. But instead he takes Geli's chin in his hands, turning her face this way and that, inspecting.

"No," he says after a moment. "She isn't. Nur eine kleine *Hure*."

Geli curls her lip and spits into his face. Now he does hit her, then grabs her hair and pulls her to her feet. He motions for someone to bring him the scissors, and to my horror, Fritz steps forward. Geli spits at him, too, and he recoils before the other officers laugh and shove him toward her.

"Careful, boy, the whore's got bite," one of them says. I whimper, wishing I could press my face into Renate's shirt so I wouldn't have to see this.

But her brother is doing this, and she has not looked away, not once.

So I won't either.

My heart is in my throat, and I watch, watch, watch as Fritz takes fistfuls of Geli's hair and begins cutting it off.

She closes her eyes. And when she finally opens them, she

looks directly at me, and I am frozen, frozen in place, before I remember that damned book hidden in my shirt, and slowly pull it out and turn it so she can see it.

She nods at me, just once, imperceptible to anyone else. Her lips move and for a second I think she's singing one of those songs, those damned jazz songs we loved so much, and then I realize I know all too well what she's saying.

Fürchte nichts, geliebte Seele
Übersicher bist du hier;
Fürchte nicht, daß man uns stehle,
Ich verriegle schon die Tür.
Do not fear, beloved darling
You are still protected here;
Do not fear, that we'll be taken,
I already locked the door.

It is the last time I see Angelika Haas alive.

Ich hatte einst ein schönes Vaterland.

Der Eichenbaum

Wuchs dort so hoch, die Veilchen nickten sanft.

Es war ein Traum.

Das küßte mich auf deutsch, und sprach auf deutsch

(Man glaubt es kaum,

Wie gut es klang) das Wort: "Ich liebe dich!"

Es war ein Traum.

I had a beautiful homeland, once.

The oak tree

Grew so tall there, the violets nodded softly.

It was a dream.

It kissed me in German, and spoke in German

(You could hardly believe

How good it sounded) the words: "Ich liebe dich!"

It was a dream.

—HEINRICH HEINE, "IN DER FREMDE"

Part IV

MAI–AUGUST 1945

Mai - August 1945

ALLIIERTEN-BESETZTES DEUTSCHLAND

THE WAR ends in May during a defeated, scorching summer, yet even before it ends, it continues to destroy the things I love, while I can only watch. Watch as my family huddles together in the cellar of our building, only to emerge and find the entire thing reduced to rubble, to ash, our belongings singed and burnt and gone, save for the few things we stashed in our suitcases. Watch as more and more Jews disappear and clouds of smoke rise over Germany, ash in our mouths we will never stop tasting. Watch as letters come in from Hans until one day they don't, as Renate holds up her family when her father dies a year later in a bombing and her mother refuses to get out of bed.

Greta and Mama and Papa and I move in with Renate and her mother, because somehow their flat is still standing, and we try our damnedest to hold ourselves together. At nights I hold Renate, because I can do nothing else.

I watch as the Zoo Greta loved so much is destroyed, listen in horror to reports of the keepers turning to eating the animals. Watch as the Russians march into Berlin and Renate, Greta, Mama, Frau Hoffmann, and I hide ourselves in the cellar, because we know what they will do to women they find. When it is safe, when we no longer worry about them coming for us in the night, Renate tells me she will never go underground again. We walk everywhere because she doesn't want to take the U-Bahn, and I am grateful for the distraction that trying to navigate through the ruined city brings.

I watch, and I remember, and I draw maps to places that no longer exist because they have been reduced to rubble, to ash.

And then the war is over, and it doesn't feel like it's over, just like that, but Hitler is dead and the Allies have come in and declared our city theirs, dividing it up like any existing borders don't matter, making liars out of our maps once again.

I do not want the maps I draw to lie, but they will regardless, because they are drawn from my memories.

But I find I cannot stop drawing them anyway. The route from Renate's home to mine, no longer straight lines but curving, winding ways around the remnants of buildings that block the way, ending in a blank point rather than in the strictly marked parameters of our old building. For Greta, I draw a way to the Zoo, but for her I draw the entire park still intact. On any paper I can find, I draw the route we will someday take to a now liberated Paris, where hopefully we can find Minna, the twins. I draw the way to my father's home back in Bayern, the route to Austria—which I stubbornly keep named Austria—for

Greta, so she can someday visit the palace where Elisabeth lived. I draw these things, drawing out our future, trying to re-create what was destroyed.

The war destroyed everything we loved, including a golden-haired girl who looked at me like I was the most precious thing she knew. She and the other captured swings were sent to Moringen, to Uckermark, names I cannot let myself think of. Some came back, unable to discuss what happened to them there.

The girl I loved did not.

There are nights I wake up, shaking, because I can still feel her looking at me, can still hear her voice in my ear.

Renate holds me, then. She tells me I could not have saved Geli, no matter how much I loved her, and I make her tell me over and over and over until I almost believe her.

Almost.

The war destroyed everything we loved, so when it ends, we set to work rebuilding. Renate and I join the other Trümmerfrauen, the rubble women, the ones left after most of the men were killed or lost in battle. We set to work rebuilding this place that we hate and love, digging our memories out from beneath the ruins. Greta helps, when she can, though more nights than not I see her studying the map with the route to Paris, practicing what little French she remembers from school.

She tells me she still dreams about the twins. They are no longer ten, she says, and she has to find them so she can be sure. I tell her I will help, that we may need to go farther than Paris. We will go together and we will find them and we will make things right, do absolutely everything we can to make things right.

I tell her this, and I know she believes me.

Sometimes at night she curls up into Renate and me, and I let her, because she is my sister, because there, I know she is safe.

We rebuild, and we rebuild, and we rebuild, concentrating on the tangible things we can fix, the buildings and streets and bricks and stones, because it's all we can do. And sometimes when we rebuild, we sing. Badly, but we sing, the tunes of those songs we listened to in the clubs. Renate whistles better than any of us and sometimes I catch her whistling "Flat Foot Floogie" the way Moritz used to. When we forget the words, or don't know them, we make up our own. Our hands become raw, our knuckles bloody, but it is better to feel this pain from something we can control than the pain that awaits us when we close our eyes at home, pain that cannot be so easily chased away with music.

One afternoon in late August, as we finish carting the last remnants of a residential building down Friedrichstraße, Renate, leaning against the wheelbarrow she's using, declares that we need a break. I sit next to her and grab my satchel from where I set it earlier, dig around in it for my lunch until my hand bumps against something hard. Greta must have slipped it in, trying to make me happy in whatever ways she can.

As my fingers close around it, I know instantly what it is, and I pull it out and press my hand to my mouth, open the tattered blue cover, read that familiar inscription—*Für Ursula. Alles Liebe, Oma.*

But when I turn the page, to my surprise, there's another inscription, one I've never noticed before. The ink of this one is less faded than the other, the handwriting intimately, painfully familiar to me.

Für Charlie. Alles Liebe, Geli.

I don't know when she did it, maybe one of the nights she came over and stayed with me, but there it is, and I find myself pressing my fingers to her handwriting, to my name, to something she touched that proves she was real.

"Was ist?" Renate asks as I lean into her, solid and steady and there.

"It . . . it was Geli's," I say, pressing the book to my chest as I begin to cry. Renate waits a long moment, then gently takes the book from my hands, opening it up to the marked page with the poem Geli wanted me to memorize so long ago, and begins to read.

ACKNOWLEDGMENTS

Everyone says the second book is the hardest, and that was definitely true for me. Luckily, I had so, so many good people in my corner who helped this book take shape and become the absolute best version it could be. It would not exist without every person named in these pages.

First and foremost, as always, to my parents. Mom, for being the best research assistant I could ask for, and Dad, for showing me the Swing Kids movie in the first place that sparked this whole idea.

Without my incredible agent, Eric Smith, this would still be a Word doc on a hard drive. Thank you for everything that you do, and for being as excited about a queer Swing Kids inspired book as I was.

To the team at HarperTeen—Catherine Wallace, for believing in this book enough to want to make it a reality (and for the many deadline extensions), and Stephanie Stein for the absolutely pitch-perfect comments and editorial notes that really make this book sing. Stephanie, you helped make this the queerest, saddest version of itself it could be, and I'm so immensely grateful for that. I'm not sorry for all the tears I caused. To Sarah Maxwell and Corina Lupp, thank you for the absolutely beautiful cover. To the rest of my fantastic Harper team, including Sophie Schmidt, Erin DeSalvatore, Mark

Rifkin, Alison Donalty, Annabelle Sinoff, Nicole Moulaison, Shannon Cox, Lauren Levite, Patty Rosati, Mimi Rankin, and Katie Dutton—thank you. So happy to be part of the Harper family.

Drafting a book about WWII in the middle of the pandemic was a challenge, to say the least, and I wouldn't have made it through it without friends both online and off. So, so much love to Geertje H., Kadan W., Rachel R., Stacy G., Sneha G., Olivia V., Alec L., Sarah P., Nell O., and the lads of the Pia and Wilma chats. Thanks for the Discord streams, the encouragement, and the general cursed chaos. To Mary Nita, thank you for letting me use your cabin regularly for retreats.

To my writer friends who've been there every step of my publishing journey with this book: Dante Medema, Rey Noble, Marieke Nijkamp, Corinne Duyvis, Cam Montgomery, Sarah Hollowell, and Tess Sharpe—thank you, thank you. To Kip Wilson, thank you for wading through so much research with me, and sharing our love of Berlin. Special thanks to the Tin House 2021 YA writers group (and the world's best Slack group.) And to my beloved Rae Bowser and Kath West: thank you for believing in and loving the girls as much as I do.

To Valeria Krabbe and Frauke Arnetzl (as well as the rest of the German Brötchen) thank you for the German help. Special thanks to the Bundesarchiv in Berlin for the help with research. Much love to Susanne Gomoluch, Brooke Shafar, and especially Dave Limburg for helping me on this path to learning this beautiful language. There really is a word in German for everything. Any remaining mistakes are my own.

Natürlich, to Hannah. Schatz, I don't know where I would be without you. Thank you for being the best cheerleader from the first draft onward, and for just truly understanding what I was trying to do with this book and letting me bounce ideas off you. And thank you for loving me.

And finally, to the readers who supported my first book. Thank you for letting me continue to devastate you with queer stories. Your support means the world, and is the reason I get to keep writing what I do. Thank you, thank you, thank you. (Danke, danke, danke.)

FACT VS. FICTION: AUTHOR'S NOTE

Though the characters of *Nothing Sung* are fiction, the Swing-jugend were a real group of German teenagers who used American and British jazz to resist the Nazis in the 1930s and '40s. The real Swingjugend were largely based out of Hamburg instead of Berlin, as they had access to the port there and were able to buy records, like Ingrid. Like Geli, most of them belonged to upper- and middle-class families, as those were the ones who could afford the records and clothing the swings adored, as well as the ones who had learned English in school. Like Minna and Max, many of them were Jewish, which put a far larger target on their backs than simply being a Swing. For many of the non-Jewish swings, their privileged upbringings sheltered them from the worst of the war.

The swings were generally left alone by the regime, more a nuisance than a threat, save for the massive raid on a swing meeting in Hamburg in August 1941. Over 300 swings were rounded up and sent to nearby Möringen and Ravensbrück, where they were subjected to torture to cure what the Nazis saw as "sexual deviancy," as the Swingjugend—particularly the girls—had a reputation for promiscuity.

While there were groups of teens who rebelled against the Nazi regime, such as the Edelweißpiraten and the Rote Kapelle, to my knowledge the real Swingjugend never actively participated in resistance the way Renate, Charlie, and Max do in the novel. Their resistance was inspired in part by the White Rose movement in Munich and by Otto and Elise Hampel, a working-class married couple who distributed anti-Nazi postcards in Berlin and were executed for it in 1943.

Nothing Sung is, in many ways, about the various forms of resistance people can undertake, regardless of their positions in life—whether that looks like Greta not indoctrinating her group of Jungmädeln once she becomes a leader, or Charlie's father listening to illegal broadcasts after dark, or Charlie and Renate distributing postcards, or even Geli sneaking out to listen to music. The Swingjugend themselves were often criticized after the war for their apolitical attitudes, something Charlie and Renate mention—that sitting on the sidelines dancing and listening to music *doesn't* feel like enough. That with their privilege in the war, they should be doing something *more*. It's something Charlie chastises Geli about after Kristallnacht—that Jewish people are being attacked and forced to flee, and all Geli cares about is the club. Charlie is right in this moment, of course: Geli's own privilege and upbringing have kept her from having to reckon with the horrors of the Nazi regime, even as she points out to Charlie that such evil lives in her own home.

But for the real Swingjugend, I would like to argue that what they were doing was certainly resistance as well, even if on a much smaller scale. Sometimes resistance is in large acts, and sometimes it is in joy. For Minna and Max and the other Jewish

Swingjugend, the simple act of going to the club was resistance, because, as Minna points out, the stakes for her being caught resisting are much higher than they are for Charlie or Renate, and certainly higher than for Geli. And yet for all of them, the risk is worth the small moments of joy they are able to find throughout the horrors of the war.

In the end, Geli's privilege cannot save her, just as it did not save the 300 Swingjugend rounded up in Hamburg in August 1941. And that is what I hoped, ultimately, to show with this novel: Not that resistance is futile or that Geli's actions aren't sometimes selfish or self-serving, but in the face of a horrifying totalitarian regime, sometimes even the smallest acts of resistance are just as dangerous—and just as necessary.

SELECT SOURCES IN GERMAN

Eicke, Brigitte, et al. *Backfisch im Bombenkrieg: Notizen in Steno.* Matthes & Seitz, 2013.

Lange, Sascha. *Meuten, Swings & Edelweißpiraten: Jugendkultur Und Opposition Im Nationalsozialismus.* Ventil-Verl, 2015.

Stölzle, Alexandra, and Gabriele Trost. "Kindheit Im Zweiten Weltkrieg: Die Swing-Jugend." Kindheit Im Zweiten Weltkrieg: Die Swing-Jugend - Nationalsozialismus - Geschichte - Planet Wissen, Planet-Wissen.de, 4 Nov. 2020, www.planet-wissen.de/geschichte/nationalsozialismus/kindheitimz-weitenweltkrieg/pwiedieswingjugend100.html.

Ueberall, Jörg. *Swing Kids.* Archiv Der Jugendkulturen, 2004.

Wuthe, Stephan. *Swingtime in Deutschland.* Transit, 2012.

Statistisches Jahrbuch Berlin, 1938.

Statistisches Jahrbuch Berlin, 1939.

SELECT SOURCES IN ENGLISH

Bessel, Richard. *Life in the Third Reich*. Oxford: Oxford University Press, 2001. Print.

Blackburn, Gilmer W. *Education in the Third Reich: A Study of Race and History in Nazi Textbooks*. Albany: State University of New York Press, 1985. Print.

Fallada, Hans. *Every Man Dies Alone*. Translated by Michael Hofmann, Melville House, 2010.

(www.dw.com), Deutsche Welle. "1945: Youth in Ruins: DW: 21.06.2014." DW.COM, 21 June 2014, www.dw.com/en/1945-youth-in-ruins/a-17721661.

Göbel, Frank. "German Swing Youth." Swing-Kids, 2003, www.return2style.de/amiswhei.htm.

Johnson, Eric Arthur, and Karl-Heinz Reuband. *What We Knew: Terror, Mass Murder, and Everyday Life in Nazi Germany: An Oral History*. Basic Books, 2006.

Kater, Michael H. *Different Drummers: Jazz in the Culture of Nazi Germany.* Oxford University Press, 1992.

Kater, Michael H. *Hitler Youth*. Harvard University Press, 2004.

Mayer, Milton. *They Thought They Were Free: The Germans, 1933-45*. University of Chicago Press, 1995.

Neuhaus, Tom. "Youth Rebels of the Third Reich." History Today, vol. 55, no. 11, Nov. 2005, www.historytoday.com/archive/youth-rebels-third-reich.

Reese, Dagmar. *Growing Up Female in Nazi Germany*. University of Michigan Press, 2010. Internet resource.

Sandor, Cynthia A. *Through Innocent Eyes: The Chosen Girls of the Hitler Youth*. Revised ed., BDM History, 2018.

White, Robert. "Swingjugend: The Real Swing Kids." Swungover, *24 Sept. 2013*, www.swungover.wordpress.com/2013/07/26/swingjugend-the-real-swing-kids/.